JAMES MATTHEWS

The Party is Over

Kwela Books

The acrylic painting on the cover, *The Party is Over*,
was done by Tyrone Appolis in 1996
The pen and ink drawing inside, *The Drift Road, Teslaarsdal*,
was done by Peter Clarke in 1956
Cover design and typography by Nazli Jacobs
Set in 10 on 12 pt Times New Roman
Printed and bound by National Book Printers;
Drukkery Street, Goodwood, Western Cape
First edition, first printing 1997

ISBN 0-7957-0044-X

Contents

The Drift Road,
Teslaarsdat
France:
nov. 1956

BOOK
ONE

1

Table Mountain, a gigantic backdrop against the skyline, loomed darkly beyond the sprawling townships of the Cape Flats.

It was dusk. Light falling from the front windows of one of the semi-detached houses faintly illuminated the lane in Bridgetown. Bright light and loud music set this matchbox apart from the other similarly constructed houses monotonously duplicated along every other street of the township.

When he entered, Steward noticed that the front room had been cleared of all furniture, except for the radio with its extending speaker stuck in the opposite corner. A recorded rock group was stridently urging the partying people to get with it. The floor took a pounding as the gyrating dancers showed that they got the message of the 'swinging sixties'.

Outside the air was cold, but the dancers were generating a noticeable heat of their own. Steward went through to the kitchen.

"She swings, man. What you need is a drink to make you mit it. Come'n, I'll pour you one." David took out a demijohn of wine from under the kitchen sink. He filled two glasses.

"Here," he thrust one at Steward. "Get this inside you."

Yvonne stared disapprovingly at him from behind the mound of sandwiches she was preparing. "I wonder what the rest is going to drink if you start off like this?"

David looked at her. The high heels made her two inches taller than his five foot two. Her long, black hair was oiled and slung across one side of her face, terminating in a plait. The red dress, tight across the waist, balconied at the breasts, the low cut accentuating her smooth brown skin.

"For God's sake, Yvonne. Knock it off! It's a damn party, isn't it? What do you want me to do, stay off the stuff?"

He swallowed the rest of the wine with a defiant gesture and refilled his glass.

Yvonne did not reply, concentrating on buttering the bread. The knuckles of the hand holding the knife were white lumps of resentment.

Steward stood sipping uneasily from his glass.

The second drink seemed to have dispelled David's flare of rage and he winked at Steward. "Grab hold of a goose inside," he suggested. "I'll help Yvonne."

Steward dutifully complied and David got himself a knife.

"Can I pour you one, Yvonne? A small one. It's not really party wine. Steward and I got together and bought a private one. It's your favourite: Frontinac. Steward insisted."

He took a glass from the dresser and half filled it.

Yvonne sipped delicately, her lips barely touching the glass. It always amused him – her feline manner of drinking.

"Please, David. Don't get out of hand tonight."

"I'm never obnoxious, darling," he assured her. "It's just that some people bring out the swine in me."

"Well, try to be nice to everybody."

He delighted in the play of her hips as she placed the empty glass in the sink.

"You certainly make everybody else's wife look the hag she is. I'd better keep an eye on you. You'll turn every man hot for you tonight."

She joined in his laughter, pleased at his words.

With unobtrusive ease he poured himself another drink and stood watching Yvonne finish the last of the sandwiches. As she was taking off the small apron pinned to her dress, he placed his hands on her shoulders and deftly swung her around.

"How about a quick feel?"

Her body tensed for a moment. Then she relaxed and allowed him to kiss her, his hands sliding down her body. He held her longer than he had intended.

The back door opened. David raised his head, not altogether releasing her. "You don't mind if I kiss my wife, do you, Eddie?" he asked mockingly.

Eddie, medium height and paunchy, said pompously, "Not at all. You hold full rights."

"I just thought I should ask you. Not being hep to these things."

Eddie grinned, revealing an expanse of gum and yellowed teeth.

Yvonne jerked her hips free of David's grip. "If you done with your nonsense, I can go inside."

"I'm sorry, darling. I didn't mean to detain you." He bowed to her, then turned to Eddie. "There she is, Eddie. Can you blame me for burning so strongly for her?"

Yvonne snorted with exasperation and click-clacked on her high heels from the kitchen.

10

Eddie allowed himself a parting shot before following her: "Now, don't overdo it, David. We don't want the host to pass out this early in the evening. You should know by now that age and liquor don't mix well. And in your case, the mixture is disastrous."

David grunted to himself.

Age? The bastard is two years older than my thirty-five and going grey, but still he thinks himself a young Lochinvar. He must be of the mind that I'm too stupid to know that he's making a play for Yvonne.

David emptied his class and slammed it down on the table. He might fool her with his pseudo-gentleman act, but not me. He's as phony as those whites who preach political equality but have the shits when you eye their woman. Well, Yvonne can play around with him if it amuses her. He's too stupid to realise that she and me are one. But then, what does he know about loving anyway? Loving that damn cow of his must be as exciting as a trip to the morgue. Shit on him!

He went inside. The shouters on record had made way for a crooner, and the dancers held each other in a tight embrace as they swayed to and fro to Billy Vaughn serenading them with *You belong to my heart*. The light had been turned off and he could only dimly discern faces.

As soon as the record ended, the light was switched on again. Eddie and Yvonne broke apart and Eddie lit a cigarette for her.

David looked around. Eddie's wife Rebecca, angled in a corner, scowled at them. Like most of the married women, she was over-dressed, her face smeared with make-up. Next to Yvonne, these older women were discarded trimmings from a Christmas tree. Yvonne outshone them. Agreed, her figure was fuller than that of the younger girls in the room, but the maturity it spelt was a stronger lure.

Most of the men were clustering around Yvonne.

David's pride was soured by anger. Yes, here she certainly was a queen among women. Here, she feels safe. Half of these married bitches spend their time thinking up filth to smear her with, warning each other that their men are not safe with her around. At the same time, they're burning up trying to be tenth-rate copies. If only Yvonne would go to the parties he attended. She could show those white bitches too what it is to be alive and a woman. But she was too damn afraid of their whiteness.

He walked across the room to claim her for the next dance.

The music started. It was a fox-trot.

"Now who the hell's put on square music?" he exploded.

"Relax," Eddie said. "This is music for the masters."

David withdrew, and together with the eighteen-year-old girls contented

11

himself with the role of wallflower while the housewives, with Yvonne in the lead, went through a series of intricate steps with their partners.

Eddie beamed at David as he whirled past with Yvonne in his arms. David turned his face away.

There was a knock at the door and two white men came in, squeezing past the dancers towards him.

David held out his hand in greeting. "Glad you could make it, Arnold. I hope you've brought something with you? And I don't mean your friend."

Arnold's friend gave a self-conscious laugh.

"Don't you worry about that. I brought my contribution." Arnold produced a bottle of brandy from underneath his voluminous sheepskin jacket. "David, this is Herman Bernstein. He is down from Johannesburg. Antique dealer."

"Hi, docco man," David said, taking hold of the outstretched hand. "Not much to look at here in the line of furniture, I'm afraid. Let's move to the back room where we can talk."

In the back room – ordinarily a childrens' bedroom, as the crayon drawings on one wall betrayed – a sideboard, moved from the front room for the occasion, served as a bar counter. Rows of bottles and glasses were lined up on top. In the middle of the floor a discarded empty tea crate substituted for a drinks table. One normal and one bunk bed were pushed against a wall.

A tall, lean form lay sprawled on one of the beds.

"Arnold, you know that bastard," David said, pointing to the body with its cropped hair and sunken cheeks. Then turning to Herman: "Charley Dickson is his name. He's a Dostoevski man. Has read every book on and written by his god. Don't get into an argument with him or else you'll still be here tomorrow morning."

Charley raised himself on an elbow. "Pour us a drink," he said, thirstily eyeing the bottle in Arnold's hand.

"Pour him one," David prompted, looking with affection at Charley, who leered back at him with bloodshot eyes.

They settled themselves on the other bed, the bottle of brandy at their feet.

"How's your writing going, Arnold?"

"I'm working on a new piece. It occupies all my thoughts. I only hope it works out the way I see it in my mind. Remember that story in the paper a month ago, David, about the people who have to leave the community they had started on the outskirts of George a hundred years back? Well, I visited them and stayed a few days."

12

"That's right, white man. Study us brown folks at close quarters. Soon you will be an expert on what makes us trot at a whip-snap."

"Come off it, David. You know it's not like that. I thought it could develop into a first-class story. I still think so, in fact. I only hope that I don't make a mess of it." After a few seconds he asked, "David, do you really believe that I'm happy about the set-up in this country? Sure I teach English at a white high school and my salary is higher than that of a Coloured teacher at a Coloured secondary school, but I haven't a choice. Same as you. You should be a reporter, not a switchboard operator. Let's not even mention Africans with matric certificates who are only allowed to be petrol pump attendants."

"Don't mind me," David grinned. "I'm just annoyed that I can't go off after stories like you can, because of that switchboard. It's damn good material for a story, that community. The stuff history's made of. Democracy at work – South African style! If you're Black, scat!"

Herman Bernstein lowered his head and sipped his brandy, avoiding David's eyes.

From the other room Chubby Checker invited the dancers to *Twist Again*.

"That's my cue," David said.

He found Yvonne before anyone else could move in. "I must have at least one dance with you before the night's done," he said.

Yvonne stuck a hand on her hip, her other arm held aloft. Then she bent her knees and swung her body to one side in time with the beat. David followed suit. For the next three minutes he tried to match her movements. She danced with complete abandonment, eyes feverishly aglow, breasts protesting against the constraining brassiere, hips undulating. He thought of her in bed, spread out naked.

He leaned forward. "Let's try that movement again in bed after they've all gone," he whispered in her ear.

She pushed him away and waggled her hips enticingly.

Rebecca's stare caught David's eye. Her face reflected disgust.

More people were finding their way to the children's bedroom now. The little artists who had created the bright crayon pictures on the wall behind the sideboard were nowhere to be seen.

Terence, narrow-hipped, tall and willowy, resplendent in an open-necked white satin shirt and hip-hugging jeans, had promoted himself to barman. Long, slender hands fluttered up and down like doves at a bird-bath, and his voice trilled as he filled glasses.

David nudged one of the younger girls towards a bunk bed. She sat down next to Herman Bernstein, and David seated himself beside her.

"What do you think of her?" he asked Bernstein, leaning across her shoulder, fingers entwined in her hair. "Isn't she just the right thing to keep you warm on a winter's night?"

"Haai, Mr Patterson musn't say things like that. What would your friend think and what would the Law say?"

"That's the Law's problem. But he'll be thinking the same thing or else he's no friend of mine."

She turned, hooked a finger in her short, curly hair, and tugged at her short skirt with her other hand, measuring Bernstein with her eyes. He blushed a deep red.

While David laughed at Bernstein's discomfort, Yvonne appeared in the doorway and took in the scene. She flashed a smile at Terence and returned to the front room.

The music resumed a moment later and couples drifted back towards the sound.

Terence joined the trio seated on the bed. He held his drink to the light. The wine shone amber through the thin glass. He took an appreciative sip and savoured the taste. "Ah, there's nothing like sweet wine. Brandy's for barbarians, and there's Tassies for the wine-swines!"

He gave Bernstein a teasing smile and told the girl, "Darling, why don't you join the rest of the girls inside and find yourself a nice young man you could burn up with your hot cookie?"

The girl leapt up and left them, pouting.

"What's wrong, Terence?" David asked. "Don't you like competition?"

"You could hardly call that competition, could you? She's only taking up space. One can hardly speak to her. Her brain is covered by her panties."

"I didn't come here for a debate," Arnold said from the door. "Whatever her brain can take in or not take in, it is just fine with me. Pardon me while I hunt her up and see what she can tell me."

Bernstein made as if to follow Arnold but Terence held out a restraining hand. "We haven't had a chance to really get acquainted. The party's not going to end yet. There's lots of time."

Herman Bernstein gave him a searching look.

"What do you think of homosexuality?" Terence suddenly asked.

"Well," Bernstein stammered, looking at David for guidance. "To tell you the truth, I've never given it much thought."

"Have you ever met a homosexual?"

Bernstein shook his head.

"You've seen one, haven't you?" Terence persisted.

14

"Yes, I've seen a homosexual before."

"Do you think I'm one?" Terence asked, his head cocked coquetishly.

"Are you?"

"That's for you to find out, friend," Terence said, laughing softly.

Bernstein, clearly uncomfortable at the trend of talk, suggested that they join the dancers.

"What about Dostoevski's Idiot Prince?" Charley had awakened sufficiently to join in. "Do you think he shows homosexual tendencies?"

"Don't bother us with your Dostoevski," Terence replied tartly. "And, furthermore, I'm not familiar with idiots."

Charley looked expectantly at Bernstein, who sat nursing his glass.

"Well, I don't know," Bernstein murmured. "I haven't read Dostoevski."

Charley, realising that neither wished to discuss the Idiot Prince's sexual inclination, appealed to David: "David, let's get pissed, the two of us, and stay here talking. What do you say, huh?"

"We could get pissed, but we could also have a ball inside."

"Aw, you know that's not for me. When are the bastards leaving so that we two can have a talk?"

"Charley, don't you ever do anything except get pissed, as you so inelegantly put it?" Terence ventured. "It's a party, and at parties people dance as well as drink."

Charley squinted in Terence's direction. "I've never been able to master the intricacies of the dance. Drinking is my department and dancing yours."

Rage flared up in David as he sat listening to them. Why the hell must they always slash at each other like this? Terence with his bright chatter is more maid than man. And Charley will never be the poet he wants to be because he's shit-scared to put words on paper.

What about myself? He grinned ruefully. Crap-arse writer.

His voice was gentle as he spoke: "Knock it off, Terence. Let's go inside and show the tourists what a real dancer can do."

"Well, if you insist," Terence said, blossoming under David's praise and glancing at Bernstein, the only "tourist" in sight.

David refilled Charley's glass before leaving the room.

In the front room Terence put a record on the player that would give him ample scope for choreography, and after the first few bars it was obvious that the other dancers would have to clear the floor if they wished to remain unscathed by his flashing feet.

As the girl he had chosen as partner proved too inept to follow his lead,

15

Terence brusquely pushed her aside and gave a solo display. At the end of his performance, he acknowledged the scattered applause by dropping his head slightly.

Herman Bernstein seemed at last to have gathered sufficient courage to approach Yvonne to partner him, but he was beaten to it by Arnold. He stood looking slightly bewildered as they swirled away.

David, who had refilled his glass, observed the incident, a sardonic smile creasing his face. He swallowed his wine in one swift gulp. His actions were sluggish as he stumbled to Bernstein's side, but his mind was detached from the awkward body.

"I think your wife's marvellous," Bernstein offered enthusiastically.

"Don't tell me you're also hot for her? Do you think you'd be able to make out with her?" David grabbed hold of Yvonne's arm as she and Arnold danced past them.

Yvonne glared at him but he did not release his hold. Despair crept into her eyes. "What is it?" she demanded.

"Don't look so outraged. Herman, here, has just paid you a compliment."

Yvonne looked at Bernstein.

"I said that you're a marvellous woman."

Her pleasure was evident in her smile. "Thank you, Herman."

"Now that you've said your piece, do you think you'd be able to make out with her all the way, Herman?" David spoke loud enough for everyone in the room to hear. "The bed's in the next room. Why don't you ask her whether it's on?"

Yvonne stared at David, her face draining of colour.

The younger girls giggled at David's words and continued dancing, but Rebecca and the other married women stood, avidly taking in the scene.

"You want to take me to bed?" Yvonne suddenly asked Bernstein, her voice matching David's in volume.

Arnold cut in before Bernstein could reply: "Don't be foolish, Yvonne. David was just joking."

A foolish smile crept across David's face. Yvonne's eyes raked him with rage and contempt. His smile froze, and he turned away and stumbled to the back room, where he collapsed on the bed next to Charley.

David's outburst seemed to have taken the heart out of the party. People took their leave one after the other until only Eddie and Steward were left.

"I'll see whether I can't wake Charley," Steward said as he left Yvonne and Eddie in the kitchen.

"Well, that's the end of another successful Patterson party," Eddie said. "Not that my host contributed much to its success."

Yvonne did not reply and stared stiffly in front of her.

"David can't help himself," Eddie continued, watching the effect of his words on Yvonne. "You shouldn't take him seriously, especially when he's had a few pots. Then he's like a little child. Must always do something to get everybody's attention."

"Eddie," Yvonne ventured hesitantly. "You think something's wrong with me? Sometime I get this feeling that David don't love me any more, that we drift apart. When first we come to stay here, I trust him with any woman, even if he sleep in the same bed with another woman and me. His hands don't stray. Now, he's like a ram after every soft-skin kid that come along. When we move in here, beer is his drink. You see how it's now. Anything goes."

"Do you and David have arguments about his drinking?"

She nodded her head.

"And what's his reply when you object to it?"

"He say he drink to forget the way I dance. He say it make every man in the room want to take me to bed. I don't see how he can say that. I don't dance different from other women."

Eddie recalled the earlier scene: Yvonne completely absorbed in the dance, withdrawn from everyone in the room, her eyes aglitter with an invitation to pleasure. That was what had drawn him to her right from the start. He was certain that she was unaware of the light in her eyes, the gleam that aroused in him a fire that his own wife's body could not light.

"No, I can't say that you dance much different from other women, except that you seem to get more enjoyment out of it. But then you should. You get a kick out of doing things. You're a go-go girl. You've got style."

Yvonne looked at the ashtrays littered with cigarette ends, the sink piled with dirty dishes, a plate with a forgotten sandwich, a woman's scarf draped on a chair.

"I'm tired. I think I go to bed and leave everything for the morning."

"What's going to happen to them?" Eddie asked, jerking his head in the direction of Charley and Steward in the back room.

"Steward say he stay. It's too late to go back to Wynberg. I don't know about Charley. He can stay if he want to, but he got a habit of waking up in the middle of the night and want people to talk to him."

"I'd better speak to him and find out what he intends doing."

Yvonne followed him to the back room.

David was seated on the bed, head buried in his hands. Steward was studiously going through a magazine and Charley was staring deeply into a half-empty glass.

"Well, well. What a mouldy collection we have here. After the ball is over, is this what we have left?"

No one responded.

"What's your move, Charley? Going or staying?"

Charley raised his head and peered at Eddie. "No. I'm not staying. I'm going home. Home is where my bed is, and whoever shares my bed is at home. But, of late, I've none to share my bed."

"I don't blame them."

David reached out a hand to Yvonne. She did not resist and sank down next to him. He took her hand and raised her palm to his lips.

Steward was embarrassed by the unexpected intimacy. Charley pretended he hadn't noticed, and Eddie gave an envious grunt.

Yvonne was stirred by the gesture.

"I didn't mean what I said about Bernstein taking you to bed."

"What will you do if I take up your offer and go to bed with him?"

"You know what would've happened. There would've been a much-bloodied white man here tonight."

"Then what make you say such a bad thing?"

David's eyes pleaded with her. "You are a red, red rose searing my soul," he said softly.

He could feel her tension easing.

"Seeing that everything is so rosy in the garden," Eddie said sardonically, "I'll push for home and leave you lovers."

He left without bothering to wait for Charley.

"David, you sure you don't want to sit up talking?" Charley tried once more.

"No. I'm for bed. You can stay if you want to talk and keep Steward from sleeping."

"No, thanks," Steward protested. "I'm far too tired. And I'm not in the mood for Charley's talks. We worked very hard at the factory this week cutting up timber and constructing desks. Had to meet a quota, and I was up early this morning. Had to go and buy the stuff for the party. Something you should've done, David."

"But I'm sure you didn't mind. You just love helping Yvonne."

"Never mind him," Yvonne said and got up to kiss Steward full on the lips. "I appreciate everything you do for me."

To cover his embarrassment Steward lowered his head behind his magazine.

David gazed at them fondly. I've got everything I want, he thought. Yvonne, the children, and the best bunch of guys one could wish for as friends. Yes, even that bastard of an Eddie.

"Let's finish off the Frontinac before going to bed," he said.

Yvonne did not object.

The wine finished, Charley left and David and Yvonne closed their bedroom door on Steward, who was still immersed in his magazine.

2

The four walls were like the sides of a prison cell. Sounds drifted through the open window: a car backfiring, the voices of people enjoying the night, and the sharp yelp of a dog. With distaste he stared at the switchboard in front of him. His stomach hurt. It felt as if someone had tied a string around his intestines and pulled it tight. A gnome had set up shop inside his head and was hammering away at a grey anvil. To think was pain.

Two lights flickered simultaneously on the switchboard. He swore in annoyance. Just as well they didn't have a telephone at home. It would drive him crazy. He did not bother to modulate his voice in the manner in which he had been instructed: "Cape Times. Can I help you?"

Both were sporting queries. He brusquely told the callers that none of the sports writers were available.

Shutting his eyes, he sank his head on the edge of the switchboard and took deep breaths in an effort to rid himself of the throbbing.

He checked the time on the wall. Half past eight.

I can ring now. She should be finished with her dinner.

He dialled a number and listened to the ringing. Then a voice: "11-4962."

"May I speak to Dawn, please?"

"Who's speaking?"

Irritation prickled him. He had to go through the same routine each time her father answered. He had angrily accused her of being pretentious, saying that the next time he would make an appointment to speak to her.

"David," he snapped.

"Hold on, I'll call her."

He ignored the flashing lights in front of him. Bloody messengers! They can wait.

"David?"

"No. Frankenstein's mother-in-law."

"I thought it was your day off."

"No, it's my turn to be on."

"Anything special to tell? How did the weekend go?"

"We had quite a party last night. Lots to drink."

"What did you do wrong this time?"

"Nothing much."

"Except for . . ."

"Hell! I may as well tell you. I did Yvonne a terrible wrong. Insulted her in front of everyone."

"Were you drunk?"

"I was, but not that much. I don't know what came over me. A white guy, a friend of Arnold Barker, paid Yvonne a compliment. Before I could control myself, I challenged her to go to bed with him. She looked as if I had spat in her face."

"You see? That's why I'll never come to your parties. Not after that Saturday afternoon at Gwen's." The plan had been to meet at Gwen's flat in Elsies River to go through Steward's drawings. David had brought along a story, but Gwen had bought a bottle of whisky…

"I didn't think it would work out that way."

"The way you started pouring should have warned me. Big tumblers of whisky with a dash of water. I'd never seen anyone drinking whisky that way. And you were so stubborn. We never even looked at the drawings."

David shifted the receiver and took a deep breath.

"You scared me so much when you stripped to the waist and threatened to jump from the balcony. And Steward locking himself in the toilet. I lost my head and fled, leaving poor Gwen to clean up the place."

"Hell, Dawn. I apologised to both of you. I even sent Gwen a big bunch of flowers afterwards. And Steward gave her a drawing."

"Being sorry afterwards doesn't help much. How many times have you told me that you're going to give up drinking? That it's no good for you? And what happens? Each weekend is just a repeat of the previous one, a series of drinking marathons. I don't think that you really want to change your ways. You've become conditioned."

"Are you trying to tell me that I'm an alcoholic?"

"If you can think of another term, you're welcome to it."

"Go to hell!"

"Do you want me to hang up?"

"No. It's just that I feel that I'm falling to pieces. My guts are busted."

"You know what causes it. Why don't you stop drinking?"

"Please, Dawn. Let's not get into that again."

"If you wish. But don't expect me to sympathise with you. How's your novel getting on? Or have you started something else? I haven't seen anything of yours in the Argus lately."

20

"I've stopped writing. Not in the sense that I've given it up altogether. It's just that I can't get words onto paper these days. I sit here at the switchboard and the paper in the machine mocks me. Hours go by and the paper stares at me. A blank sheet. And when words come, it's so much puerile muck that it sickens me."

"Perhaps you're thinking too much about the novel. Why don't you drop it for a week or so? Start something new. Start a story for the *Argus*. What did you do with those notes you read to me on the phone a month ago? I like the idea about the bergies acting as parking attendants on Riebeeck Square. It should make a good story."

"I've still got them. Maybe you're right. I'll forget about the novel and work on the story ... "

"Hey, David. I'll have to ring off. I've brought some work from the office that I want to finish."

"Okay. I'll ring you during the week, as soon as I complete the story. So long."

He felt invigorated, as he always did, no matter what his mood, after having had a talk with Dawn.

She was so unlike Yvonne. Six years younger than Yvonne's thirty-three. From a completely different background. Yvonne had been born in the Bo-Kaap and had grown up in Chiappini Street, a slum as bad as any section of District Six. Formal schooling had held little interest for her and she had left school as soon as she could, continuing her education on street corners and darkened doorways, passing out with an illegitimate baby before her seventeenth birthday.

He had tried to get her interested in the books from the library. At first she had dutifully read them all, but she had soon given up. Faulkner was too heavy to absorb. Picture love-stories and the *Golden City Post* with its weekly close-ups of rapes and robberies, were easier to assimilate.

She showed the same lack of interest in his writing. She was bored when he spoke of his ambition. A writer with their background was a foreign idea to her. The more his writing drove him into moods, ranging from elation to despair, the further she retreated behind the covers of her picture magazines.

Not Dawn. She didn't find his urge to put words on paper strange. From the moment they had met at the National Library in the Gardens more than a year before, where he had gone in search of a collection of Balzac's short stories. She had encouraged him to continue writing. He started sending her his stories. He respected her judgement, even though he didn't always agree with her. Dawn had gone from kindergarten right

21

through to university, chosing librarianship as a career, which landed her the position of head of the children's section at the Hyman Lieberman Library, the only library in District Six. She still lived with her parents in Walmer Estate, almost walking distance from the library. He assumed that Dawn was still a virgin.

He loved Yvonne, but how he wished she would show more of Dawn's qualities.

3

"Cynthia, would you get the books ready? I'll read to you children as soon as I've finished helping your mother. Get Shirley and Thelma into their pyjamas so long."

He took a plate from the basin and wrapped the drying cloth around it. With a quick circular movement it was dried and transferred to the kitchen dresser where the other crockery was stacked.

"This is what I like about being off-duty, even if it's only for one night. Helping you, reading the girls a story before putting them to bed. It really gives me the feeling of belonging, of being a family."

Yvonne smiled and for a moment no one spoke, the only sound the clatter of cutlery as she rinsed a handful of knives and forks.

"Daddy, when is Daddy going to read us the story?" Thelma called from their bedroom.

"Thelma's getting terribly bossy," David said fondly.

"It's your fault. You the one spoiling her."

"I can't help it. She's my favourite. She's going to look just like you. At times, I don't know which one I love most. You or her."

Thelma made her appearance before Yvonne could reply. She was freshly washed and dressed in pyjamas, her feet in felt slippers and her long, black hair, like her mother's, done into two plaits with little bows. She surveyed her parents.

"Thelma, go to bed now," Yvonne scolded her.

She stood her ground. "I'm waiting for Daddy to tell us the story. Daddy said he was going to tell us a story when we finish with washing. We all washed and we still waiting for Daddy."

"Don't you argue with me. Go to bed!" Yvonne dried her hands and made as if to advance on Thelma.

The little girl flashed an appeal to her father, then scampered from the kitchen.

"Leave the knives and forks. I'll do it. You get on with your story-telling or else we have all your daughters trooping to the kitchen."

"Now don't tell me they are getting you down?"

"It's that Thelma child! The other two are quite okay. You know what she did this morning at the shop? I buy her a sweater, a yellow one, and she, all of five years old, made me change it. Don't want it, she said. She want a red one. And she had her own way. I didn't want people to see her beat me down in front of them."

David snorted with laughter.

Yvonne joined in his laughter.

"I didn't feel like laughing this morning, but still, when we come home, I didn't give her a hiding."

"I know what you mean. But she's worth every moment of torment. All three of them." David looked at Yvonne, her hands dripping with soap suds. "There'll never be another woman for me!" he said.

She blushed and, to hide the pleasure his words gave her, said, "What about the young girls who come here, fluttering around Mr Patterson?"

"You know it doesn't mean a thing. It's just an act on my part."

"Well, just don't let the act turn serious. I don't share my man!"

David pressed her close. She playfully shoved him away. "Scat! You don't want to start something now, do you?"

"Why not?" he said, patting her posterior as he left the kitchen.

The children made room for him on Cynthia's bed. Thelma insisted on sitting on his lap. Cynthia gave her little sister the superior smile of an eight-year-old. Then she and Shirley settled themselves on either side of their father.

Yvonne in the kitchen listened to David's words rising and falling, pausing only to explain a word to Thelma. I can't really complain about him, she thought. He's given me more than all of the men in Chiappini Street could give their wives.

She ticked off in her head the washing machine, the refrigerator, the stove, the radiogram – all new, nothing second-hand. All bought since they had moved in here. And that was not counting the bedroom suite, the furniture for the children's room, the kitchen dresser, the table and four chairs that came with it, brand new from the store. He had said that he would give her a home, that she wouldn't need to go out and work, and he had kept his promise, sticking to his job at the newspaper even though he hated to work the switchboard.

She recalled visits to her former home with the children. She would bask in the envious looks of her childhood friends. They were married and still stuck in the area she now realised was a slum. She could not help mentioning to them all the wonderful things David had bought her.

Some congratulated her, but she knew that out of earshot they would maliciously conjure up her past. Even her mother only grudgingly admitted that she seemed to have cast aside her wildness and appeared content in the role of mother and housewife.

Yvonne pulled out the plug and the water gurgled down the drain. She removed her apron, put it with the next day's washing and joined David and the girls.

She sat cross-legged on the bottom of the the bed, half listening to David reading a story while glancing through a woman's magazine he had bought her. She knew he was still trying to steer her from her picture love-stories.

When Thelma's head finally drooped on her father's shoulder, he got up and cradled her in his arms while Yvonne quickly prepared the bed. Shirley climbed into her upper berth. Cynthia, with blankets to her chin, wanted to read in bed. At eight she was a good reader.

"You'll have to switch off the light when done."

"I will, Daddy," she promised.

David and Yvonne kissed the children in turn and retired to their room. Yvonne collapsed into bed. David went to his wardrobe. After briefly rummaging in it he casually tossed a slab of chocolate at Yvonne's feet. She gave a squeal of delight and sat up. Mouth full of chocolate, she kissed him. Lazily she broke off a strip. "Open your mouth."

While she leaned back against the cushion, contentedly savouring the chocolate, he slipped into bed next to her. She rested her hand on his head, fingers caressing his ear. He stirred impatiently under her touch, then got up. He lifted one side of the curtain covering the window. It was peaceful outside. The lane was clear of people, with light shining from all the windows in view.

He turned from the window, picked up a book, flipped its pages, then replaced it on the table.

Yvonne watched him, an amused smile on her face.

"What's the matter? Why so restless? A few moments ago you were so happy to be home. Now you act like a tom cat itching to go on the prowl. Is it impossible for you to be with us all evening when you off on a Friday?"

He gave a self-conscious laugh but avoided her eyes.

"Why don't you get into bed? It look like rain coming. Tell you what," she smiled seductively, "you come to bed and I give you a treat. I'm in the mood."

24

The front gate squeaked loudly before he could reply. He hastily moved towards the window.

"It's Terence," he said almost gaily.

The door opened and a moment later Terence joined them. "Good evening, Mr and Mrs Patterson," he said breezily. "And how are you this fine and frosty Friday evening?"

Yvonne smiled at him while David looked at him inquiringly.

"Have you been over to Eddie's place?"

"Yes, I've just come from the Williams's residence. The court is in session. Charley and Steward are there, and the court clots are in attendance as usual."

"What's that suppose to mean?" Yvonne asked.

"That some of Eddie's workmates have turned up and brought liquor with them. The people's wine. It looks as if they're in for an evening of stultification. That's why I left after the first drink."

"I'll just go over for a little while," David said casually.

Yvonne flashed him a quick glance. "You better take the key with you," she said tartly. "I know all about your little while. I'm not going to get up and unlock the door for you. Terence can go out by the back later."

"Terence, you sure you don't want to go back with me?" David tried.

"No, thanks. They were playing dominoes when I left. Dominoes, drunks and dumb talk is too deadly a combination for me. I'd rather sit here and exchange gossip with Yvonne."

"But there's nothing to drink."

"Not to worry," Terence said, producing a half-jack of gin. "I haven't forgotten my Girl Guide training."

"Don't you get my woman drunk," David joked.

"That shouldn't bother you. I'm perfectly harmless."

They joined in laughter.

"Let me go and face what you escaped from," David said as he left Yvonne and Terence, without saying goodbye to either of them.

He closed the gate behind him and walked up the lane. Two dogs were frenetically barking at a man with a stumbling gait coming towards him. He waited until the man was almost abreast of him before greeting him. The man responded with a loud belch.

David eased his leg over the wire fence around Eddie's yard and entered the house through the kitchen. Steward, Charley and two strangers were seated on the couch in the lounge. Eddie and another stranger sat at the table, facing a circle of glasses which Eddie was filling from a demijohn of white wine.

"I was just going to send one of the kids to call you," Eddie said as David entered.

Eddie introduced David to his friends. From the way they reacted, David surmised that Eddie must have told them earlier that he was a writer. He resented Eddie always doing that. More often than not, it created a barrier between him and others. But he said nothing, just nodded.

Eddie passed the glasses around and one of the strangers said, "Cheers, Mr Patterson."

David winced as he swallowed the wine.

"Where do you get that mister business from?" Eddie asked the speaker before David could respond to the toast. "There're no such things as misters here. He is David and you're Tommy and I'm Eddie."

David felt that Eddie's remarks were made not to put his friends at ease but to make it clear that there would be no special form of address for him.

The voices got louder as the night stretched, David's as loud as the rest. The demijohn was drained and replaced by a full one. Eddie's wife Rebecca, dressed in a lurid pink nightgown, showed her displeasure by entering the room occasionally to glare at them. "You are disturbing the neighbours," she would shrilly point out before disappearing into an unlit bedroom. Of Eddie and Rebecca's three sons there was no sign or sound.

When the game of dominoes was resumed, Charley made his contribution by bellowing out the words of a song.

Earlier Steward had removed himself to a corner of the room where he was listening to the old wireless in the corner. He was trying to get some comfort from a Mozart piece for strings that was being broadcast. He glared his annoyance every time a domino was slammed onto the table.

Almost at midnight, with repeated loud good nights and a promise that they would get together again the following week, Eddie's workmates departed.

Steward, who had switched to another station, was now listening to a jazz composition by the Modern Jazz Quartet.

Charley lay sprawled on the couch.

"Let's pull out the couch," Eddie suggested.

"I'm not going to stay over," David replied, remembering Yvonne's offer. "I'll just stay a little longer, then push for home."

"What about you, Steward?"

"I'm staying. There's no chance of getting a bus from Bridgetown to Wynberg this late."

A relative quiet settled on Eddie's place.

"Give me a hand with the corpse," he said as he took hold of Charley's shoulders. "I want to turn the couch into a bed for the two of you."

Charley came to life – a robot switched on. "Come'n, you hounds. Let's talk," he announced. "But first let's have a drink."

David stumbled his way home.

He swore as he struggled with the key, and then swore again as he skinned his knuckles. He stumbled towards the back. He bumped his hip against the refrigerator on his curving path through the darkened kitchen.

He switched on the light in the bedroom. Yvonne did not stir. He stared at himself in the mirror. His hair was dishevelled, his eyes mere slits. He grinned crookedly at the message scrawled in lipstick across the mirror.

I left you a nightcap.

Terence

A red arrow pointed in the direction of the bottle on the dressing table.

David uncorked the half-jack and drained what could have been a shot of gin. His lips puckered at the bitter burn. Slightly shivering, he undressed and dropped his clothes on the floor.

He moulded his naked body around Yvonne's sleeping form, slipped his hands inside her nightdress and fondled her breasts. He continued caressing her until her nipples stood taut under his fingertips. Like a cat she stretched herself and turned towards him. "What kept you so long?" she murmured as their lips met.

4

"What are your plans for today?" Eddie asked, squinting at Steward through a haze of cigarette smoke. It was Saturday morning and they were sitting in Eddie's lounge.

"I'm going through to town. There's a new exhibition on at the Argus Gallery. I was at the opening but you could hardly take it in then. Also, I'm meeting Virginia Metcalf at the Gallery. I said I'd be there at about 11.30."

"Is that another of your white friends?" Eddie asked, his voice edged with sarcasm.

"Yes, that's right. It's another of my white friends."

"Do they ever visit you at your place?"

"Sometimes."

"How come you never bring them along to visit us?" The sneer on his face broadened. "Or are we not good enough because we're not artists?"

Steward ignored the jibe. Eddie resented most of them for being creative and taking their artistic capabilities seriously. Eddie was frustrated with himself. He had a flair for drawing, but he insisted that any schoolboy could draw just as well. Charley was the only one safe from Eddie's tongue. Nothing would be coming from him, it seemed, because of the way he abused liquor to escape having to put down his poems on paper. As for Terence, Eddie showed him an almost affectionate contempt and delighted in mimicking his postures and affected speech.

Eddie's flow of reproach would certainly increase now that Steward was seriously working at his drawings, encouraged by David. David was supportive of anyone who displayed artistic merit. Before he came to live in Bridgetown, Eddie had always assumed leadership of the group. But David's arrival had changed all that. It was David's idea that they should hold discussions, not only on art but any topic of interest – politics, film, music, history . . .

Steward smiled to himself. Their discussions reached no great intellectual heights, but their intelligence made the talks stimulating enough.

It was David as well who had instigated the impromptu parties for which they had now acquired a reputation. Taking them to Cape Town to a shebeen run by a friend of his had brought an end to their earlier Saturday afternoon talk-and-drink sessions at Eddie's place.

David was the main target of Eddie's castigation. It galled him that David had taken over the group without even noticing the effect on the members. Now that some of David's short stories had been published in the *Argus* and *Cape Times* magazines, the cancer of envy gnawing at Eddie's soul would probably intensify . . .

"Charley and myself are going to town," Eddie interrupted Steward's thoughts. "Where do you want to meet us? I can't see us marching from gallery to gallery in search of culture."

"What's this about culture?" Charley asked entering the room.

"Hell, Charley," Eddie said with relief. "I was afraid that you'd taken up residence in my toilet."

"No fear of that. The place's too awful. What's all this talk about culture?"

"I intend doing the rounds of the galleries in town," Steward replied. "Eddie said that culture is not for the two of you."

"Eddie's right," Charley joked. "Galleries are filled with white man's culture. Coloured culture comes in bottles."

Dragging her feet, Rebecca came into the room. With her back against the frame of the bedroom door she asked Eddie for money. The boys wanted to go to the cinema later, and she would like them to have a little extra to buy some sweets as well.

Eddie reluctantly gave her the money. "Isn't it enough that I'm paying for their tickets? Must I feed them too? Why not ask me for bus fare as well?" he barked and turned to Steward and Charley. "Let's go over to David before I go bankrupt."

David had finished his breakfast by the time they arrived.

From the front room Ravel's *Bolero* evoked a gypsy woman dancing, her skirt flared above her knees. The music climaxed in a crescendo of drum beats just as they entered the kitchen. Not completely surprised, Steward noticed the glass of Tassenberg next to David's plate.

At times Steward felt close to David, and they would have long discussions about their work. But David never really opened up completely. David was a puzzle to him. One moment he was filled with the fervour to write, and Steward would be amazed at the animation with which he spoke of a story he was working on. The next instant he would either call writing so much intellectual crap, or else insist that it was just a matter of luck that he was able to put down emotions and experiences in words. And then the constant drinking . . .

David indicated seats and pointed at the glasses lining the kitchen dresser.

"Bernstein's doing Ravel proud. He certainly knows the score, and that for an American," Eddie said to parade his knowledge.

The statement was made in a tone stamped with finality.

"You mean it's surprising that an American should be a first-rate conductor?"

"That's right, David. What do Americans know about classical music?"

"You're being damn presumptious!"

"Not at all. Have the Americans produced the likes of a Beethoven, a Mahler, a Verdi?"

"That's crap! South Africa hasn't produced anyone either but that doesn't mean that South Africans or Americans are ignorant when it comes to classical music. Just because America hasn't yet produced a Beethoven, it doesn't mean that America cannot produce first-class composers and conductors."

Neither of them know enough about the merits and demerits of American conductors to come to a conclusive understanding, Steward thought to himself. It was just one more pointless argument between David and Eddie.

"Is Yvonne at the back?" he asked David.

"No. She went to the butcher. But she'll be home soon. Thelma and Shirley went with her."

Eddie, smouldering, grabbed a chair and sat himself down in the doorway with the sleeve of a record, absorbed in the notes on the back.

"Are you going to town with us, David?" Charley ventured.

"I have to go. Who else's going to look after you?" David joshed him. "You know you're a farm boy. The guys in town will have a ball working you over." He smiled good-heartedly. "We can push as soon as Yvonne gets back. I don't know about Terence."

David walked to the kitchen window and called Cynthia. "Darling, run up to Uncle Terence and tell him that we're going to town, and that he must hurry if he's going with us."

"Do we have to wait for Auntie Terence?" Eddie asked in annoyance.

The front gate squeaked before anyone could respond, and Yvonne, preceded by Thelma and Shirley, came up the cement pathway. Eddie rushed forward to relieve Yvonne of her parcels.

"Daddy, Daddy," Thelma piped. "I carried the cabbage all the way from the shop." She turned towards her mother.

"Yes, Thelma. You did."

David, without getting up from his chair, hoisted her shoulder-high and planted a kiss on her lips.

"You're all grown up. I think one of these days you could do the shopping on your own."

Thelma crowed with delight. When her feet regained the ground, David picked up his glass. "You know what I'm going to do?"

She shook her head.

"I'm going to let you have a sip of my wine."

The five-year-old looked at her mother. Hearing no objection, she eagerly turned with parted lips. David raised the glass.

Thelma's lips pulled back at the tart taste of the Tassenberg. "I don't like it," she wailed. "It's not nice."

They all laughed at her discomfort and David took five cents from his pocket and placed it in her hand. "Ask Shirley to go with you and buy sweets. It should taste better than the wine."

Shirley, on hearing her name, hurried to her father's side. David produced another five cents and gave it to her.

"She didn't drink the nasty wine," Thelma protested.

"It doesn't matter. Everybody has the same rights. If I give you money then Shirley must also get some."

"But Shirley didn't drink the wine . . ."

David turned Thelma around and lightly slapped her on the buttocks. "Run along before I change my mind and take my money back."

She scampered ahead of Shirley, already loudly arguing over what she was going to buy.

"How long do we have to wait before Terence makes up his mind?" Eddie growled.

"We don't have to wait any longer," David replied. "Here he comes."

"Hi," Terence greeted them. "What's the rush? I haven't had any breakfast yet."

"We're leaving," Eddie replied. "You can have your breakfast, and if you still feel like coming to town with us, you'll know where to find us."

Terence sat down and pulled at the crease of his trousers, which stood out like the blade of a knife. He shaped his face into a non-committal mask and spoke in an affected voice:"Eddie, my dear, don't let me delay you one instant from swilling at the trough of the tavern of your choice. Depart, and perchance when we meet once more you will be in your cups and in a more amenable mood."

"Go get stuffed!"

"I think I'll find myself more charming company," Terence said and walked to the kitchen.

"Come'n, let's go," Charley urged, quiet till now.

In the few seconds of silence that followed, Terence could be heard complimenting Yvonne in the kitchen.

"Yes," agreed David. "I think we should leave."

The three made an odd combination as they walked down the lane, David in front, flanked by Eddie and Charley.

Yvonne, watching them through the kitchen window, felt a momentary pang of regret at David's lack of inches. Eddie was a head taller than him, and Charley towered over both. Then she comforted herself with the thought that despite his diminutive stature, he was the one who led, while others followed.

She went to the lounge. Sitting next to him on the couch, Cynthia was shyly discussing with Terence a book on ballet which she had brought from the library. On one of the kitchen chairs, Steward sat sipping the coffee she had poured for him, looking at her attentively.

She knew that he was very much drawn to her, and perhaps secretly in love – a fact he would probably not admit to himself.

"You still planning to have a exhibition?" she asked, returning his intense look.

"I don't know, Yvonne. I've done quite a lot of work but I don't think it's any good. David gets all excited about it, but then he doesn't know much about art."

She recalled the drawings he had shown her. She was moved by his depictions of people in slum areas, but she would have been unable to tell him why she liked them. If pressed, she would have said that they appealed to her because the subjects were close to her, so real, almost like people she knew.

She smiled encouragingly.

"I'm taking the stuff to the Argus Gallery this morning. I'm meeting someone." In response to her raised eyebrows, he continued: "Virginia Metcalf. You don't know her. She wants me to show the drawings to the owner. She thinks he'll be impressed."

"I'm sure he'll like it." She turned to something more in her line. "You had something to eat?"

Steward shook his head.

"I fix something for you." She left him seated in the front room and went into the kitchen.

"Terence," she called. "I suppose you want to eat as well?"

"Yes, darling. Thanks."

Later, Yvonne watched Steward as he ate. His smooth, brown face was without a line of worry. His hair was neatly brushed back, his eyes calm and withdrawn. The hands holding the knife and fork were square, the fingernails trimmed.

The Royal Crown was crowded. Drinkers stood two deep around the counter and all the small tables scattered around the bar were occupied. The hum of voices created a deep drone.

They forced their way to the counter and each ordered a pint of Lieberstein. "And a bottle of beer!" David added.

Holding their glasses close to their chest, they edged their way free and found a place against the front wall. There they squatted with their glasses, the beer protected by their angled limbs, and stared into the deep red interior of the watering hole.

Their voices automatically adjusted pitch in order to be heard above the crescendo of noise around them.

A man stopped in front of them, one hand sprouting a bunch of plastic combs, his voice a whine: "Wanna buy a comb, cheap? Only ten cents."

There was a strong odour of dried urine.

"Goddamn bum!" Eddie muttered sourly.

David looked up and studied the face. The man could have been white. He had the ruddy complexion of a farmer or a sailor. His clothes, a long army coat and faded blue jeans, looked as if he habitually slept in them. There was no collar to his shirt and his shoes, only centimetres from David's own on the grimy tiles, were cracked across the uppers.

I wonder what set him on this road? David mused. I'm sure if I got him to talk, I'd really have something to write about.

"Here," he thrust twenty cents at the vendor.

Two combs were given in return.

"They good combs."

"I don't want them. Keep them. Buy yourself a drink."

"Thanks. God look after you."

For a moment it looked as if the man would break down in tears, then he shuffled towards the counter.

"Did you have to do that?"

"Look, Eddie. No man should be made to beg. Okay, so he's a wine-swine, but that doesn't make me any better."

Charley was staring into the depths of his glass while they spoke. As if to rid himself of some unpleasant thought, he suddenly said loudly, "Come'n, finish your wine so I can order the next round."

With his second drink inside him, he announced, almost aggressively, looking at Eddie as if challenging him to dispute it: "I've been working on my poem the last few days."

Surprised, David looked at him. A glass of wine in his hand, Charley looked at them with satisfaction. He glowed with confidence. "When do you think you'll finish it?" David asked.

"I don't know. I don't work at it often enough but I'll get it done. Don't you worry. The second draft is sitting on the table in my bedroom."

Ever since David had come to know him, Charley had been working at this poem. It was an epic, he said. Inspired by some obscure battle fought by the early Boer settlers against an African tribe. David had not seen a single line of the epic.

Steward and Terence took the lift to the third floor.

The walls of the Argus Gallery were ablaze with colour, the paintings executed in bold, vivid strokes, paint smeared heavily on the canvas.

As they stopped to read some reviews pinned on a board, a middle-aged woman came up to them. Virginia Metcalf.

"Hello, Steward."

He returned her greeting and introduced Terence.

She peered at a tiny watch on her wrist: "Unfortunately, something else has come up and I'll have to leave in about half an hour. But Frank Redick's waiting for you."

Leaving Terence to peruse the reviews, she led Steward across the hall to a small office partitioned off in a corner. The partitioning was only waist-high. The office contained a desk and three chairs.

"Frank, this is Steward Thompson. He's brought the drawings I want you to have a look at." Virginia Metcalf smiled at Steward to put him at ease.

Frank Redick, after the formality of shaking hands, cleared a space on his desk and took the parcel of drawings from Steward.

Across the floor, Steward noticed, Terence had moved away and was inspecting the paintings on view.

One after the other the drawings were displayed on the desk. Finally Frank Redick placed the last one on top of the pile and leaned back in his chair, hand stroking his hair, not saying a word. His silence unsettled Steward.

"What do you think of his work?" Virginia Metcalf asked impatiently.

"Have you completed any more drawings? These are not bad. As a matter of fact, some of them are damn good. You show a good command of line in your drawings, and you've certainly captured the spirit of the characters and the scenes. Have you been working on the lino cuts for some time?"

"No, I've only recently started on them. This is all I've done so far," Steward replied, a strange tightness in his throat.

"I thought as much. You don't always pull it off. I'd suggest you work on them some more. You have the right approach, and continued practice should make you more sure of yourself. Tell you what: You do some more work, particularly drawings. Keep in touch and I'll try my best to book you when there's an opening."

It was more than Steward had hoped for, and for a moment he almost said so. But he kept his face a blank mask. "I will do that," he said.

Virginia Metcalf felt cheated by his lack of enthusiasm. "Aren't you absolutely thrilled?" she asked Steward peevishly.

He nodded his head.

"Well, I must be off." She glanced at her watch. "Come for lunch on Wednesday."

Her high heels tapped a tattoo on the tile floor as she walked out of the gallery.

"Do you think I could hold on to these over the weekend?" Frank Redick asked. "I'd like to show them to some people."

"Fine. I'll pick them up on Wednesday afternoon."

"Thanks. I'll see you here on Monday at Pamela Blake's opening."

Still not smiling or showing any emotion, Steward walked over to Terence.

"Was he impressed?" Terence demanded to know.

"He liked it."

"So?"

"He said that if I turn out more stuff then he'd book me for an exhibition."

Terence looked at Steward and touched him lightly on the shoulder. "I can just see it on the social page: 'Promising young artist has first exhibition.' They'll print your picture as well. I must wear something new that day, and stick close to you when the photographers set up their cameras."

Steward could not help feeling pleased at the scene conjured up. "I must tell Yvonne," he said. "She'll be so pleased." Then almost guiltily: "And David. I'll tell him the moment I see him."

"I wish David would drink at a more civilised place," Terence said bitingly as they passed through the swinging doors of the Royal Crown.

They hovered for a moment. When their eyes were accustomed to the gloom, they spotted David, Eddie and Charley at a table in the far corner. Several empty glasses were clustered around two empty beer bottles on the table.

David gave Steward and Terence a broad smile which Steward, after one look at David's eyes, knew could easily turn into a scowl, spelling trouble for all. Charley, Steward noticed, had reached the stage where he hovered between sobriety and inebriation, slipping from one to the other with an ease that never failed to surprise Steward. Eddie was leaning back, surveying the rest of the drinkers with smug superiority.

I can't tell David, not in front of the others, Steward thought. David did not share Eddie's snootiness or Charley's self-centredness. Instead Steward feared the exuberance he would display at the news.

"You may buy us the next round, Terence," Eddie said condescendingly. "We've run out of money while waiting for you."

"It's a pity you couldn't restrain your thirst!" snapped Terence.

"To drink. To drink," mumbled Charley before lapsing into silence.

"Buy the booze, Terence," David said, still smiling. "And cut out the crap talk!"

5

Monday evening, the Argus Gallery in Burg Street swarmed with people. Their talk was like the amplified buzzing of bees. Groups would split into smaller groups while some individuals were left stranded on the periphery. Most were dressed as if for the theatre, some of the women sporting short fur coats. They stood with practised ease, casually posed for the arrival of the society-page photographers. The long-hairs present and their female counterparts wore jeans and fisherman jerseys, their voices boisterous – casually-clad hippies who had found a haven.

David and his party were the few black islands in a sea of white.

Steward, with Terence in tow, was frequently stopped by people who wanted to know how his work was progressing.

Terence avidly lapped up the introductions, appraising the smooth faces and elegant clothes, cataloguing them for future reference – clothes a cut apart from those worn by the customers of the men's shop in Waterkant Street where he was employed as an assistant. It wouldn't be long before he launched off on his own.

As soon as they arrived, David had found himself a seat near a window. He sat there impassively, clutching a glass of wine in his hand, his mind filled with the argument he had had with Yvonne before setting out for the gallery with Steward and Terence. Over the weekend he had managed to cajole her into accompanying them. But then, shortly before they were about to leave, she had announced that she was not going. He had looked at her, restraining his rising anger.

"Why aren't you going? What has happened? Tell me what's wrong?"

"Nothing's wrong," she had said stolidly. "I'm just not going, that's all."

The more he had ranted, the more she had retreated into a shell of obduracy. His angry words had frightened only the children.

"Stupid bitch!" he said under his breath.

A woman standing nearby raised her eyebrows. She quickly turned her back on his vicious, level gaze.

David surveyed the gallery and its patrons. It was like a fashion show with each model battling for the spotlight. He turned his attention to the conversation. It sounded like an exact repeat of what people had had to say to one another at the last exhibition.

David's face pulled into a wry grin as he glimpsed a slim, short woman on the opposite side of the gallery. She was dressed in a plain black dress, her blonde hair piled high on her head, and even from this distance he could see that her face was devoid of make-up. He watched her as she moved around.

"What do you find so amusing?"

He looked at Arnold Barker and pointed his chin at the woman. "I was looking at the blonde beast."

"That's Zelda Ulrich. She's German. Deals in African art – masks and sculptures. Interesting woman. Very strong personality. I've met her on and off at exhibitions. I could introduce you to her. But then you're not very much into white females."

David clucked his annoyance. "Christ! Most of them give me the shits! They think they're doing you a favour just talking to you. And as for sleeping with them, I haven't met one yet worth going to jail for."

"But what are you doing here? I thought you'd given up going to exhibitions?"

"It was Steward's idea. I told myself I might just as well come along and finish off their liquor. Have you ever thought of writing about this set-up?" His hand made a sweeping motion. "The white social rat race!"

"I've never really given it a thought. But now that you mention it, I certainly think it has possibilities."

They were silent for a moment.

A Coloured youth bearing a tray tightly packed with wine-filled glasses stopped in front of them.

"We might just as well stock up," David said removing three glasses from the tray. He winked at the youth. "You must look after your brown brothers."

"You know then, my bra," the youth responded.

Arnold followed David's lead and added another three glasses to David's on the windowsill.

"Hey, what's this?" Terence demanded. "A covey of conspirators? Or are you just being unsociable?"

They turned to face a grinning Terence.

Arnold studied Terence's Italian-styled suit and pointed shoes. "Is it your going-to-exhibition outfit?"

"This is nothing," Terence said, waving a disparaging hand at his clothes. "I just grabbed the first old thing out of my wardrobe." He made a half-turn. "Do you think it becomes me?"

"I don't care very much for the tie," Arnold said. "It's just a little bit too loud. What do you think, David?"

Terence agitatedly stroked his tie.

David took a sip of wine, then peered at Terence through his glass. "You're absolutely right, Arnold. It doesn't strike the right balance."

"I think you're altogether wicked. Both of you," Terence giggled nervously.

"I was wondering when Ron Brink would make his appearance," David said, jerking his head in the direction of a mixed couple.

The man spoke animatedly, one hand fluttering up and down. The woman listened attentively.

37

"I wonder which suffering son of a bitch Ron Brink will produce for milady's table."

"I think you're too hard on Ron, David," Arnold objected. "He's not bad, really. He's frightfully intelligent."

"His sort of intelligence I could do without."

"Who is the woman?" Terence asked.

"Get Arnold to introduce you. He most probably knows her."

"Don't you ever let up, David?" A shade of annoyance clouded Arnold's face. "Yes, I know her."

"Come now, Arnold. Tell me, have I insulted white womanhood?"

"Go to hell! What Ron did to you, happened ages ago. Don't take it out on every white person."

"As you say, it happened ages ago. But Ron Brink hasn't changed his habits. And I'm most certainly not going to allow myself to be added to any white's collection of artistically inclined Coloureds!"

Terence, who had not dared to say a word during their exchange, nudged Arnold: "I think she's trying to get your attention."

Arnold looked at the white woman with the Coloured man at her side. She smiled at him. He placed his glass on the windowsill and walked over to them.

"That's right," David said softly. "Assure her that her white womanhood is still secure." He finished the last of his drinks. "I'm going off to my prison cell. If you people feel like coming over after this, then do," he told Terence, not even trying to conceal his anger.

He left the gallery, avoiding Arnold, Ron Brink and the white woman.

He was stopped by Steward in the passage before he could get to the lift.

"There's someone I'd like you to meet before you go."

David turned around to meet the cool gaze of the short German woman in the black dress.

"Zelda, this is David Patterson. David. Zelda Ullrich."

Her hand was even colder than her stare.

"I'm having lunch with Zelda two Saturdays from now," Steward said. "She'd like you to come as well."

David shrugged his shoulders. "I'll think about it. That's if I'm not too pissed."

She gave an amused laugh.

"I'll have to rush," David said. "I've got to go to bloody work."

Not another collector of talented Coloureds? he asked himself in the lift going down.

6

The coal-burning stove filled the kitchen with a cozy warmth. An unusual calm settled among the four people round the table.

"A kitchen with an electrical stove is cold and clinical, robbed of its homeliness," Eddie said.

David grunted in agreement, tossing a card on the table.

"Rummy!" Yvonne cried triumphantly, placing four queens, three tens, and four fours on the table.

"I'm caught without a set," Charley groaned as he handed in his cards to be counted. "This puts me out of the game."

The front door opened and a cold draught whipped through the kitchen. A short, almost plump girl entered. She placed a large bag on the floor, and in greeting kissed all the men in turn.

Yvonne's lips pulled into a thin line as the girl flung her arms around David's neck. Then she faced Yvonne. "Good evening, Mrs Patterson," she said, the words tumbling out fast. "It's my day off. Is it all right if I stay over? I only have to go back to Sea Point at four tomorrow."

Yvonne spoke slowly: "It's quite all right, Paula. Thelma can sleep with Shirley. You can have her bed."

Paula cleared the table of empty cups and put them in the sink.

"What've you got in the bag?" Charley asked.

"It's some stuff for tonight."

She opened the bag and produced a bottle of brandy, two bottles of beer, and a bottle of dry white wine which she handed to David.

"Thanks, Paula."

His hands slid up her arms, gently stroking the smooth skin.

His actions did not escape Yvonne's notice. She caught the gleam of pleasure in Paula's eyes before she lowered her eyelids.

"I also got some groceries."

Paula casually opened a cupboard door and placed a tin of cocoa, a packet of biscuits, a tin of jam and a box of cereal on the shelf, oblivious to Yvonne's eyes stabbing her in the back.

Yvonne had always hidden her dislike for Paula, suspecting that of all the girls that came to the house, Paula, in her early twenties, was the only one capable of holding her own with her when it came to men. Yvonne secretly believed that girls who worked as domestic servants were not of quite the same class as herself, a married woman who didn't need to slave in the kitchen of a white madam. Moreover, she was convinced that domestic servants were willing bed-companions of whatever male came along. Just look at Paula's behaviour!

"Thanks, Paula," she said, her voice as smooth as silk. "We don't really need it. David more than provide for this house."

"I know Mrs Patterson don't need the stuff I bring but I bring it because whenever I come here I feel as if I'm home. Besides they don't even miss it."

"Don't give up the job," Charley said. "I like the old man's taste in brandy."

"You don't have to worry about that," Paula said, laughing gaily. "I'm from the country but I'm no cabbage. I'll never take a job in a factory."

"Why not?" Yvonne asked innocently. "You be free every night."

"I know. But it means I got to pay board with the people I stay. At Mrs Barton and the colonel I get a room free and food don't cost me a cent. I even have a shower for myself and I don't have to bother about clothing as I wear an overall all the time."

"How do they treat you?" Eddie asked.

"I can't complain about the people I work for. There's only three in the family. The colonel and his wife and their daughter. She's about twenty and at varsity. It's no bother. I don't work for shit whites who think just because you Coloured they can shout you around."

Yvonne shoved the cards aside.

"I better dish up soup," she said to hide her resentment.

"No, don't get up Mrs Patterson," Paula said. "Sit down, I'll dish up." She filled five bowls, placing one in front of each of them.

"What about the children?"

"No. They gone to bioscope," Yvonne replied.

"Before I forget: I also brought them a bag of popcorn."

"Thanks," Yvonne said without much enthusiasm.

"The soup is delicious," Paula enthused. "Try as hard as I can, my soup never turn out like this, Mrs Patterson. You must show me how you do it."

Yvonne glanced at Paula's face. Who she fooling? "Yes, one day when you off then you come around and slave in my kitchen while I rest," she said, trying hard to mask the malice she felt.

"Ah," Charley grunted. "A drink would do me good after a nourishing plate of soup." He reached for the brandy. "KWV – brandy for the connoisseur. My palate's certainly being given an education with the colonel's money and selection."

"In your case," Eddie sniped, "it's an education wasted. Alcohol is alcohol to you, regardless of quality or price."

Charley swallowed slowly before replying, "Eddie, as always you're

40

right. Wine or spirits, it all serves the same purpose, and that's to get me drunk as quickly as possible and render me immune to the criticism I so richly deserve. I shall seek my salvation in a bottle. For who knows the agony of my soul?"

David understood what Charley meant. Despite the warmth in the kitchen, a chilling anxiety gripped him that one day he, too, would have to admit that he was unable to put words on paper, that he would never complete his novel. Perhaps, for him as well, in time to come, wine would become a substitute for words, and Dawn's fear of what he was doing to himself would be justified.

The raised, chirpy voices and the opening of the front door announced the arrival of the children. David was grateful. Their return at once dispelled the sombre mood Charley's words had cast him into.

"No, please, Mrs Patterson, let me wash the dishes," Paula insisted, and Eddie, with a flourish, took a drying cloth from a rack. David filled their glasses.

The dishes done, everyone moved to the front room. The rug was pushed aside, the table and chairs moved against the wall and a record put on the gram.

Yvonne pretended that she did not notice the way Paula clung to David as they danced in the darkened room.

Later, after Charley and Eddie had left and Paula had gone to sleep in the back room, Yvonne, without turning her head, whispered sharply to David, "It look as if Paula is after your blood."

She did not respond when his arms reached out for her. She kept her eyes on the ceiling instead.

7

Yvonne was shaking him by the shoulder.

"Here's a letter for you."

Confused, he lifted his head and tried to focus his sleep-flushed eyes on the oblong envelope with the multicoloured borders she was waving in front of his face.

When she was satisfied that he was awake, she handed it to him. He pushed a finger under the flap, tugged, and a sheet of paper fluttered onto the bed. He skimmed the few lines, then reread them slowly and reached for Yvonne with his right hand, pulling her onto the bed. She looked at him quizzically.

"They've accepted my story. It's going to be used in their anthology at the end of the year!"

Yvonne looked at him blankly.

"It's the one I sent to London!"

"How much they paying?"

"Twenty pound."

"How much is that?"

"I don't know. But I'm sure it's twice, or even three times more than what I get from the *Argus*."

She looked at David's radiant face.

"Then why don't you send all your stories to them?"

David sighed. "Yvonne, I wish you'd get it into your head that it's not the money," he said wearily. "The stuff I've sold to the *Argus* and *Times* is mainly crap. But this story was different. I worked very hard at it. It's the sort of thing that'll show whether I really can write."

"But you know you can," she said with a tinge of impatience. "The papers all take your stories."

"Yes, I know I can write the sort of shit they want. What I want to know is if I can write really well. I'm sick to hell of churning out stuff that people read in their shit-house and which goes down the drain with their crap. I want to write worthwhile stuff."

"You think you be able to sell worthwhile stuff?"

"Look, Yvonne, why can't you understand that the money I receive is not the most important thing when I sell a story? I want to write about things that concern us deeply, but somehow I don't have the words. I should've stayed on at school. I'm damn sorry now. Words are my tools and my tools are blunt."

"But you do write."

David lay back against the pillows. He closed his eyes and slowly opened them. He avoided looking at Yvonne who was staring at him with wide eyes.

"Yes, but it's not the kind of stories I want to write," he said staring at the sunfilter curtains that only half managed to keep out the bright morning light.

His words were wistful and she could feel his distress.

"What about your book? I don't hear you speak about it much any more."

It was in his mind to tell her of his fears, but it would be futile, so he said, "I haven't forgotten about it. It's just that it isn't coming alive for me at the moment."

"Never mind. There's always the *Argus*."

A crooked grin creased his features. "Yes, there's always the *Argus*."

"You getting up?"

"Could I first have breakfast?"

"In bed?"

"Why not? It's not every day that I'm included in an overseas anthology. If there's any wine in the house then let's drink a toast. I'd say a celebration is in order."

"Isn't it a little early for drinking?"

"Come'n, Yvonne. I don't want to fall out with people today. The world is a wonderful place. My story is going to be published. The sun is shining. And my love is a thing of fire."

"You trying to sweet-talk me?"

He looked at her as she strutted from the room. It's a pity her mind doesn't match her shape, he thought.

He had put on his shoes and trousers by the time she returned with the tray.

"I thought you going to have breakfast in bed?"

"Sorry, I had to get up. I just couldn't stay in bed any longer. Not after such good news." He had to get out and speak to someone – Dawn or Steward. They would understand.

"What about eating?"

"I'll have breakfast in the kitchen after I've washed."

"Yes, master. Can I come and scrub master's back?"

"No, madam. None of that! One scrub will lead to another, and before you know it we'll have a session."

"David Patterson, you go to hell! I wasn't thinking anything like that." She slammed the tray down on the dressing table and made for the door.

But he blocked her way and pinned her hands to her sides. "My love is truly a thing of fire!" he whispered and pressed his lips on hers. Slowly her body began to relax.

"Daddy," a voice interrupted them.

He released Yvonne and turned around. He bent down and kissed Thelma on the cheek. "Hello, darling."

"I want to say morning to Daddy but Mummy didn't want me to."

"I was still sleeping but you can say morning to me now."

"Morning, Daddy."

"Ask your mother if there's any fruit in the fridge for you. I'm going to wash."

Thelma was gone when he joined Yvonne in the kitchen.

"There's some vermouth left," said Yvonne. "Want me to pour you a glass?"

"What about yourself?"

"And who you think is going to do my work? Did you see the pile of washing in the children's room?"

He did not reply and sat down. He hurried his meal down, quickly drank the vermouth and rinsed his plate and glass. After replacing it in the green dresser with its glass partition, he paused at the bathroom door. "I'm going up to Athlone."

"Bring back something nice."

Thelma stopped him at the gate. "Take me with you, Daddy," she begged.

"I can't, darling. You must stay in case your mother needs to send someone to the shop."

Her lips rounded into a pout.

"Here's a cent," he appeased her.

Consoled by the coin, she called out after him: "Goodbye, Daddy."

Yvonne held David's letter in her hand. "David get a letter from England this morning," she announced to Christine and Cora who, like Rebecca, were neighbouring wives, all sitting with her in the kitchen. Each morning, their washing completed, the four women took turns turning their kitchen into a coffee bar while their washing fluttered on the line outside.

Yvonne looked at their faces, knowing that none of them had ever received mail from beyond the border of the Cape Province, let alone from overseas. Like her and David's, their mail usually consisted of monthly bills.

"From England?" Cora echoed.

Yvonne nodded her head. What do you think of that, Rebecca Williams? she silently challenged.

"Yes, from England. They going to put one of his stories in a book with other writers."

"That's nice," Christine commented.

"Will he get a book when it comes out?" Rebecca asked.

"They say they send him one. I'll show you when it comes."

"What's the story about?" Cora asked. "You know, I read all Mr Patterson's stories in the papers. It must be wonderful to be able to put down in words the things you see in your mind."

Yvonne hesitated. She was not quite sure of the contents of the story.

"Don't you read your husband's stories before he send it off?" Rebecca asked, casting Christine a meaningful glance.

"Of course," Yvonne snapped. "David show me all his stories the moment he finish them, and ask me what I think of it. Yes, I can remember it now. It's the one about the old man going to jail and his son go fetch him."

"He read it to us one night," Rebecca informed Cora and Christine. "Eddie don't think much of it. He say David must stop writing about Coloured people. If he must write about Coloured people, he must stop dragging in how poor we are, as if life's just one, big struggle."

"Oh, Eddie do!" Yvonne retorted. "What do Eddie know? All he know is getting up a ladder and putting a light on a pole."

"He always read the books he bring from the library," Rebecca said. "Thick ones with hard covers."

"Well, he may read books, but he don't write books," Yvonne snapped. "Anyway, those people in England don't think he mustn't write about Coloureds. They say his story is one of the best in the book."

"You must be proud of Mr Patterson," Cora said.

Yvonne favoured her with a smile.

Rebecca's pursed her lips together and glanced briefly at Yvonne's face.

"I always tell people that I know Mr Patterson," Cora said.

"David like you. He always say how nice you are to him when he passes your place. I hope you not trying to steal him away from me."

Cora gave a coy laugh.

"I think I better also start reading David's stories," Christine chimed in. "Perhaps he go for me as well."

They all laughed, except Rebecca. "I don't think David go for you. He go for the young ones," she said looking Yvonne straight in the eye.

You so right, you bitter bitch! Yvonne acknowledged to herself. Aloud she said, "I don't mind David working himself up with the little bitches. It only make it that much nicer in bed when we go it."

"I agree with you," Christine said, smiling to herself. "When my old man's already heated up, it's like when you just starting out and can't do it often enough."

Cora sat with hands demurely folded, not voicing her opinion. But Rebecca could hardly conceal her chagrin at Yvonne's refusal to be baited. "You hear what that little Harris girl been up to?" she said, selecting a fresh target.

"Which one?" Cora asked with concern.

"The younger one."

"Well, what she do this time?" Christine asked without much interest.

That's right, Yvonne noted to herself. Since you can't get your satisfaction from me, why not dig your claws into someone who is not going to fight back? Poor girl, she don't know you like I do.

David sat looking with unseeing eyes at the scenes flashing by and the passengers entering the compartment. The day had been a complete letdown. He had thought there would be some company to celebrate the good news, but in the Beverley Bar only the framed mirror had greeted him on his entry.

He hated drinking alone, so he had offered the barman a drink.

Sam was wiping a tall beer glass. "I'll have a small Torino," he answered impassively. "Thanks." He turned and poured some vermouth in a glass. "What about yourself?"

"Make mine madeira. A pint."

The wine had the colour of blood and it warmed him.

Sam allowed him to use the telephone. He dialled Dawn's number, but the conversation only added to his frustration: "Hello, Dawn?" – "David." – "Busy?" – "I won't keep you long." – "No, they've accepted my story." – "Yes, that's the one." – "The anthology is coming out at the end of the year." – "Thanks." – "You have to ring off?" – "I'll ring you tonight. So long."

It was ten-thirty on the clock mounted on the wall behind the silent barman. He would hang around a bit longer. He felt like spending some more time there, but drinking on his own did not have much appeal, so he eventually left for Wilton's Corner Shop and bought the girls some chocolate bars and sauntered back home.

Thelma, as usual, had been the first to waylay him.

"What did Daddy bring me?" she asked, eyeing the small plastic bag swinging from his hand.

"Am I supposed to have brought you anything? I remember giving you a cent before I left."

"But that was this morning, Daddy."

"You mean every time you see me, I've got to give you something? Well, I think you'd better grow up quickly and find yourself a boyfriend who will spend all his money on you."

"I don't want a boyfriend. Daddy's my boyfriend."

The thought had amused him.

Shirley and Cynthia had already arrived back from school and were sprawled across their beds in the back room, Shirley reading a comic and Cynthia *Black Beauty*.

A quiet surging went through David as he recalled how absorbed Cynthia had been in her book. She hadn't noticed him until the bar of chocolate had landed next to her on the bed.

Sitting in the train, he smiled again at the thought of his bookworm daughter. He defended Cynthia whenever Yvonne scolded her for burying her nose in a book and not helping with the household chores.

The train jolted to a halt in Cape Town Station. Crossing the empty Grand Parade, David glanced up at the clock in the tower of the City Hall. Quarter to seven. It was going to be a long night.

He could not rid himself of his despondency as he walked up Church Street and turned into Burg Street. The streets were almost deserted in the early evening. Only a few office cleaners were still scrubbing doorways, saying goodbye to late workers as they deftly twirled their wet mops around. David looked at a departing car and imagined the two men stopping at a bar before going home. It made him even more depressed.

He phoned Dawn the moment he sat down in front of the switchboard.

"I'm sorry, David," she apologised. "I couldn't speak to you longer this morning, but I did intend phoning you later this evening."

"That's all right. I thought you'd lost interest in me."

"What brings on this little-boy-lost act? You sounded on top of things earlier."

"I'm sorry, Dawn. It's just that it turned into such a helluva let-down. You know how it is with Yvonne. I can't seem to get through to her any more."

"It really was impossible for me to speak to you this morning. I had a pile of books to sort out. And, of course, one girl had to take sick today! Congratulations. I knew they would take it. I think it's one of the best pieces you've written so far."

"Do you really think so?"

He needed reassurance because the novel wasn't going anywhere. In the meantime, he'd started on a new story. He'd toyed with the idea of putting some stories together for a collection. He had three in draft form but it would take him some time to complete them, and was not sure whether they would match the one in the anthology. He confessed to Dawn. "I guess I was lucky with that one."

"I wish you'd come off it. You've written a very fine story, and it's up to a publisher to decide if the rest of the stuff is of the same calibre. You can't deny that your writing has improved a great deal since you started out. Your first stories in the *Argus* and *Times* four years ago had only one thing to recommend them: the authenticity of their setting. But you've gone beyond that. You're not writing sketches any more. You're showing that you're capable of developing characters, not just depicting a situation. And your feeling for words is much better."

"I'm not so sure of that. There are so many things I want to say but I don't have the words to say them with. Sometimes, when I think of writing,

I get scared. I read Dostoevski or Shakespeare and I get drunk on it. Then I read my own stuff and I feel like vomiting. I wonder why I still try."

"You keep on trying because no matter how much you doubt yourself, it is something you can't stop yourself from doing! If you'd stop worrying about your background, your lack of schooling, and concentrate on your writing, you'd see that in the end those things are not so important. You're certainly not the first writer to emerge from a slum. Think of Genet. Stop fretting about your past, use it. Put it into writing."

"Jesus, Dawn. What am I going to do when you get married?"

To change the subject, she asked, "Did you and Steward go to the exhibition on Monday?"

"Yes. Terence went with us."

"Anyone else turn up that I know?"

"I've told you about Arnold Barker. We stood around discussing the set-up and decided to each write a story with the exhibition as background. That's the one I'm working on now. I'll let you have the first draft as soon as it's finished. Oh yes, and dear old Ron Brink pitched up as well. Pimping, as usual."

"The two of you still at odds?"

"I've not spoken to him since he took me to Colin Ashworth's party. I don't think I'll ever forget ..."

"Sorry, David," Dawn interrupted him. "I have to ring off. My date has arrived to take me to the flick. I can hear him hooting. My father doesn't like him, so he has to hoot and wait outside."

"Your father doesn't seem to like any ..."

"Let's not get into that again. I may ring you when I get back. So long."

David listened to the drawn-out purr on the line for a while, then pulled out the cord and let it drop into its socket on the switchboard. The memory of Colin Ashworth's party flooded back into his head.

The room was huge. All of his own house in Bridgetown – two tiny bedrooms, dining-living room, kitchen, minute bathroom – would easily fit into it. After a bewildering while he eased himself onto the couch and surveyed the place: a lush cream carpet underfoot, the end wall covered with a large tapestry and paintings, gilt-framed mirrors on the facing wall.

Enormous as the room was, it could not contain the many people crowding into it and they spilled back into the passage. Someone nearly knocked an ivory carving from its pedestal near the door.

He gave what he hoped was a polite smile when a woman squeezed in next to him on the couch. Her thigh pressed against his. He wanted to edge his leg away, but that would be too obvious, so he shifted his haunches to raise himself.

She turned to him and smiled. "Don't get up, please. I know it's a bit of a jam but we should manage."

He remained seated but shifted his body. "It's my fault," he said. "I'm taking up too much space."

"It's kind of you to say that, but I'm afraid it's my fault really." She patted her hips.

David nodded his head as if to assure her that he also had his troubles with a body that was not always what he would have liked it to be.

"Quite a crowd."

"Yes," he replied.

"I wonder what's happened to the drinks? Have you been served?"

"No."

"Hold onto my seat and I'll see what I can do about it."

He changed his position and spread his legs so that he occupied his neighbour's space as well as his own.

For the first time he had a proper look at the people in the room. The women outnumbered the men. And the women were all white. Of the men only four, including himself, were not white. He knew Ron but not the other two.

Although everybody spoke the same language, he felt a stranger amongst strangers: his colour set him apart.

His eyes searched the room for Ron. He needed some assurance.

He spotted him just before the crowd engulfed him again. As always, Ron was dominating the conversation, the centre of attention. He envied Ron for his calm, cool manner, his ability to mix, seemingly without any restraining thoughts about his colour. He admired his talent to bridge the divide as if there was none at all.

His envy, at that stage, was without malice. He was hoping that with time he would acquire a similar smoothness of manner and be forever rid of the unease he felt in white circles.

The room was loud with speech. He could not distinguish individual voices. The gruffer tones of the men merged with the shriller pitch of the women, and above the roar, like clanging cymbals, female laughter. Snatches of conversation came to him like so many broadcasts from different radio stations.

"Jack's done it again!" Laughter. "Would've thought he had more sense." Sniggering. "Going to Margo's place on Friday?" "Yes, darling." "Who will she have on show this time?" "God alone knows!" "Bet it'll be another genius with talents only Margo can detect." "You going?" "No, thanks – not that hard up for a meal."

He felt a tightness in his chest. Was this what he was up against? How would he find his way in this jungle of polished manners and sharp tongues?

Ron had insisted that he come along to celebrate the publication of Colin Ashworth's new book, his third. Critics had hailed it as a new direction in South African writing. Fiction in a similar vein to that of the new Latin American writers. A South African Gabriel Garçia Marques.

David knew the writing. He had become an admirer of Ashworth's with the publication of his first book and had read everything he had written since. But he wanted to back out when Ron told him that he would be meeting the author.

"Look, David," Ron had said, "I went to the trouble of getting you an invitation to the party so that you could meet Colin Ashworth. It's about time that you start meeting other writers and going to places."

So he went, and was introduced as soon as he and Ron Brink stepped into the intimidating room. "Colin, this is David Patterson," Ron had said. "He swears by you as a writer."

David stiffly put out his hand to take that of a guy a head taller than himself. "How do you do?" he said, hating himself for the conventional inanity.

"Good to meet you. Ron tells me that you also write, David. Would you let me have a look at some of the stuff you've done?"

He looked into a pair of understanding blue eyes, a choking heat engulfing him. "Yes ... yes," he had stammered.

"Excuse me for a moment." And Colin Ashworth left them to welcome a couple he obviously knew well.

Ron greeted several other people as they crossed the room, repeatedly stopping to speak to someone before passing on. Somewhere in the centre of the room he got separated from Ron and made for the couch.

"A drink?"

Startled, he reached for a glass of sherry. Doing so, he glimpsed a bare bosom. He blinked and stared. Never before had he seen breasts so temptingly displayed. But the woman sedately moved to the next person without so much as a glance in his direction.

He looked with fresh interest at the women in their revealing dresses with low neck-lines. They belong on a cinema screen, he decided. Their chatter provided the script.

One woman in particular intrigued him. He kept losing and finding her in the shifting pattern of the crowd. She was no longer young but a regal bearing compensated for her lost youth. She could play the part of a queen or a duchess. The game of watching her delighted him and he pursued it in earnest, counting how many times he could find her before finally losing her.

But he became aware of someone looking at him. Guiltily, like a small boy caught eyeing forbidden things, he raised his head.

It was the woman who earlier on had offered to get him a drink. She was approaching with a tray on which she was balancing a plate of snacks, a bowl of nuts and two glasses of red wine.

He jumped to his feet.

"Please, sit down," she said after making herself comfortable, moving her body to make space for him. "I've brought us something to nibble on. I don't think you've had anything to eat since you arrived. I see you've got yourself a drink, at least. Oh well, you can have this one, too."

"No, thank you."

"Do have it," she urged. "Besides, I've been here longer than you."

He took the second drink, carefully placing his empty glass on the side of the tray.

"What do you do?"

The friendliness of her smile soothed his wariness. "I write. At least, I try to."

"Have you had anything published?"

"Six stories." He stopped, dismayed at the schoolboy eagerness he was displaying.

"Where were they published?" she prompted.

"Locally." He rattled off the titles.

"Wait a minute. I think I've read all of them. They were used in the *Argus*, weren't they? I loved them. So you're David Patterson," she said nodding slowly.

A glow of warmth swept over him. She remembered the name of the writer!

"'The Char's Birthday Wish' and 'The Golden Penny' were my favourites. I always thought those stories couldn't have been written by a white man. They were too authentic, too close to the heart." She touched him lightly on the shoulder. "You know what I mean. I must say it's a pleasure meeting you after enjoying your stories so much." She held out her hand. "I'm Margo Pearce."

He gingerly wrapped his hand around hers. It was soft to the touch. Could she be the same Margo who invited the dullest people to her dinner parties?

As if to confirm it, she said, "You must come to dinner at my place. There we could have a proper talk. I'd like you to meet some people," and she mentioned a few names – writers, artists, a sculptor. People Ron had talked about. Names that were not too well-known yet but who would be in time.

He burst out laughing at the thought of the conversation he had overheard earlier. How wrong those two women must be. If these people Margo Pearce had just mentioned were dull, then the company those two moved in must be the wittiest and most talented in the land.

Margot Pearce gave him a puzzled look. "Is it so funny, my asking you to dinner?"

"No, it's not that. I'm sorry. I just thought of something someone had said." He imagined the dinner would be served in a big house, at a long table covered with starched white damask on which would be arrayed costly chinaware and heavy silver cutlery.

He smiled to himself. When he and Yvonne had stayed with his mother after their marriage, dinner was always served in the kitchen. Only on religious holidays did they eat in the dining room.

"When would you be able to come? Would next Friday do? I could arrange for someone to pick you up. Or, if you prefer, you could come out by bus. I live in Three Anchor Bay. St John's Road. You can't miss it. It's a small house with a block of flats on either side."

He searched for an excuse. There was a difference between a big party like this and a sit-down dinner. At a party there is the safety of numbers. You can withdraw into yourself and be lost in the crowd, but a dinner party would be more intimate. Would he know what to do? What if he should choose the wrong spoon or fork? Would they laugh at his ignorance outright or cover it with their talk? Both ways would be painful for him. No, it would be best to refuse the invitation.

But he hesitated. He very much wanted to be in the company of the people she had mentioned. He needed to mix with those with the same yearnings as himself.

He looked up to see Ron briefly waving at him from across the room, before being swept up in the crowd again. He felt reassured. He would go.

"It would be less bother if I came by bus." He hoped he sounded firm.

"It's no bother, David."

"I'm sure I'd be able to find the place on my own, Mrs Pearce."

"I shall be very angry if you don't call me Margo. Everyone else does."

He rolled the name on his tongue a few times, savouring it before saying: "Margo."

"Margo, dear. I don't think I've been introduced to your friend."

A tall, slender young man hovered in front of them. A study in black and white. Dark hair brushed flat against the skull contrasted sharply with a pale face. Black eyes glowed under dark eyebrows. He sported a black suit, white shirt and pencil-slim black tie.

"Edward, meet David Patterson. He's going to be a first-rate writer. Remember I'm the one who told you." She turned to David. "David, this is Edward Blakely."

The name and face were familiar. Then he remembered: Blakely was a member of the Progressive Party. Again he felt that awkwardness when he shook hands.

"David's coming to dinner next Friday. You're still coming, aren't you?"

"Of course, Margo." Then to David: "Would you excuse us for a minute? I'd like to introduce Margot to some people."

"Not at all." David felt bold enough to add: "Then I'll see you next Friday, Margo."

"Yes, and do bring some of your work."

He leaned back and took a deep breath. Doubt washed over him. Would she have asked him to dinner had he not been the writer of the stories she had found enjoyable? How would she have reacted had he told her otherwise? The doubt resurrected old doubts he had done his best to bury. These people, Ron had assured him, made no fuss about the colour of one's skin, accepting one for what one was. But were they really so open or was it a pose they assumed?

"Do you intend sitting on this couch for the rest of the evening?" Ron demanded. "What's happened to Margo? I saw her speaking to you a little while ago."

He got to his feet. "She left with another chap, Edward Blakely, who said that there were some people who wanted to meet her."

"Oh, Edward. Looking like a corpse with his pale face and black eyes. What do you think of Margo?"

"She seems to be quite nice. She's ..."

"I know. She's invited you to dinner. She fancies herself as a patron of the arts. She should've lived in the eighteenth century, then she could've turned her house into a salon. At least you are making progress. It's about time that you crawl out of your shell, David. It's at parties like these that you meet people, important people. People who can help you a lot if you go about it the right way."

He did not reply, silently wondering what the right way was.

He was not sure whether he should be grateful to Ron. Until nine months before, Ron had scarcely spoken to him. Although they sometimes hung around the same crowd, Ron had never introduced him to any of the white friends he spoke of so intimately and who regularly featured in the social pages of the local papers. It was the publication of 'Barrow Boy's Moon' that had brought about the change.

"I've read your story," Ron had said the next time he had met him with Steward at the Artists' Gallery in Adderley Street. "It's not a bad effort. Is it your first?"

"No, it's not. I've written several stories but it's the first one to be published."

"Why all the secrecy? Why didn't you tell me before that you're writing? I could've introduced you to some people if I'd known. Influential people. Established writers."

With a second and third story published, he had found himself among the select few that Ron favoured. Suddenly Ron urged him to accompany him to parties and exhibitions. "Come along with us tomorrow night," he would insist on the phone. "Tom Hopkirk is having a party at his place in Devil's Peak."

"No!" David would reply.

The idea of mixing socially with whites had filled him with dread. But the more Ron spoke of the parties he had been to and the people he had met, the weaker David's resistance had become. He had finally capitulated when Ron told him about Colin Ashworth's invitation.

"Let's join the others," Ron now urged.

"No. I'll sit here a little longer, if you don't mind. Perhaps Margo will come back and we can continue our talk."

He felt pathetically grateful to Margot for her friendliness and to Colin Ashworth for the understanding he had shown.

Ron shrugged his shoulders and moved away.

Another woman sank down beside him. It was the "duchess".

She gazed at him as if he was some curio. She lacked only a lorgnette. When finally she spoke, her voice was cool and condescending: "Tell me, what do you do?"

"Do?" He felt an instant dislike.

"Yes."

"I work in an office. I'm a messenger."

"I don't mean the type of work," waving it aside as if it was a distasteful object. "Do you paint or write? I can be very helpful if I like what you do."

"Neither!"

"Come, now. I bet that isn't true. The others do either one or the other."

There was no need to ask who the others were. And it was clear that she was one of the "influential people" Ron had boasted about.

"I've told you the truth. I don't do a thing." He was not worried about deceiving her. It would be just too bad if she were to check with Ron. She was not going to add him to her collection.

"You don't paint and you don't write and you're a messenger?" Her eyes and voice jabbed at him.

"That's right."

"Then what are you doing here?"

"The same thing you're doing." His dislike for her strengthened him, stilled his trembling. "I'm here because I was invited."

"I don't want any of your damn cheek," she said, her voice jumping several octaves.

People seated to the left of David on the couch, and those nearby, turned and stared. A horrified Ron pushed his way towards them.

"What is the matter, Mrs Meredith?" His voice dripped with concern. "What has happened?"

"I've been insulted by this impertinent messenger boy!" she said, pointing a trembling finger at David.

Ron faced him. "Get up and apologise, David," he commanded.

He stared at Ron whose composure was crumbling with the effort to placate Mrs Meredith. David felt sick. Ron had betrayed him! Then his unease gave way to anger. She would have accepted me if I'd told her that I'm a writer, he thought, and Ron, without bothering to find out what's been going on, has taken her side.

His admiration for Ron turned to contempt. He realised then why Ron had been so ingratiating. His talent, and that of the other "painters" and "writers" was on display for Mrs Meredith and her kind. And Ron was their pimp, without compunction procuring virgin after virgin for their inspection.

To walk in the shade of a Mrs Meredith and other "influential people", Ron had snubbed him, denying that he was one of them. He had always envied Ron for his ability to converse and move with ease among white society. Not any more.

His anger had sent a rush of blood to his head, making speech impossible. He had got up from the couch and blindly pushed his way through the animated crowd.

"Damn pimp!" he now said angrily, glaring at the mocking eyes of the round sockets of the switchboard.

8

David glanced at the City Hall clock as it sounded two o'clock. On a Saturday afternoon Cape Town's business centre quickly acquired the forlornness of a sport stadium deserted of players and spectators, with only debris left behind.

The stall-keepers on the Grand Parade were clearing away the remains of their wares – fruit, vegetables, dried herbs, samoosas, cooldrinks – and locking up. As their vehicles moved away, the large square near the station was emptied of the last signs of life.

Long lines of people stood at the bus stops bordering the Parade. Coloureds leaving Cape Town for their weekend stay in the townships.

David joined a waiting circle.

An elderly African man in a tight black jacket, striped trousers and grimy white shirt with frayed collar was pleading with his listeners to cast aside the materialism of the world and work for spiritual wealth in God's Kingdom. Tiny froth bubbles edged the corners of his mouth. His listeners looked at him blankly, not bothering to interject even when his exhortations became a loud shriek.

The man's seemingly pointless preaching embarrassed David. Why the hell doesn't he stop? Nobody's a damn interested in what he has to say. David stopped to buy a bag of fruit at one the mobile fruit stalls at the bus stop.

"Return to the Lord," the preacher's voice pursued him as he crossed Adderley Street into Shortmarket Street. At Riebeek Square commercial buildings gave way to the Bo-Kaap and its terraced town houses.

Shortmarket Street, beyond Rose Street, had seen some changes since he and Yvonne had moved to Bridgetown with Cynthia and Shirley four years ago. Thelma had been born in the township. All the houses on one side of the street had been renovated while the three remaining houses on the opposite side stood looking on like poor relatives. With peeling paintwork, rusty roof plates and raw side-walls where other semis had once clung to them, they braved the wide spaces of derelict ground between them, strewn with papers and a harvest of weeds.

David stopped in front of the first of the three houses, a double-storied structure, and opened the door. The old, familiar smells enveloped him. A mustiness coming from the staircase at the end of the passage, a closeness of air which told of too many people inhabiting too few rooms. Even now that he and his two sisters had moved away, the air was still as stifling, the stale odour of countless meals fried in fat as overwhelming, the smell of dogs long unwashed as strong. The house that once had been his home.

He paused in the passage, waiting for the rush from the yard of whichever dog had grown to full size since his last visit. When no warning bark came, he continued.

His mother was in the kitchen, ironing. On the table in front of her a pile of clean clothes waited. Two old-fashioned irons were perched on a small primus stove that gave off an occasional asthmatic splutter.

He took in the Dover stove, gleaming from its weekly polishing, a bag of coal nestling under its brick stand. The kitchen dresser, bought on hire-purchase. The walls had been whitewashed, and he wondered which of his two brothers were responsible. He stood watching his mother, legs spread, her weight resting on the palms of her hands clamped to the edge of the table.

"Good afternoon, Mama."

She turned slowly. "Good afternoon, David."

He scanned her face. She seemed to have aged each time he saw her. The lines in her face were etched deeper than on his previous visit and the grey in her hair more visible. Her eyes had the rheumy look of the aged. She was still two years short of sixty.

"Where's the children?"

"They've gone to bioscope."

He hid his annoyance. He had often told her that he did not want the girls to go to the cinema when they came to visit her. He no longer approved of the bug-house the neighbourhood patronised.

"It's for you, Mama," he said, putting the bag of fruit on a corner of the table, adding a rand to it. "Is Papa home?"

"Your father's upstairs, sleeping."

He walked past her and seated himself on a low stool in the doorway. He didn't ask about his brothers. In one corner of the yard a dog's kennel had been constructed from corrugated sheet metal. A dog's collar, attached to a chain, lay next to the kennel.

"What's happened to Sally?"

"The SPCA come and fetch her. She got full of sores and her hair fall out. Willie's getting another dog on Monday."

He thought of the many dogs they had had in the past. He could still remember Rexie, the first dog he'd ever owned, not to be confused with the family dog that had belonged to everybody. He had not needed his father to tell him that nothing could be done when he'd came home from school that day. Rexie had been run over by a car. He hadn't bled much, but each time he'd taken a breath his sides had heaved convulsively and blood had trickled from his nostrils. He'd refused to leave Rexie's side, even to eat, and when Rexie had finally died, his tongue licking at his hands, David's face had been wet with tears.

"You want something to eat?" his mother asked, looking at him curiously.

"No thanks, Mama. I don't want any mince curry."

He knew she never could understand him, even as a child. She had always complained that he withdrew from the rest of the family. She was always puzzled by his fascination with books. She had once admitted that she had secretly hoped that he would become a teacher, that she could not understand why he always wanted to write down things on paper. She could not understand why he was so obsessed with something so alien to their family and to the neighbourhood. But that was long ago. Now she just searched his face every time he told her that one of his stories had been published and talked about everyday things.

"How do you know it's that?" she asked, amazed.

He pointed to a curry-coated spoon on the pot.

"I'm going to the bar. Tell the children they must be ready when I get back. I'd better leave some cigarette money for Papa."

He deposited another coin on the table.

Each street corner he passed had its congregation of youths passing their time in the usual manner. They don't ever seem to learn, he said to himself at the sight of the many girls in their early teens wearing tight skirts and breast-bulging sweaters.

He caught snatches of conversation in passing. Loose talk that revealed their knowledge of carnality. Some girls showed signs of that knowledge having been put into practice; with the boys it was not so easy to detect.

9

David was intrigued by the Victorian houses with their bay windows and broekie-lace verandas and flower-bordered lawns. He didn't often come to Tamboerskloof, and the co-existence of the elegant old houses and the square modern blocks of flats, for which some of the old structures had recently made way, always pleased him. Compared to the cramped, overcrowded townships of the Cape Flats from which he and Steward had just come, the City Bowl, even on a Saturday morning, seemed only half populated.

"Is this it?" he asked surveying the block of flats facing them. Steward answered by crossing the street and entering the lobby.

The lift deposited them on the second floor. Steward had hardly pressed the bell at number 23 before the door swung open and a short, thick-set man with a florid face confronted them.

"Miss Ulrich," Steward said, "She's expecting us."

"Ja. Come in. This way."

They followed him down a short passage into a spacious lounge. The room was like a page in a glossy magazine. David sat down on the short side of an L-shaped couch. Steward chose to study the abstract painting above the fireplace.

With a murmured apology, the man left the room.

Zelda Ulrich, dressed in black tights and sweater, glided soundlessly into the room. David glanced at her bare feet and red-coated toenails. The same colour she wore when he'd met her at the Argus Gallery two weeks before. She reminded him of a couger.

"Hello," she greeted them. "I'm glad you could come, David."

Steward shook hands with her and David gave a little wave from the couch.

"Ernst Völker," Zelda introduced the fat man when he reappeared.

The name, the accent and the handshake were unmistakeably German.

"Ernst, would you please bring in the drinks?" she asked when the formalities were completed. "Everything is on the big tray."

He returned with an enormous tray laden with some pickle dishes, three bottles and four glasses.

David was delighted by what he saw. Time and thought had obviously gone into arranging the cold meat, cheese, pickles and biscuits on the dishes. He glanced past the silver ice bucket at the lables on the three bottles. Italian vermouth, Monis Sherry and KWV Port.

"In between working for Sherman & Withers advertising agency as a copy-writer, Ernst writes," Zelda explained. "But his work is of a more scholarly nature. He's busy with a book on German theatre and playwrights at the moment."

David looked at the man with new eyes. He could have been a baker or a butcher!

"Are you familiar with German theatre?" Ernst asked him.

"I don't know very much about theatre. German or otherwise," David confessed. But he couldn't help saying: "I've read most of Shakespeare, and on the more contemporary scene I've read Miller, Tennessee Williams, John Osborne, and one or two pieces of Brecht."

"Well, then you *do* know German theatre," Zelda laughed.

"I find Brecht very exciting and I'd like to read more of his work. In translation of course."

"You know that Brecht is a communist?" Ernst observed.

"That doesn't bother me. I'm attracted by his concern with working class people. I feel his plays could have been inspired by conditions here in South Africa. And probably in any other country where there is an oppressive ruling class. But I think Brecht's plays go way beyond political pamphleteering."

"Ja?"

David wanted to smash the man's cold academic approach. "Look at us," he said, "born and bred here, but because of the colour of our skin Steward and I have fewer rights than you, a stranger in our land."

Ernst dabbed at his face with a large navy-blue silk handkerchief.

"Are you a member of a political party?" he asked.

"Since the government banned the ANC and PAC three years ago, there hasn't been any Black political party. One can hardly call the Federal Party one. In fact, very few Coloureds voted for it even though it is tolerated by the government to represent the Coloureds."

Steward had buried his head in a magazine. Zelda, trying to steer the conversation in the way she had intended it to go, said to David, "Have you tried the American market? They pay fabulously well for a story."

Confused for a moment, he shook his head.

"You should. Magazines like *Esquire*, *Playboy* and the *New Yorker*, but especially *Playboy* ... I don't as a rule read the local papers. Too parochial. Or listen to the radio, for that matter. Too much advertising. I know Ernst must earn his living, but really I find the silly little jingles very boring. However, someone showed me one of your stories the other day and I was curious enough to check the paper's back copies. Having read three of your stories, I think that you shouldn't find it difficult to sell to the *New Yorker*. You just need to develop those stories a little more."

She mentioned the name of a friend who had sold two stories to the *New Yorker*. David had read one of the stories. The characters had all been Coloured. The writer was white.

"Now, you are more intimately acquainted with the subject and I think a better writer, David."

Then Zelda proceeded to tell him that she could send off a few letters to London and West Germany if he prefered magazines of a more literary nature. She knew quite a number of important people on the top magazines. She concluded with: "A word from me could make it just that much easier for an aspiring writer to get his foot in the door."

He grunted noncommittally, concentrating on the wine in his glass. There's never an end to her sort, he thought. Important people who know important people, and always on the look-out for a Black artist to be led around by the balls so that he would forever after have to bleat his thanks to his benefactor.

"These people that you've mentioned," he asked, "do they judge work on merit or has the colour of the writer's skin become the criterion?"

A faint blush skittered across her face. "Of course," she snapped. But she quickly recovered her composure and said, evenly, "Of course they judge work on merit. But knowing the right people does facilitate matters." She smiled at David. "You must admit that getting published is the most important thing. A writer needs to communicate with an audience, or else he might as well stop writing."

A chill was settling over the luncheon. Steward's discomfort was obvious. Probably blaming himself, David thought, wondering whether he should've warned Zelda that I wouldn't accept her help. Probably petrified that I might blow my top.

He spoke deliberately slowly between sips of wine: "I've had some stories published without any strings of colour attached. I'd like to keep it that way. If I'm going to succeed, I want to make it because my writing is good, not because the market is hungry for Black writers from Africa. In any case, I can't really be classified as a Black African writer."

"Why not?" Zelda was perplexed.

"Let me put it this way: I don't come from a tribal background, neither do I speak an indigenous language. I'm not white, but I am not African either." David fell silent. It would be a waste of time to try to explain to these misguided people that he sometimes felt that the Coloureds had become the new lost tribe of Israel.

"Are there *any* Black writers?" Ernst asked. "I mean … South African writers that are … not white?" he stammered in an effort not to offend.

"Disappointingly few. Since Peter Abrahams fled these shores, God knows how many years ago, no one of his quality has come to the fore."

"Surely, you writers have only yourselves to blame," Zelda challenged.

David reflected before replying, "You're right. The fault is ours. We all seem to be suffering from an inertia that shames me when I think of the West Indian writers. It has always amazed me: a story gets published, BBC interview follows, then a book. Next stop London. Like flowers transplanted, nurtured and blossoming in the abundant sunshine and rain of publishers and a responsive public.

"We, too, could blossom," he continued, "but our writing is sterile be-

61

cause most of us are obsessed with the political situation. As a result, we turn out political tracts instead of good literature."

"Wait, wait," Ernst said excitedly. "Earlier, you said that you admired Brecht ..."

"Exactly. But the writer should show how people are affected by the political system, not rant and rave about the system itself with the people becoming props. We don't seem to be able to create living characters, like Mother Courage. At best we produce excellent reportage, at worst clumsy propaganda. But enough of this," David interrupted himself. "Do you think I could have some more port?"

Zelda, reluctant to terminate the conversation, pointed at the bottle on the tray and asked Steward: "Do you share David's feeling of isolation?"

David swirled the wine in his glass, sniffed it and set about drinking steadily. He let their words wash over him. With only half an ear he listened to Steward saying that there were more Coloured artists than writers, that most of them were art teachers and that their work was anything but exciting. That most artists in Cape Town were white but that he got on well with them.

"Hell, I can't say the same for myself," David broke in.

But Steward hardly noticed. He was bewailing the fact that nowhere in Cape Town there was an area where artists could live and mix freely. It was a matter of seeing someone at an exhibition or sitting around someone's table sharing drinks and talk, then not seeing each other again for months.

The amount of liquor David had consumed had warmed his belly and he could feel the skin stretching tight across his cheek bones. He registered the first stirrings of recklessness. He wanted to say that Cape Town, too, had its little Chelseas, but that they were for white artists only, and that their main occupation seemed to be making it into the social pages of the newspapers. That he, in fact, didn't consider them artists at all but arty-farty show-offs.

But he kept quiet, telling himself to cool it. It was time to go before he said or did something that will close another door on him.

"I think it's time for us to leave," he announced. "I still have to go to a few places."

Steward gave him a perplexed look but said nothing. Silently, he watched David gather his coat and drape it over his shoulders. When David started for the door, he got up from his chair, thanked Ernst and followed Zelda, who was walking David to the door.

At the lift she held out her hand and David shook it briefly.

"If you should change your mind about letting me help you, then let me know."

"I'll do it my way," David said with a broad grin.

10

Despondency settled on David the moment he closed his front door and walked down the lane towards the bus stop. He pretended not to notice Eddie waving at him from across his fence.

Gloomily he watched bus after bus jerk to a halt at the opposite bus stop, disgorging loads of workers. Men and women whose work was done, free to enjoy whatever the night had to offer.

He bathed in self-pity. Jesus Christ! Another night, like the hundred nights before and the hundred nights to come, cooped up in a box, a prison cell, plugging and unplugging wires, answering and putting through calls, making his voice syrupy to hide his revulsion at the insipid pleasantries he was forced to listen to. His only consolation was the quiet times in the dead of night when he could write.

The beauty of the evening increased his dejection. It was June. Not the June of storm-tossed heavens and rain-drenched earth which caused the first Portuguese seafarers to name this place the Cape of Storms. It was a June of soft warm breezes. Cape of Good Hope. The sky had deepened to a dark hue, with just the faintest sliver of a crescent moon breaking its evenness. From the minaret of the mosque in Cornflower Road at the far end of Bridgetown floated the voice of the muezzin calling the faithful to prayer.

When a bus finally approached and David stepped off the pavement to hold out his hand, the driver accelerated and roared past.

Son of a bitch! Why the hell did he have to do that? I wanted to go to Mowbray! That's what's wrong with these bastard drivers – put them behind a wheel and they think they're doing you a favour if they stop.

The next driver skidded grudgingly to a halt. David got in and sat down in the first empty seat, consigning all bus drivers to a region of agony where they would be forever without transport, their limbs maimed, hobbling around on crutches. And I'd be behind the wheel of the only bus, he gloated. I'd slowly cruise up and down past them while they frantically waved their crutches in the air.

He burst out laughing at the idea. A woman sitting in front of him raised her head from the prayer book on her lap to look at him. His hilarity did not displease her, and with a smile she returned her attention to the printed page.

At Athlone station he cast the bus driver one last nasty look and ran for the train which was just pulling in. The familiar smell of stale sweat and cheap tobacco welcomed him to the third-class carriage.

He settled himself at a window seat.

Steward had arrived at their place an hour before David had left for work. After the luncheon at Zelda Ullrich's place, Steward had spent a week in Franschhoek, painting and drawing. He had returned with a number of new pictures of which he was very proud and which were to Frank Redick's liking. They were damn good, David thought.

So Steward was finally having his own exhibition. He and David and Yvonne had sat talking about the opening in the Argus Gallery on Thursday. The prospect of facing the critics for the first time made Steward quite nervous.

"I see you're into *Of Mice and Men*."

The conductor's words made David jump. He thrust his monthly ticket at the man who, after glancing at it, sat down next to him.

"Steinbeck's a very good writer. I'm busy with *Grapes of Wrath*."

But David didn't want to be drawn into conversation, not even by a conductor, who, unlike most white conductors in third class, was speaking to him as if he wasn't aware of his colour, someone who was clearly interested in literature.

When he got out of the train at Cape Town Station, David regretted not having talked to the man. I hope I see him again, he thought. We could have an interesting chat.

But his fleeting sense of good will had evaporated by the time he reached his place of work. An even deeper despondency gripped him as he stepped into the steel coffin that would ferry him up to the third floor.

Shit!

11

David had deliberately arrived at Steward's exhibition after the opening speech. Yvonne had gone in the company of Eddie, Charley and Terence. Steward had set off for the gallery much earlier, hiding his nervousness behind a nonchalant pose.

At the entrance of the Argus Gallery, David quickly surveyed the scene.

Yvonne and the others stood clustered in a corner. Only here and there a brown face stuck out among the whites filling the gallery.

He threaded his way through the crowd towards them. He had a glimpse of Steward surrounded by three elderly white women and a man, attentively listening to what he was saying.

Yvonne stared with suspicion at David. He returned her stare with a look of innocence. Placing his right hand on his chest, he held up the left, palm facing his audience, and said, "Scout's honour! Never touched a drop. So help me, God!"

"It's a pity that you've come so late," Terence said. "We've had our pictures taken by the *Post*." He glared at a photographer taking shots of groups of well-dressed women. "That bloody photographer from the *Times* is taking pictures of society bitches only." Then, petulantly: "He took one of Steward, though."

"What's wrong with appearing in the *Post*, Terence? It's our paper, isn't it?"

"Yes, but it loves to parade the robberies and rapes in the townships."

David looked around and recognised some familiar faces from previous exhibitions.

A blonde woman stopped in front of them. She looked intently at David. "Hello, Zelda," he said.

"I thought I recognised you but wasn't altogether sure because of the dark glasses."

David took off the glasses to reveal two black circles around his eyes.

"What in heaven's name happened?"

"The spirit was willing but the flesh couldn't take it." He did not elucidate further. He was in no mood to talk to Zelda Ullrich. There was no need for her to know that his drunken sprees sometimes ended in a punch-up.

David noticed that Yvonne had moved to the back of the group, isolating herself from them. Why the hell does she have to do that? There's no need to be fearful. But I suppose I should be thankful that she came to the gallery at all, finding it so difficult to mix with whites.

He moved to her side and touched her wrist. He could feel her tension. "Do you think I could have a drink?" he asked, smiling at her.

Yvonne nodded her head and returned his smile, grateful that he was at her side.

"How do you like it?" he asked.

She looked at the crowd, most of the women fashionably dressed. Everyone seemed to know each other. "Its all right," she answered, unconvincingly.

"Here comes our friend Samuel," Charley said. The gallery cleaner, dressed in a white coat for the occasion, approached them with a tray laden with glasses of sherry.

"The barman cometh," David said as he took a glass for Yvonne and one for himself.

The others in the group each took a glass in turn. Samuel assured them he would see to it that their needs were satisfied, then moved on.

"Is Arnold seeing Paula on the sly?" David asked as Arnold Barker came up to them with Paula in tow..

"It don't surprise me," Yvonne said cuttingly.

"Arnold see me standing outside in the street, looking for the place," Paula said, reading the query in their eyes.

"Wait, don't tell us," Arnold said, pointing at David's dark glasses. "You're a member of the Special Branch. Agent Triple X."

"Sorry, sir, you're wrong. Let me reveal my identity: I'm the reincarnation of King Farouk. And this is my harem."

"In that case, Monarch of the Moon, Despoiler of Virgins, I have a new woman for you. I found her struggling in the slave market, surrounded by pig-eating infidels."

"Ah, faithful Bedouin, Warrior of the Desert. Your reward shall be great. From now on Jasmine is yours."

"Your generosity stretches wider than the Sahara, sire, but I would settle for a glass of wine. My vows forbid me the pleasures of the flesh."

"So shall it be. Major Homo, serve him at once."

Charley turned sideways and took a bottle of brandy from an inside pocket. He poured a generous amount in a glass for Arnold and a smaller one for himself.

Arnold and David burst out laughing. Charley only shrugged his shoulders. "You never know at these places," he explained. "I'd hate to run dry. Besides, we can take it with us when we go to the café afterwards."

"Damn it!" said Arnold. "This government with its damn, degrading laws, making it impossible to sit down in a proper restaurant to have a meal and drink together. I'll see you at the party in two weeks' time, though. It's still on, isn't it?"

"Of course. We're going to give Steward a real party when the exhibition's over."

Yvonne swallowed her annoyance at Paula's arrival, secretly grateful for her presence because it made it easier to handle to the situation. She feigned interest in Paula's chatter while watching Eddie and Terence move around the gallery and Charley furtively pour some brandy in a glass.

"How's your writing going?" Arnold asked David. "The last time we met, you were very bucked-up with the novel."

David stared at his feet. What should he tell him? "I'm still struggling with it. The damn thing is going very slowly. I just can't seem to get to grips with it. I also gave up on the piece set in a gallery. But I read yours in *Contrast*."

"What do you think of it?"

"It's well-written but it's too magaziney. You missed out on the point you said you were going to make. Instead of concentrating on the artist anxious about the integrity of his painting, you came up with a story of local boy made good. By pleasing others and not remaining true to himself."

"I knew you'd say that. I started out all wrong. Rather than sticking to what I had in mind, I wrote with the idea of selling the story to the magazine. I know that's fatal."

"At times I also have a problem with that. But the stories I submit to the *Argus* and *Times* I keep as true as possible to my original idea. You can get away with a lot of social protest that way. But then it's easier for me, writing mainly about people in slum areas."

"Have you ever considered the overseas market?"

"I'm thinking of it. You know, of course, of the short story in the anthology coming out later this year. One gets very little money for all the effort one puts in, still, it's more than what the *Argus* or *Times* pay. And it's all right from the prestige angle. But, I wish publishers would be more generous. All you get is a flat fee. So even with a successful anthology, you're still out of pocket."

"I agree. But why not concentrate on both? If a story intended for the *Argus* or *Times* turns out very well, you can always flog it overseas instead of giving it to them."

Arnold pointed to the paintings around them and said, "The exhibition seems to be going well. I notice a few red tags have appeared."

"I only hope that they're not buying out of curiosity. You know what I mean? A Coloured man's attempt at art. Nothing infuriates me more than the sick, patronising attitude that most whites adopt when they're confronted with Black artistic expression. It's up to the critics to show whether they too suffer from the same sickness."

"Here," Charley interrupted their conversation. "We don't have to be so sparing with it now that Paula has brought some more brandy."

David took the drink and looked around the gallery.

Paula was clearly more interested in what was going on around them than Yvonne, and was commenting quite loudly on the women's fashions. Yvonne did not participate much in the conversation, but she too was watching the people crowded around Steward. Neither of the women spared the paintings a thought.

David waved at Steward on the far side of the gallery. When he turned back to Arnold he saw Ron Brink staring at a canvas. David nudged Arnold. "I see our cultural attaché, has condescended to grace the occasion with his presence. Or is he bent on procurement?"

"I wish you'd stop your act," Arnold admonished him. "In his way, he was only trying to help you."

"I now know I don't need his help!"

Charley, under the spell of too many brandies, had retreated into a corner, mumbling incoherently. Unaware that part of the gallery's decorative scheme, a layout of cacti and rocks, was directly behind him, he tripped and sat down unceremoniously. His face contorted and bewildered, he pressed back with his arms but was unable to raise himself.

His feeble croaks brought Arnold and David to his side, but they could not restrain their mirth as he looked pleadingly at them, the outstretched palms of his hands covered in fine thorns. Laughing, they took hold of his arms and pulled him erect. Charley bent forward to reveal a posterior bristling with thorns.

Frank Redick came hurrying over. "What happened?"

Terence, whose vivacious rounds of the gallery had been brought to an abrupt end, walked over, disapproval written all over his face.

David could not reply, tears of laughter wetting his face.

"It was an accident," Arnold explained. "He lost his balance."

"I hope he didn't hurt himself," Yvonne said anxiously.

She and Paula started to clean the palms of Charley's hands carefully with a pair of tweezers and some handkerchiefs that Paula had magicked out of her make-up bag.

Without a word, Frank Redick replaced a small rock that had fallen to the floor and strode away to his office.

The crowd thinned out and shortly after seven it was mainly people that David knew who remained. Like most art exhibitions it had lost its earlier air of liveliness and had now adopted the almost forlorn look of a church fête with only the priest and parish committee left. The barman and a helper were collecting empty glasses while Frank Redick collated names and addresses on a list, checking them with Steward.

David waved a hand at Samuel and pointed to their empty glasses.

A fresh tray was served. Terence saw to it that Charley was left without a glass.

"I'm leaving," Arnold said, checking his watch.

Steward, who had just joined them, said, "We might as well all leave," and led the procession down the stairs.

"See you at the party," Arnold said as he got onto his scooter outside and roared off.

Charley was supported by Paula and Yvonne. While vociferously maintaining that he was capable of controlling his own movements, he stumbled along between them on unsteady limbs. Getting onto the bus proved trickier. To stabilise himself, he held onto the pole in the middle of the platform inside, blocking the entry of the rest.

The conductor demanded that they clear the platform.

"Have a seat," Charley gallantly offered Yvonne and Paula.

He moved a few steps down the isle and stood swinging with the jerking of the bus, hands hooked through the straps above him. He belched alarmingly a few times.

Terence, fearful that if he removed a hand, the motion of the bus would topple Charley and unleash the vomit that had to be bubbling inside him, hastily paid for both of them before the conductor could approach.

Finally the bus stopped in Sir Lowry Road, and with relief Terence slithered past Charley to gain the safety of the pavement. The rest followed suit.

David, Yvonne and Paula entered the Medina Café in Russell Street first, Terence and an unsteady Charley just behind them. Eddie and Steward brought up the rear. They walked past the front section to the back where some tables had been reserved. Hester was seated at a corner table.

"What's our school teacher doing here?" Eddie asked.

"I told her to reserve a table and order food for us so long," Steward replied. "I hope you don't mind?"

Eddie did not reply. His mind went back to the two previous occasions that Hester had been in their presence. After striking up an acquaintance with her at an exhibition opening at Wolpe's Gallery in Strand Street, Steward had taken her to meet David and Yvonne. Eddie had disliked her air of superiority right from the start. The second time, again at David's place, he had suggested that she joined them for drinks at his place. "I don't think so," she had replied. "I have things to do." Her tone of voice made it clear that whatever she would be engaged in would be more important than being in his company. Later he had discovered she was a teacher.

Steward looked at Eddie, realising that Hester's presence would further compound Eddie's resentment at the success of his exhibition. He'll get his chance when the critics flay me, Steward thought.

As soon as they had taken their seats at the table, three waiters entered, carrying trays with plates of mutton curry, a salver of steaming rice, side plates stacked with roti, and numerous small bowls of spicy salads.

Knives and forks were placed next to the plates. "For tourists," David said, disdainfully glancing at the cutlery and breaking off a portion of the roti on his side plate and wrapping it around a piece of meat and some rice. He dipped the small parcel into the oily curry and transferred it to his mouth.

To show that he, too, knew the correct procedure, Eddie followed David's lead. The others decided to use knives and forks, except Charley who, observing David and Eddie, put down his knife and fork and with a flourish broke his roetie in two.

"This is the way to do it," he announced, scooping up a potato and some rice. The potato slipped free as he raised it to his mouth and tumbled back onto the plate. A line of curry marked his wrist and sleeve.

"How, now?" Charley asked, contemplating the mess.

He carefully replaced the roetie on his plate, pushed back his sleeves, unmindful of the yellow stains, and repeated the performance with exactly the same result.

Hester, seated next to Charley, was disgusted but tried to hide it. Yvonne smiled and savoured the thought that Hester would have preferred to be alone with Steward, quietly celebrating his success. How easy it would be to oust Hester from Steward's affections, she thought. Terence, sitting on the other side of Charley, had bilious tremors each time Charley tackled his food. As Charley yet again tried to fill his mouth with food, leaving a trail of oil across his cheeks, he hurriedly got up from the table, excused himself and rushed to the toilet.

"What's the matter with him?" Charley asked with concern, staring at Terence's retreating back.

"I suppose the curry's too strong for him." David nonchalantly filled his roti with meat and rice, transferring it to his mouth without spilling a grain of rice or a drop of oil.

"I'd better go and see what's wrong with him," Charley volunteered.

No one deterred him.

Terence had splashed cold water on his forehead and was standing wiping it off with a handkerchief when Charley entered.

"What's the matter?"

"Nothing! Nothing!"

"David said something about ..." But Charley could not speak any further. Hurriedly pushing Terence aside, he leaned forward and unleashed a torrent of vomit.

Terence gave one look at Charley's shuddering shape and gulped once or twice, then hastily turning away, he lowered his head and spattered the tiles in turn.

Their stomachs emptied of food and wine, they rinsed their mouths and returned to the table.

The wine and food had taken effect on the others. Their speech was innocuously gay, and even Eddie's repartee had lost its sting.

David held his glass up as Terence and Charley approached. Terence shuddered visibly. "No more! No more!" he pleaded.

12

Although he didn't say it outright, Steward was more than pleased with the critics' reviews of his work. The two-week exhibition period was over and the paintings had been taken.

The party to celebrate the end of the exhibition was Yvonne's idea, but David supported it wholeheartedly. He and Steward were seated on opposite beds in the children's bedroom.

"Tell me, Steward," he said, raising his glass to his lips. "Are you cooking up something with Hester? I think she's got some sort of idea that there's an attachment between the two of you."

After a few sips of wine the answer came: "Let her hang onto the idea, as long as I don't have to share it."

"If you're happy, I'm happy." David said, pressing Steward's shoulder affectionately.

Yvonne appeared in the doorway. "Why don't you give Charley a hand, David?" she demanded. "He's busy in the kitchen stacking glasses."

They rose from the beds. "Not you, Steward. You the guest of honour. Tonight, you don't do a thing." She lifted her head so that the new string of imitation pearls caught in the light. "And thanks for the present. It's more than I can expect from my husband."

"I'd better get out there before my sins are reeled off one by one," David said and left the room.

Steward looked at Yvonne. He longed to draw her, to capture her lazy sensuality on paper. He'd draw her with hair disarrayed, blouse open and breasts bare.

"Has David told you that I'm going to do illustrations for his stories once he has completed the collection?"

"No. And the way he's working, he'll never finish it. David don't seem to finish anything these days. I think he'd sell a story to the papers but all I get from him is 'I'm busy working on one'. Also, I wish he give up this night-shift job. I'm sure he can get another job with the same pay. He's away from home every night except Saturday night or when he's off. I don't ever go anywhere at night. I feel I'm buried inside these four walls."

How do I tell her that David complains that he can't talk to her about his writing?

"You know how David is," Steward proceeded cautiously. "His moods change all the time when he's writing. There are times when his writing has him by the throat and he can't spare a word for you. And if he speaks then it's about the story. Then there are times when nothing works for him. I believe he suffers terribly then."

"But you not like that. You take things one at a time and finish it. You never throw a fit. At times David's like a child who can't get his way and every small thing upset him."

David's return made it unnecessary for Steward to reply. "Should I open the soft drinks?" he asked.

"Yes. And the tins of sardines as well so I can prepare the biscuits. I already cut the tomatoes. What's happened to Terence? Is he still going to be barman?"

"Don't worry about him. He'll pitch up any moment. I like the pearls. They match the sparkle in your eyes," David said, pretending to measure the shine of the pearls against that of her eyes.

"Sweet talk is all I ever get from you ..."

Steward left the room as David said, "My purse might be too empty to buy you treasures, but never let it be said that I was stingy with compliments."

As always, Yvonne bloomed under his praise. She reached forward and kissed him lightly on the lips. "Thank you, lover boy. See you later."

David settled back on the bed. Yvonne. A soft, warm feeling filled him. He had loved her since they were children in the Bo-Kaap. During adolescence his feeling for her had grown stronger and he had married her, even though someone else had fathered a boy by her. Walking out of the magistrate's court that day, it was as if everything he had ever hoped for was granted to him.

David shifted uncomfortably. Lately he had begun to occasionally lust after another woman. But that lust never diminished his longing for Yvonne. Dawn was different. He needed her understanding. Every now and then he needed to talk to her. Like two weeks ago in the teashop at Cape Town Station ...

"That's right. Take a rest," Charley said, cutting into his reverie. "I've already poured the minerals. When do we start drinking?"

David smiled. "I don't know. We're supposed to be on our best behaviour tonight. Yvonne has warned me that she doesn't want me to upset things again."

Charley's expression changed. "Can't we make a plan, huh?" he asked anxiously.

The thought of the first glass of wine stirred David. But his need was different to Charley's. Charley consumed glass after glass until he sank into a somnambulant state. He, on the other hand, would first be filled with geniality, then hilarity and finally vulgar aggressiveness that he would vent indiscriminately.

"I think we'd better wait until Yvonne gives us the word," he said.

Charley lapsed into silence. "I'm going out for a minute," he said after a while.

"Where to?"

"To the smokkie to buy a bottle."

"Why?"

"You want me to die of thirst?"

But Charley didn't leave. At that moment, Trini Lopez started belting out *La Bamba* in the front room, charging the air with excitement.

"How do I look?"

David swung round. Paula had walked into the room, a shopping bag in her hand. She dropped it on the floor, kissed Charley and then him, hugging him tightly.

The shiny Chinese-style dress clung to the curves of her body. On each side a long slit revealed an enticing strip of leg.

"Good enough to take to bed," David said softly.

Charley's eyes were fixed on the bag. "Anything in that for us?" he asked.

"Why not have a look?"

He reached inside and took out two bottles of brandy, a half-jack of peppermint liqueur and three small jars of olives.

"The olives for the party," Paula explained, "the brandy for Steward and the peppermint for us."

"You've saved my life," Charley said with fervour. "I'll dedicate my next poem to you."

"Where's the glasses?"

"In the kitchen. But you'd better fetch them, Paula," David said. "I've been banned until further orders."

Paula looked at David and then at Charley. "I suppose we can drink without glasses," she said, shrugging her shoulders.

"Why not? Ladies first," Charley agreed enthusiastically, unscrewing the top and handing the bottle of peppermint liqueur to Paula. She took two sips and passed the bottle back to Charley. He swallowed deeply. Another mouthful and the bottle was reduced to half.

"Bang goes another resolution," David said as he swallowed his share.

One more round and the bottle was empty. David opened the window and tossed it into the weeds along the fence. "How do you feel now?" he asked Charley.

Charley, his eyes half-closed, sent his tongue over his lips. "I think I should be able to hold out until the next round."

"Better put the brandy with the rest of the stuff," Paula cautioned. "I'll put the olives in the kitchen and go and see what the rest of the men look like."

"Yes. Give them a good time," David said, giving her a farewell pat on the buttocks.

The drink and Paula's appearance had infused him with a feeling of well-being. He turned to Charley, who was already reclining on the bed. "It's a pity you don't like going to the cinema. I saw *The Idiot* in town."

Charley's interest quickened and he raised himself.

"It was a Russian film. In colour but with none of the garishness of the technicolour crap that the Americans turn out. The acting was superb."

"Who played Muishkin?"

"I'm sorry, I can't remember the name. But he was excellent, whoever he was. And trusting like a child. He was almost Jesus-like, the way he accepted everything that was done to him."

Charley's eyes narrowed. To David it looked as if he was praying.

"Tell me, what have you two been up to?"

Terence had appeared in the doorway and, like an actor, bedazzled them with the splendour of a shantung suit. He stood as if waiting for a roll of drums or a fanfare of trumpets. Eyes stern and one arm outstretched, fingers pointed accusingly, he said, "I spot bottles. Where are the glasses?"

"Don't tell a soul," David confided. "We've ate them!"

"Enter, Bella Lugosi of the fashion plate," Charley added caustically.

"You're just jealous of my sartorial display. No one could be nearer a vampire than you. But I've not come to engage in chit-chat about corpses and coffins. The bar is my domain and I shall rule it with justice and might!"

"Here I shall lie," Charley replied firmly. "I've dug my grave and will not vacate my ghoulish couch."

"What must be, must be. But do not hinder me in my task, and perhaps, just perhaps, I shall fill your cup with gore."

"Do that, and I shall be your willing slave. Just point out your enemies and my fangs shall feast at their throats."

"Now that the two of you have come to such a genial arrangement," David said, "I'll take my leave and join the festivities within."

Hester was hovering at Steward's side. Eddie and Yvonne were dancing – under the watchful eyes of Rebecca.

David crept up behind Paula, who was sorting through the records, and poked a finger in her ribs. She gave a little yelp.

"Let's have a quick squeeze before you have them all lined up and waiting."

He took her in his arms and slowly circled the floor with her. He loved the moment.

The record ended after just a few turns and David reluctantly released her.

The next record was a twist number so David stood aside and watched the dancers. But the beat was infectious and he found himself hopping to it and murmuring, "Nicely, nicely."

A feeling of discomfort made him turn around. Eddie was looking at him, a hint of derision on his face. "I don't know what gave me the feeling that you would not be here," David said.

"How could I stay away on the night we pay homage to our friend's triumph? Or were you going to do me out of my share of wine, David?"

At that moment, the front door opened and Arnold Barker entered, followed by Herman Bernstein and three girls. The girls, two brunettes and one blonde, seemed to have visited the same hairdresser: all three sported a page-boy haircut. They could also all have been to the same dress-maker: they wore silk dresses with hem-lines just above the knee. Only their heights differed: the blonde stood half a head taller than the dark-haired girls.

David ushered them to the back room. Names were called out and Arnold and Herman were relieved of their two bottles of wine.

"Any of the ladies want something to drink?" Terence asked, his voice dripping obsequiously.

The three girls looked at each other and nodded their heads in unison.

David studied them. He didn't catch their names, but he knew: Kenilworth or Constantia liberals doing their thing – fraternising with the brown folks.

They looked at Terence attentively when he addressed them again and replied politely.

"May I also have a drink, please?" David asked Terence, mimicking their posh accent. "And a drink for each of my friends, as well. That is, if it's not too much to ask."

Charley got up and handed Terence an empty glass.

"What would you like, Arnold?" Terence asked, ignoring Charley's gesture. "And what about you, Herman?"

"The same as they're drinking," Herman said, pointing at the women's glasses of wine.

"For me, as well," Arnold added.

"I don't care a damn as long as you fill the glass," David said. "And don't forget Charley."

He emptied his glass in one long gulp, and before Terence could stop him reached for the bottle and refilled his and Charley's glass.

David answered the three girls' dismayed look with a mocking stare.

"Let's go dance," Arnold suggested to the girl next to him. Herman partnered a second girl. The blonde remained seated on the bed.

A sudden silence settled on the back room. The girl was uneasy. She shifted about, gave two slight coughs, looked at their faces then back at her empty glass.

"I think she needs another drink," David said and nudged Terence.

She smiled almost gratefully. "I think I do," she said, holding out her glass. "This is the first time that I've been around with Arnold."

"You mean this is the first time you've come to a Coloured party. How do you like it?"

"I think it's jolly nice."

"Shall we dance?" Terence suggested.

She smiled at him, eager to be free of David's discomforting stare.

"Goddamn tourist!" David said as he sat down next to Charley.

"Undoubtedly!" Charley agreed. "So let's drink to the damnation of all tourists."

"You're so damn fucking right!" David said, filling their glasses.

"Why don't you come and join us?" Yvonne taxed David from the doorway. "We need more partners."

"As my love calleth, I come," he said, smiling at her petulant scowl. He straightened up from the bed, put his glass down and lumbered to the front room.

"Are you in the mood for white meat?" Paula teased as they later danced together.

"Shit!" David replied with annoyance, then added, "Brown pussy tastes better."

She moved one leg so that their thighs caressed while they danced.

Despite Yvonne's disapproval, Terence's had moved the wine to the sideboard in the front room so that he could join in the dancing. Yvonne feared that the close proximity of the liquor would lead to a change in David's present good mood. It did not, for although he and Charley made frequent stops at the sideboard as the party progressed, David's spirit soared higher and higher. Only Charley was affected in the usual way. He sank into a lethargy that later lulled him to sleep in the back room.

At about midnight, Terence resumed his role of barman. Talk switched to Steward's successful show as everybody stood around drinking. The three white girls had also visited the gallery and were enthusiastic about it. One had bought a drawing.

David wanted to choke on their patronising praise.

The girl he had earlier suggested needed a drink turned to him, unsuspecting. "Arnold has shown me two of your stories. One can't deny its sincerity. I think I've also come across one in the *Argus* or *Times*. Have you done much writing beside that?"

There was an explosion in his head. "Yes, I've done quite a lot of writing, all done sincerely and all unsaleable! If you want to read it, go right ahead. My shit-house walls are smeared with rejections, and you won't need a laxative afterwards."

Shock flushed her pale cheeks. She pulled in her breath sharply.

"Cut it out!" Arnold said, an edge to his voice.

"David," Yvonne pleaded.

Their voices were meaningless echoes. The only way to demolish the pent-up frustration that was suddenly threatening to suffocate him was to slash at the three pale female faces huddling together in front him.

"Goddamn tourist bitches!" he screamed. "Is this the slumming section of your grand tour? Well, watch carefully so that the next time you have tea and cake in your genteel homes, you will have something to relate."

He grabbed a bottle from the sideboard and stormed towards the back room. He pushed past Rebecca and her affronted stare and collapsed on a bed. In anger he raised the bottle to his mouth and swallowed.

A trickle of wine eased down his chin and he wiped it off with his shirt sleeve. "Who the hell do they think they are?" he muttered.

13

Yvonne was sitting with her back to the gate. It was an exceptionally balmy winter's day.

Eddie paused, taking in the picture. A wide straw hat covered her head, showing only a thick lock of hair creeping out under its broad brim. Yvonne's legs were thrust out in front of her. His eyes travelled from her ankle to her rounded calf and thigh.

He swung his leg over the fence so as not to disturb her by opening the squeaking gate. His footsteps were silenced by the thick sand in which even the hardiest plant could not survive.

On tiptoe he peered over her shoulder. She sat with eyes closed, lips slightly parted.

Eddie moved round and squatted in front of her and watched the rise and fall of her chest. A shiver shook him as he visualised her naked.

Goddamn David! What has he done to deserve her? Underneath this woman's friendliness lurked a sensuousness that would leap alive at a touch or be awoken by a word spoken at the right time.

Eddie knew he had often awoken that feeling in her, but never strongly enough for her to succumb to his desires. Afterwards he would return home and bed Rebecca with a savagery that turned her into a rigid lump of silent protest.

If he could have her only once. Just once! What the hell did he care if Rebecca threw a fit or walked out? It would be worth it.

Yvonne stirred in her chair.

It took all of Eddie's self-control to keep his hands from touching the heaving breasts. He swallowed and cleared his throat.

Yvonne opened her eyes and looked straight at him.

There was no time to change his expression. It would be clear to her what was on his mind. He could not stop the faint flush tinging his features.

"How long have you been here?"

He did not trust himself to speak. He shook his head in an effort to clear his thoughts. Then he blurted out, "I don't care what you say. I sat here looking at you and I couldn't get my mind off taking you to bed."

Yvonne did not reply.

He scanned her face. She was not displeased. This time he did reach out. Her thigh was warm and inviting beneath the soft dress material.

Her blood seemed to flow faster at Eddie's touch. She sat silent as his touch became more urgent, surrendering to the caress, exhilarated.

"You know how I feel. I want you so much that I don't care any more."

Yvonne looked around in alarm, got up and hurried inside.

Eddie picked up the chair and followed her.

She was standing next to the refrigerator, sipping from a tumbler. "Want some ice water?"

Eddie gave her a crooked smile and shook his head. "No, thanks. I don't think that will cool me off."

Yvonne walked over to the window. "David got no sense of shame," she said, staring into the lane. "I don't know where to hide my face when he insult those girls the other night. It always happen when he's drunk, and the more people around, the more sick his performance. There was no need for him to say those things."

Eddie knew it was a ploy to divert his attention. "You should know David by now," he replied in conciliatory tones.

"It's no good standing up for him. I know David, but the way he go on, I don't want to know him. When he's like that, you can't do anything with him. It's all the damn drink! I don't understand why he can't take wine like you and the others. As soon as he got some wine in him, he start acting up. The party was going so nicely and he go and spoil it! Poor Steward must be disappointed, although he of course don't say a word. Arnold was mad. Sometimes I wonder why people still come here? I hate David when he performs."

Eddie refrained from defending David, even half-heartedly. It would upset Yvonne to know that he was in full agreement with David more often than not. It was just that he rarely indulged himself like David did.

"If you only know how I feel about it," Yvonne continued. "He's slowly turning me away from him. And when he start arguing, I can scream. Everybody's wrong but not him. He don't care if he know anything about what they say. As long as he can have his say. I never forget that day he argue with Arnold. That was when Arnold come back from London.

"Arnold is telling us how long it sometime take for films to come to small bioscopes away from London, and that white bioscopes here also got to wait their turn. David keep on saying that Arnold is wrong, that white bioscopes see the pictures at the same time, and even before London. Arnold was very angry when he left. David almost finish two bottles with Charley. Now, what do I do with a man like that? You tell me?"

"You shouldn't have anything to do with a man like that. He doesn't deserve such a beautiful woman as yourself."

His words made Yvonne swing round.

"Now, if it had been me, I would treasure you. You're a jewel that needs constant rubbing to bring out its sparkle, not rough treatment that would mar it."

He approached slowly and placed his hands on the outside of her arms.

Yvonne, suddenly smiling roguishly, challenged, "Would you now, Eddie?"

His hands slid from her arms and cupped her breasts. He leaned forward and whispered, "Yes, I would."

She raised her head. This should teach David.

Eddie's tongue parted her lips. One of his hands found her breast. She could feel her nipple stiffen under his touch.

She withdrew to search Eddie's face but he pulled her closer, his lips pressing down on hers. Waves of desire made her body mould itself to his.

"Wait a minute," she said, her voice husky. "I lock the front door."

She locked both front and back door.

Eddie followed her into the bedroom.

The rattle of the front door and a shrill voice froze their movements.

"Mummy, Mummy, I want to come in!"

Why the hell did she have to come back now? Eddie silently raged, easing himself off Yvonne. Yvonne took a deep breath and motioned to Eddie to leave through the kitchen door. Pulling her dress back on and quickly twisting her hair into a plait, she moved to the window and opened it. "I'm coming," she shouted. "Why don't you stay outside? It's such a nice day," she admonished as she unlocked the front door. "I'm cleaning the place."

"I want some bread, Mummy."

"I got no time to cut bread. Take an apple from the basket. Next time you want something, say please. Do you hear?"

"Yes, Mummy."

Yvonne glared at Thelma as she closed the front door behind her. If the child sensed her mother's tension, she did not let on. She sat down at the gate, pushing it to and fro, taking tiny bites at her apple.

The creaking of the gate grated on Yvonne's nerves where she stood with her back against the kitchen wall, trying to quieten her wild, racing heart.

14

David had at first thought of asking all the others to accompany him to Mavis's place in Cape Town. It was more than two weeks since the party for Steward, and he needed to get out. But in the end he had decided to take only Paula. He had told Yvonne that he would not be coming home, hinting that he would stay over at Steward's or one of his other friends in town. She did not raise too much of an objection as she had invited Christine and Cora over for the evening. "Just don't get too drunk," she had warned before he left.

In town he waited impatiently as bus after bus from Sea Point emptied itself of its passengers at the terminus in Adderley Street. Each time the stares of the women made him feel self-conscious: they could sense that he was waiting for a member of their sex. Irritated, he finally turned his back on the street and watched the passengers and passers-by in the reflection in the OK Bazaars display window.

A hand tapped him lightly on the shoulder.

"Hello, David."

His eyes lit up. "Paula."

She kissed him on the mouth.

"Come'n, let's go," he growled. He hated the way people stared.

"You don't even say you like my outfit?"

He gave her a sidelong glance. The thick, baggy green jersey obscured the fullness of her breasts. The tights clinging to her chubby lower limbs, however, left nothing to the imagination.

He squeezed her arm and smiled.

As they walked, she bumped her hip against his and related her day's activities. But his mind was on Yvonne. He did not feel that he was being unfaithful by taking Paula out. In the past he had often asked Yvonne to go with him, but she always refused if she did not know any of the other people going.

"What's wrong?" Paula suddenly asked. "Why you frowning like that?"

He blinked. "I was thinking of Yvonne."

Paula, as always, remained silent when David spoke of his relationship with his wife. The man was obsessed with his wife. He should never have married her. It can be a long time coming but she will leave him for another man. Yvonne wants to change him into Mister Perfect. If she had her way, she'd force him to take another job with more money. Then she could change her dining room furniture every second year, and get him to wear a black suit and tie and take her to hotels for dancing at weekends.

He would never be content with me either, Paula thought as they walked up Wale Street and turned into Loop Street. I know even less about books and writing than Yvonne, but I'd be more sympathetic at least. David's so generous. To all people, never mind what they do.

She gave his arm a squeeze and smiled at his distracted face.

I wouldn't be disgusted when David tells me stories of how he talks to the people in third class on the train and the drunks in the street. I'd be quite happy . . .

"This is it," David said.

They had come to a halt in front of a low, flat-stoeped house in Loop Street, boxed in by a warehouse on one side and a garage on the other.

David mounted the steps and knocked. After a short wait the door was opened. The woman had a strikingly pale face. She wore no make-up, only her eyes were accentuated by a glitter of green.

"Hello, Mavis."

"It's fifty cents each," she replied in a flat voice.

"Here," he said, offering her a rand note. She thrusted it into the pocket of her jeans and waited for them to enter.

"Things must be swinging," David concluded under his breath. "It looks like Mavis has been on tea all evening."

"Tea?

"Dagga." David replied.

"Where can I leave my bag, David?" Paula whispered anxiously.

"Could I dump her bag somewhere?"

"Give it to me," Mavis said. "I'll lock it up."

Paula passed the bag to Mavis after taking out a half-jack of brandy, which she handed to David.

"Want a drink, Mavis?"

Mavis looked at Paula. She nodded her head and turned round. "There's some glasses in the kitchen," she said, locking the front door.

She led them through a lounge and down a passage, where she stopped to wave them on and entered a room. The passage ended in the kitchen. David took three glases from a shelf and filled them with brandy and water. He passed a glass to Paula.

They stood in front of the window and waited. The yard was filled with people, some sitting on crates, others squatting on their heels. Almost everyone was clutching a glass, and the air was heavy with the tang of dagga.

"I think we'll join them," David said when Mavis finally reappeared.

"You go. I've got to watch the door."

David and Paula found seats for themselves, David responding to greetings. Some of the embracing couples were not of the same race, the Immorality Act for the while ignored. Conversation was unrestrained.

David gazed at them with a warmth that was not altogether the result of the brandy. They are my brothers and sisters, all of them, he thought affectionately. Here we sit, all together, one happy family.

He swallowed swiftly and refilled his glass. "This is how it should always be," he told Paula, pointing to the scene around them. "Universal acceptance. But you'll only find it here and among artists. Of all kinds. Here a Black jazz musician has no problem, but it's the back door for him should he play at a white night club."

The brandy was taking more effect and David became more ebullient. "Hi, docco man. Sit you down," he called out and thrust the bottle and glass at the tall, gangling blond man in dirty jeans and a fisherman's jersey. "Drink and share my happiness."

The man exchanged his dagga zol for the brandy.

David took a deep puff and blew the smoke in Paula's face. The sharp tang caused her to cough. David gave a deep laugh. "Frans," he said. "This is Paula."

Frans looked at Paula speculatively.

Playfully David pushed against his shoulder. "You keep your hands off her."

"I'm paying her a compliment with my eyes. You don't mind, do you, Paula?"

She shook her head and David tugged gently at a curl on her cheek. She lifted her head and listened. Through the upstairs window came the sound of a trio bashing out a bossa nova.

"See you, man." Frans said as he joined a group.

They had finished the brandy and David got up to return the glasses to the kitchen. "I'm going up there where the music blows."

Laughter mixed as freely as talk. Paula was completely at ease now. David led her through the throng in the yard and up the wooden staircase.

Upstairs consisted of one large room. It was packed with people. Those dancing had hardly space to manoeuvre.

David pushed his way into the pack and staked out an area for Paula and himself. He placed his hands on her hips. They could go neither backwards nor fowards and were compelled to sway to the rhythm of the music, rooted to one spot.

The musicians strung out the bossa nova, improvising as the mood moved them. With animal-like grunts of pleasure, the dancers cajoled them to intensify their efforts. David found the heavy concoction of dagga fumes and body sweat intoxicating. He closed his eyes and took deep gulps.

Paula sensed him drifting from her and drew closer, rubbing her body against his. David opened his eyes and saw the mocking look on her face.

"Bitch woman!"

He gave up all pretence at moving and stood still, straining against her. She responded to the pressure, his desire awaking hers.

The music ended and they broke apart.

They changed partners often as the night progressed, but always found each other again, both aware of the urgency to possess each other. David knew that he was going to ask whether he could stay with her for the night.

When the closeness of air became just too oppressive, Paula asked David to take her downstairs.

Frans was sitting with his back against the wall, feet sprawled at an angle, mouth agape with a silver trickle of spittle drying across his chin. Mavis sat at the kitchen door, a zol dangling from her right hand.

"Any tea going?" David asked.

"I've got two but I'm not selling. Here, have a blow."

David filled his lungs. He sank onto his haunches and blew a cloud at Paula. The dagga made him feel lethargic."Sure, you don't want to try it?"

"No."

"Could I buy some wine, Mavis?"

She looked at him, her face expressionless, raised herself slightly and reached for a bottle of muscadel behind the chair. The bottle was three-quarters full. She handed it to him.

"You don't have to pay. Give her some. I've been using this cup."

David carried the cup to Paula, and after she had emptied it, refilled it for himself.

He replaced the bottle and the empty cup behind the chair. "Thanks, Mavis."

She did not acknowledge his words, her face hidden behind a screen of dagga smoke.

The zol passed from Mavis to David and then back and forth until it was just a shred of paper with a burning coal. Mavis took out another zoll and gave it to David to light. With slow movements she filled the cup with wine and handed it to Paula.

Wonder what's up? Paula thought. Mavis don't talk much and for once David say nothing and yet it look like they communicate.

She sat back and relaxed.

Suddenly the party was over. People were leaving in twos and threes. David got up and roused Frans.

"Everybody's blowing," he slurred.

Frans rubbed the sleep from his eyes and peered around. "Jesus! I could do with some tea." He looked hopefully at David.

"Sorry, docco. I made out with Mavis. How you getting home? Any chance of bumming a lift?"

"I thought you live out of town."

"I do but I'm taking Paula home. Same way you're going. Just past Three Anchor Bay."

"I'm walking. I turn off at Mouille Point."

David grinned at Paula. "We're walking."

"It's all right. I don't mind."

"See you, Mavis," David said.

84

Frans waved a hand in farewell.

"Thanks," Paula said. "I enjoyed myself. It was a lovely party."

"Ja," Mavis replied, handing Paula her bag. Her response was as bleak as her face.

The chill in the night air made Frans shiver. He looked at Paula and pinched her arm through her jersey. "Good material," he said, and with a leer at David: "I sure wish I was getting what you're getting tonight."

A cat, hotly pursued by another, darted from an alley. With a bound, the second cat pounced. A few moments later an agonising howl was heard.

"Even the cats are at it. Everybody's in line for loving, except me," Frans said wryly. "I don't mind being a motherless child but I'm sure missing my pie."

"It is a night for loving," David reflected. "Why didn't you stay over at Mavis? You never know, you might be lucky. She looks as if she's carrying the blues of the world."

"That one's too far gone. I stayed with her once but it was a no go. All night she played Bones's *Moonlight in Vermont*. Over and over. She doesn't say a word."

Frans looked at the moon behind the scudding clouds. "She just drinks and smokes tea. Not that she's mean with the stuff. I touched her once but man, her flesh was as cold as the look she gave me. Then she wept. Not loud like a woman bereaved but silent tears running down her face, just running. I got drunk as quickly as possible and passed out. She had tossed a blanket over me when I woke up the next morning."

"How long ago is it since Bones got killed?"

"Almost two years. It was a mess. I was at the Coba that night. Bones and the boys were having a blow. Nice Swazi stuff. They were high as kites. There wasn't much of a crowd. Bones was soloing *Moonlight in Vermont* for Mavis. It was all soul. He made the notes come out soft and trembly. Then they had a break and Mavis joined him in the alley, where they sat smoking tea. You know how Bones was when he had a gig at a white club. He didn't like people around him. It was always Mavis and himself sitting around by themselves. The next moment Mavis came up to me and said Bones was fighting in the alley. Bones was leaning against the wall when I got outside, his shirt soggy with blood. Mavis held his hand. He couldn't speak. He just looked at her. For the two of them it was *Moonlight in Vermont*. This time he was giving it to her with his eyes. When the cops and the ambulance pitched, Bones was gone. There was no sense in her getting involved. A Coloured man stabbed to death and a white woman involved!"

"I've tried to get her to speak about it but she always refuses," David said.

"That's the trouble. She's keeping it bottled up inside her. One of these days we'll hear Mavis knocked herself off and Bones's record was found on the player."

Paula clutched David's arm. Now she understood Mavis's silence. It is something that men will find difficult to understand, a woman's grief for her man. Men will sorrow, but while sorrowing their eyes will wander for another woman to share their sorrow in bed. Women ...

A pair of bright lights approached from the front as they turned into Somerset Road. It was a police van. The van idled up to them slowly, keeping its headlights on. It stopped a few metres from them.

"Where are you going?" the driver demanded.

"Home," Frans replied.

The driver did not bother to ask David. He just leaned out his window and cocked an inquisitive eyebrow.

David suppressed his anger. "I'm taking my girl home. She works in Three Anchor Bay," he said.

The policeman sized up Frans's raggedy appearance and David and Paula's neatness. He gave a good-natured laugh and said, "On your way, and watch out for the Immorality dodge. It's gone up six months now."

Frans looked over his shoulder at the departing van. "Our morals are thus safeguarded by the paternal arms of the Law stretching over us."

"Yes," David agreed. "With loving care our White Father takes care of us. Even our sins ..."

"The police are not all that bad," Paula interrupted him. "Some of them, when they see one of the girls who work for a madam talking to white men at night, warn her that she will find herself at the police station."

After a few blocks Frans said good night and sauntered away, hands dug deep into the pockets of his jeans.

"David, how long you know Frans?"

"A couple of years. I met him at one of the jazz joints in town that I occasionally visit with Steward. He always looks as if he's starving. We smoked some tea in a lavatory. He's quite intelligent. Spent three years at varsity, then gave it up. Said he couldn't see himself stuffing himself with knowledge to come down on some unfortunate bastard."

They had scarcely walked another hundred metres when the same police van passed them again.

David waited until the van was out of sight before commenting, "You're right, Paula. They certainly keep their eyes on things. But then I'm no white boy."

86

They turned down towards the sea-front. Paula stopped and unlocked a gate fitted into a high wall. The path led up to the back of the house where Paula's room waited next to the garage.

Like all lovers who slept in the backquarters of a white man's home, David was roused much earlier than the master of the house. Like the master, however, he was also served coffee in bed.

Paula was dressed and ready to start her day's work. David watched her as she tidied the room, putting last night's outfit away, washing an un-matched cup and saucer.

With the light of dawn arrived a feeling of guilt about the pleasures shared in the dark. Taking Paula to Mavis's place had been another of his impulses that once executed brought no satisfaction. He finished his cof-fee, got up and put on his clothes.

"You'll have to wait for a bus," Paula said.

"I don't think I'll bother. I'll walk to the station."

She raised her face to be kissed. He gave her a perfunctory peck on the cheek. "I'll give you a ring," he said, then left through the gate in the high wall.

David saw more clandestine lovers leaving by back gates. They looked at one another knowingly. Those who were more than nodding acquain-tances formed a group. David ignored them and walked on his own.

Another group had gathered at the bus stop.

David appraised their smart clothes. Yes, that's right. Sport the sweat of their labour. Exploit these girls. Girls fresh from the country and ex-ploited by body-speculators, and, at times, unscrupulous employers. Their end will be prostitution – and a crop of illegitimate children.

The girls were still in bed when he got home, but Yvonne was absent.

"Where's your mother?" he asked Cynthia.

"Mummy's gone to church, Daddy."

He went to the kitchen and checked the pots on the stove. A roast was in the oven. He heated water for tea.

Thelma was asleep, a doll cradled in her arms. He eased himself down next to her and gently blew in her ear. She twisted her head and opened her eyes in bewilderment.

"My ear, Daddy."

"What's wrong with your ear?"

"I don't know," she said rubbing it. "It's you!" she accused.

"It's not!" he denied. "It's Greta," pointing at the doll. "She tried to wake you, to tell you that your daddy's home."

"It's not true. I know it's Daddy."

Her sister's laughter assured her.

David embraced her and kissed her on the mouth. "Did you miss me?"

"Yes, Daddy. Daddy didn't tell us a story last night."

David looked at them sternly. "No one greeted me."

"Good morning," they obediently chorused.

"Tell us a story now," Thelma pleaded.

"First, I'll have to see to the tea. Anybody want some tea?"

Three hands shot up into the air.

He fetched four cups of tea and a plate with Yvonne's home-made cookies from the kitchen and was telling them a story which he made up as he went along when the front door opened and Yvonne walked into the room.

"So, you've come home," she greeted him.

"Yes, the prodigal son has returned."

A snort of disgust erupted from Yvonne. "You think I run out and go kill a calf 'cause you home? Well, let me tell you, this is not Bible time."

David gave a lopsided grin. "This prodigal son doesn't want a feast arranged in his honour. The roast in the oven would do."

Yvonne sniffed the air.

"It's all right. I've checked the roast. Do you want some tea? I've just made a fresh pot."

"Yes, pour me some while I change."

As David left the room, Thelma called after him: "What about our story, Daddy?"

"I'll finish it tonight. Don't you think you should get up or is it your intention to spend the day in bed?"

They scrambled for the tiny bathroom.

David helped Yvonne in the kitchen while the children played outside. "Anyone been here last night?" he asked as he whipped three eggs in a bowl.

"Charley was here. He was very disappointed. He say he want to speak to you. He left soon."

"Anyone else?"

"Eddie. He kept me company while I do the ironing. Christine and Cora didn't come over."

"He would. Depend on him to look after my interest."

"What do you mean by that?" Yvonne asked sharply.

"Nothing," David laughed. "What was he expounding on this time?"

"It don't interest you."

Yvonne averted her face as she thought of the previous night. Eddie had adroitly steered their talk to the afternoon they were disturbed by Thelma, and with artful phrases intimated that now that the children were asleep and David would not be coming home they could resume what was interrupted. She had allowed his hands to explore her body, his talk and caresses to excite her. She had refused to put out the light in the front room, though, and the fear that one of the children might wake up deterred her from letting him make love to her in their bedroom.

"Charley invited you to his place after lunch," she said to prevent any further questions. "He had a bottle of vermouth with him."

"If I know Charley, there won't be much left by the time I see him."

After lunch David dried the dishes while Yvonne prepared the children for Sunday school. They watched with pride as the three girls walked through the gateway, dressed in their Sunday best. Then each reflected on the previous night's events with different partners and were filled with shame.

David reached for Yvonne's hand. She responded to the pressure. He kissed her, and she guiltily opened her lips, recalling Eddie's fervent kisses.

"What about a quicky before I go to Charley?"

Yvonne smiled her approval, hoping that their love-making would erase her transgressions. Sliding his body onto hers, David wondered whether Yvonne suspected that he had spent the night with Paula.

After a fifteen-minute walk, David stopped in front of the semi-detached house in Plum Crescent. He opened the gate and walked to the front door. He had not been here for quite some time and noticed that Charley had transformed the sandy wasteland in front of the house into a neatly trimmed lawn. A few fuchsia bushes were flowering along the front of the house.

Charley's mother opened the door. "He's in his room," she said.

David walked through the living room with its walls decorated with Dickson-family portraits, different shapes and sizes all arranged around a large picture of a thorn-crowned Jesus.

The door of Charley's room was ajar.

Charley was sitting on the bed, his back against the head-rest, eyes closed. A bottle, almost empty, and a glass sat on the small table next to the bed. A bookshelf stood in one corner and a drawing, a gift from Steward, hung on a wall. There was nothing else in the room.

David shook Charley by the shoulder. He blinked his eyes, trying to focus. "Hello, old pal," he said, raising himself and patting the mattress. "Sit down. Have the last of the Libby."

Charley poured some Lieberstein in the glass. "Hell, there's not another glass," and hollered: "Mummy, could I have a glass for David?" He nudged David in the ribs. "She doesn't like me drinking on Sundays."

"The glasses are in the kitchen and you can get one yourself!" his mother called from her bedroom.

Charley lumbered to his feet and shuffled away to the kitchen. He returned with an undried glass and opened his wardrobe to take out a bottle of vermouth.

"I thought you'd be here earlier. I had the two bottles and then decided I might just as well start on the Libby while I wait."

He thrust the bottle of vermouth at David.

"Open it and pour yourself a shot."

David filled both glasses.

"What's so important that you wanted to see me?"

"I wanted to talk with you. About my poem. You know I can't talk with the other bastards about it."

"What about Steward? Surely you can speak to him?"

"I know I can. But then he's not around all the time."

"Have you finished it?"

"No."

"What's holding you up?"

Charley refilled their glasses before replying. "It's me." He took a sip and closed his eyes. "Each dawn ushers in that pain that will one day break me. I look at your writing and I envy you because the blossom of creation does not have to struggle through the aridness that is my mind."

He sank back against the head-rest. "Dostoevski makes it clear, man is filled with doubts and torments. So I find solace in wine. Wait, how does it go, the line that thunders in my head?"

No! David's hands tightened around his glass. The irony of Charley looking to him for help!

"My soul is a candle weakly fluttering in the night."

"Is that a line from a new poem you're working on?"

"It's more than a week ago that I wrote it, and like all the other lines, it will gather dust in my drawer."

David did not comment, knowing too well of stories started and abandoned.

Charley raised two imploring eyes. "David, does it happen to you as well?"

"It happens to all of us," David said softly and gave a bitter laugh. "Come'n, let's fill our cups with cheer," he said. Then to himself: Hell! I should've stayed at home.

The Drift Road,
Teslaarsdat
Crance:
nov. 1956

BOOK
TWO

1

It was just after noon and the Kewtown library was still quiet before the rush of school children who would congregate inside it after school.

David had walked the few blocks from his house. Transfixed, he stood in front of the shelves of English fiction. The pleasure he got from looking at the books, some surely still smelling of printer's ink and freshly pulped paper, was headier than that of a glass of sweet wine.

He took a book at random from the shelf. He stroked the spine lovingly before opening it up. The assembled print intoxicated him and he quickly replaced the book. Oblivious of the people around him, he eyes ran along the shelves, devouring the names of authors and titles.

They've made it, each of them. All these books are filled with happiness and horror, dreams and despair, triumphs and tragedies. There isn't a single emotion man has experienced that has not been recorded between the covers of some book. Somewhere in the future someone would be reading his story in the anthology, and perhaps his novel. He too would have contributed his mite.

He gave a self-conscious laugh and turned around to see if he had disturbed anyone.

A tall, well-built young man near the librarian's desk was gazing at him. David returned the stare, then turned his back and continued his examination of the shelves. He selected Bud Schulberg's *Disenchanted* – the cover intrigued him: a man with a glass and a bottle in his hand – and settled himself at one of the small tables in the reading room.

But he couldn't concentrate. He sensed someone's eyes on him. In the end, he raised his head and noticed that the same young man had now positioned himself so that he could watch him.

David searched the broad face. The young man, for an instant, held his gaze. It was a face free of guile, eyes clear and appealing.

David formed a picture that threatened to convulse him with mirth. Hell! The guy looks as trustworthy as one of those St Bernard dogs on a travel poster. All he needs is a miniature cask of brandy hanging from his chest. He would most probably wag his tail and offer me a paw if I went over and patted him.

David suppressed a laugh, lowered his head and watched the young man out the corner of his eye. I'll play it his way, he decided as the young man edged nearer to his table.

He waited until the young man was within touching distance before he looked up.

"Please excuse me," the voice surprisingly soft and well-modulated. "Are you David Patterson?"

Taken aback, David took his time to respond. He noted the carefully selected outfit – light-grey suit, white shirt with faint blue stripes, a blue-striped tie, king-size brown brogues on his feet. The hair was neatly parted and the face clean shaven. A faint aroma of bay rum revealed the young man's taste in aftershave lotion.

David nodded his head.

"Are you the David Patterson who writes for the weekend papers?"

Again David answered with a nod of his head.

"I have enjoyed all the stories," the young man said with a seriousness that David found totally disarming.

The young man had not yet made any motion to occupy the chair on the other side of the table.

"Sit down," David invited, pointing at the chair. "It will be easier on my neck." The young man perched on the edge of the chair.

"I've read most of your stories, I think, and I've always hoped that some day I'd be able to meet you."

David found the respectful tone and the almost adoring expression in the eyes gratifying.

"I'm glad you've found the stories enjoyable. I'm still feeling my way around."

"I don't think you should have any fears, Mr Patterson. From what I've read, you've got the talent for writing."

"Thanks." The young man's sincerity and words were giving him a strange, heady feeling.

"Are you writing full-time, Mr Patterson?"

David looked at the shelves of books surrounding them before he said, "No. I'd like to write full-time but I've got a wife and three daughters to support and my talent has not developed enough for me to earn my living by writing." His eyes strayed back to the shelves filled with books. "My name is David. Stop calling me Mr Patterson. What's yours?"

"My name is Melvyn. Melvyn Francis."

"I work as a night telephonist at the *Times*," David continued. "It allows me some time to write, that's if the damn public doesn't bother me wanting to know when the next satellite is due to soar across the sky. You'd be surprised at the amount of crap I'm forced to listen to at the switchboard. What do you do, teach?"

"No. I work in a shop. A supermarket in Klipfontein Road. Assistant manager. It's my lunch hour."

"Interesting?"

"It depends on whether you could call checking prices and maintaining a profit interesting. But I can't complain pocket-wise. The pay's all right, and there's scope for advancement. Our annual bonus of course varies according to how much profit we've made that year. I'm studying business control part-time because I believe one must be prepared for whatever job one takes on."

David could not help smiling at the earnestness and detail with which the answer was given.

"What do you do when you're not pirating the smaller shops with your cut-throat practice, Melvyn?"

"I go to the cinema, I read a lot, and I listen to records. I used to play rugby but I gave it up."

"Why?"

Melvyn explained that there wasn't much apart from playing rugby that he shared with his team mates. They read mainly westerns and crime novels. Music, for them, was pop songs and twist numbers.

"It must've been a distressing situation for you, feeding the muscle and starving the mind," David mocked.

But Melvyn did not notice. "That's right," he agreed solemnly. "I tried my best but it didn't work out. I'd end up in a bar with them getting drunk after each match."

David raised his eyebrows. "I hope you're not against drinking?"

"Well, no ... " Melvyn drawled after studying David's face.

"We're strong on drinking," David continued. "We've not terribly intellectual, but we do manage when it comes to talking about the arts. But all talk and no wine makes for a parched throat. And we certainly don't want that. Oh yes, and we also don't listen to pop shit."

He deliberately did not mention their dancing and the type of music they danced to.

Melvyn sat like a little boy who had been shown a plate of cookies and whose hands itched to reach out and taste what was on display but who didn't dare.

"Come and visit us on a Saturday evening when you have the time." David wrote down his address. "Bring a bottle with you. Sweet."

"Thanks, Mr Patterson ... David. I'll do that." He looked at his watch. "I'm sorry but I'll have to leave. I've got to be back at the shop."

"See you."

It's not often I meet a fan, David mused as he walked home. Must tell Yvonne about this.

2

The laughter and shrill voices of children passing down the lane floated through the window.

Yvonne was agitated at David's preoccupation with the unopened bottle of wine in front of him on the kitchen table.

"You got the tickets?" she asked.

"Yes, and I wish Terence would hurry up before Thelma starts her nonsense. She's been at me since she got up this morning."

Yvonne laughed softly. "I tell her all week she got to behave herself or else she don't go to the ballet. It was hell for her. There was times she almost burst from stopping herself trying her stunts on me."

"Cynthia," David asked his daughter who sat completely engrossed in some book. "Have a look what's happened to Uncle Terence."

But Thelma came rushing through the front door before Cynthia could even move. "Uncle Terence is coming! Uncle Terence is coming!"

"It's about time," David rebuked Terence when he joined them a few minutes later.

"I first had to go to the tailor to pick up my trousers." Terence raised the hem of his jacket to display the cut. "How do you like it?"

The trousers, green corduroy, fitted snugly across the hips and backside, tapering to a very narrow bottom. "You'd better not bend over or make a sudden fart. I don't think your seat would hold."

Terence pulled his mouth in a pout and turned towards Yvonne.

"What do you think?"

"I say it suit you very well. I like the colour."

"Do you? I was going to have it in brown."

"No, green is just right. What you need with it is an avocado-green jersey. It will make a nice combination. Add to it a pair of light-brown suede shoes or boots."

A dreamy look shimmered in Terence's eyes as he visualised himself dressed as Yvonne described. A snort of aggrevation erupted from David. "Beau Brummel, we could leave when you're finished admiring yourself."

"I wish you take half as much care with your clothes as the way Terence do, David," Yvonne chided.

"My craving lies otherwise. I dress to cover my body and not to dazzle others. I could use the money Terence spends on clothes to buy books on the Parade."

Thelma tugged at her father's hand. "Are we going, Daddy?" she asked hopefully.

"Yes, sweetheart. We'll leave as soon as Uncle Terence and I have had a spark for the road."

Thelma glanced at her mother and started fidgeting anxiously.

But Yvonne said nothing as David filled three glasses with Frontinac. She sipped her wine in silence. After all, it was her favourite wine.

"Now we're all set to go," David said, boisterously replacing his glass on the table and taking Thelma's hand.

"Don't go rushing off to a bar when you get to town," Yvonne warned while she straightened the young one's bonnet, Thelma stirring impatiently under her ministrations.

"You know I wouldn't do a thing like that when I've got the children with me," David said, biting back an angry retort.

Thelma kept up an incessant stream of chatter all the way to town. David's initial irritation was replaced by pride when he saw the attention Thelma's patter was attracting from the other passengers on the bus.

On the Parade, scatterings of people were still looking for bargains while the stall-keepers had already started to stack their trestles. A flock of pigeons was industriously cleaning the ground of left-over food. Occasionally one would flutter up from between the legs of those walking by.

Cynthia pulled on David's sleeve to draw his attention to a bergie fast asleep on the edge of the pavement, his head resting on his chest and his legs clamped around a red orange-bag holding all his earthly possessions.

It was Thelma's first visit to the City Hall, and she gazed in wonderment at the Grecian statue next to the broad staircase. Terence, flanked by Cynthia and Shirley, was telling them of other ballets he had seen there.

When they reached the door, David gave Thelma the tickets. She shyly handed them to the white usherette. Without even looking up, the girl took the tickets, tore them in half, and said, "This way, please."

Their seats were in the front row of the balcony. David looked down at the rows of whites seated below. Bloody apartheid seating arrangements! But what could he do? Cynthia loved ballet and was taking lessons at Silverlea, the school she attended with Shirley. He simply had to repress his disgust and bring his daughters here where Cynthia could at least watch the University of Cape Town ballet company.

Thelma had never seen a ballet performance before. With wide eyes she stared at the gigantic blue velvet curtain partitioning off the stage. "When are they going to dance?" she whispered, her thumbnail eating into David's palm.

"It won't be long," he replied, handing her the programme he had bought. Quietly he explained to the other two: "We're going to see a story without words. It's about a young man and a girl who fall in love. From the music and the way the dancers dance you will be able to tell who the girl's mother and father are, and who the boy's mother and father. The two families don't like each other and they don't want the girl and boy to marry. But the girl's servant helps her ..."

The dimming of the lights cut off further speech. The members of the orchestra had taken their places, and applause greeted the conductor as he walked to the podium.

Thelma clapped her hands, eyes sparkling.

After the overture the curtains were raised to reveal the wonderland in which Juliet moved around like an elegant sprite.

Without uttering a single word, Thelma watched the first act. Even during interval she did not speak. Afterwards, too, she sat, completely transported, clasping her hands over her eyes during the duelling scenes and peeping through her fingers, her breath catching at each sword thrust.

Near the end of the ballet, David wanted to whisper something to Terence, but Terence was as absorbed in the performance as Cynthia. David could not take his eyes off him, because at the hauntingly sad music which heralded the death of Romeo, Terence leaned forward and bowed his head, weeping silently.

Outside, Terence explained to Cynthia the movements in the principal dancers' *pas de deux*. He listened attentively as she in turn told him what the ballet teacher at school taught them. Then, without warning, Terence placed his hands around Cynthia's waist, swiftly raised her to his shoulder and as quickly sat her back on her feet.

Cynthia was breathless. Terence seemed oblivious of the bystanders' laughter.

Something was niggling David. At the bus stop he asked Terence outright why he had never joined a ballet school.

He avoided David's gaze. "I could never tell my father that I wanted to be a dancer," he said looking at the mountain. "My father was very much an athlete in his day. Boxed, played rugby, swam. Things that left me cold. So he was terribly disappointed in me. Regarded me as a moffie. The thought was intolerable to him."

Images flitted through his mind. His father's angry castigation. His mother fearfully looking on. Himself seated, head buried in his hands, shoulders shaking as he wept on a late-night, deserted Woodstock beach. Later watching the rolling waves turn into a dance company, washing away the sting of his father's words.

"I couldn't escape my father's hold until it was too late. When I finally nerved myself to attend classes, I was too old."

"It's tough, isn't it?"

"It's not too bad really," Terence replied, laughing without mirth. "I can always get ballet music from the record libary. And then there are the performances at the City Hall."

3

Yvonne was ironing in the kitchen when she heard a knock at the front door. The children were asleep in the back, so she switched on the light in the front room as well as the one outside above the door.

"Yes?"

"May I please speak to Mr Patterson?" The voice was soft and deferential.

Yvonne did not reply immediately. The young man who towered above her matched David's description of Melvyn Francis. She noted that despite the bite in the air, he had on a navy-blue blazer, grey flannels, a drip-dry white shirt and sky-blue tie. His hair was neatly brushed back and his shoes shone. A canvas bag dangled from his wrist. David didn't say he was also good-looking, she thought.

"Mr Patterson's not here."

A look of disappointment passed over his face. "My name is Melvyn Francis," he introduced himself. "Mr Patterson said that I should pay him a visit any time I was in the neighbourhood. Would you tell him that I called?"

"I know. David said you be coming around."

Yvonne disagreed with David's assessment of the young man. Her woman's intuition told her that he would be the sort to open a door for a woman, the sort never to remain seated in a bus or train while an older person was standing. She could see that he had not grown up in their kind of background. What a shame that Melvyn had come here with David waiting across the lane, she thought. She would have liked to speak to him a little longer.

"David's just across the way. He told me I'm to bring you along when you show up."

She closed the door and Melvyn moved aside for her to lead the way. But he rushed forward to open the gate for her. She smiled to herself: she had been right. She nodded her acknowledgement of his courteous behaviour and again walked ahead of him. As they approached the pool of light under the street lamp, she swayed her hips even more. She knew it would attract his attention. At Eddie and Rebecca's fence she turned her head and caught him looking at her posterior.

"This is the house," she said, enjoying the embarrassed look on his face. "You better knock first, and watch out for the dogs."

"Thank you, Mrs Patterson." His voice was low and respectful. "Good night."

Yvonne returned his greeting, turned on her heel and swayed back in the direction of home, sure that Melvyn would not be able to resist having another look at her as she walked away.

I hope David's not going to drive him away with his usual rudeness, she thought. He never invited anyone quite as nice before.

After a slight hesitation, Melvyn knocked at Eddie's door.

"Come in," a loud voice responded.

He cautiously opened the door.

The first thing he noticed was a demijohn of wine on a table, then a large colour print of a landscape on the back wall, and below it a couch which had seen better days.

"Let's see your face," the same voice commanded.

Melvyn entered and closed the door.

"What can I do for you?" Eddie asked, and in the same breath: "Rebecca, I think here's a salesman to see you." He pointed to a chair. "Sit down. My wife won't be long."

Melvyn refused the offered chair and cleared his throat. "I'm sorry, but I'm not a salesman."

"Salesmen are also people," Charley said from the couch.

Eddie was puzzled now. "You're not one of the Baptist bunch from Hester's church, are you?" he demanded to know.

"No. I'm an assistant manager at a supermarket," Melvyn replied with a touch of pomposity. "Mrs Patterson said that I'd find Mr Patterson here."

"Oh. Take a seat, David's in the shit-house."

Melvyn sat down and braved the curious stares of the three men. After a while he shifted his gaze to take in the rest of the room.

The place was crammed with furniture: the couch; the centre table with

102

a chair at either end; a wooden pot-plant stand against the left wall between another two matching chairs. Centred above the chairs hung two framed charcoal drawings. An old wireless squatted in a corner near the window.

"Do you drink?"

Melvyn nodded his head.

"Then pour yourself a drink," Terence said, pointing at the demijohn.

Melvyn carefully placed the canvas bag on the floor. He moved to the table and tipped the demijohn, the wine swirling halfway up the glass. He sat down again, taking small sips and looking at the gleaming linoleum on the floor.

He was still sitting like this when David entered the room.

He replaced the glass and hastily got to his feet, holding out his hand. "Good evening, Mr Patterson."

"Hi, docco man," David answered. "Glad you could make it. Sit down."

David introduced Melvyn to the others. Charley and Terence immediately seemed more relaxed and Eddie said, "Take off your jacket. Make yourself at home."

Melvyn draped his jacket neatly across the back of his chair. He hitched up his trousers as he sat down as if not to disturb their neatly pressed crease. David took in the performance with an amused smile.

Hell, Eddie thought, don't tell me we're saddled with a tailor's dummy. I hope his conversation isn't going to be as wooden as he looks. Terence was envious of the stranger's clothes. Only Charley was not interested in Melvyn's garb, the fact that the man had shown himself ready to partake in their drinking was enough for him.

"Who's the artist?" Melvyn said, pointing at the two drawings.

"Steward Thompson. One of our friends. He had his first solo exhibition recently," David replied. "He won't be here tonight."

"He's visiting his white friends," Eddie explained sourly.

"Melvyn, don't mind Eddie," David said. "He's like a woman who follows fashions, and at the moment it's very unfashionable to have white friends, especially as Eddie doesn't hob-nob with whites."

"Since when do you stand up for the damnn tourists?" Eddie demanded, pushing his shoulders forward pugnaciously.

"Only when I'm sober," David teased.

"As Omar Khayam might have said," Charley intervened, "come, fill the cup with wine, and fling the garment of strife to the swine."

"I second the proposal," Terence said, fearful that an argument between David and Eddie might erupt and scare off Melvyn.

David hooked a finger through the eye of the demijohn, raised it and tilting it across his shoulder filled his glass.

Melvyn had never witnessed this method of pouring wine. He was tempted to try it, but he was afraid that he would stain his shirt, so he held out his glass for a refill.

In the meantime Eddie had placed a record on the player. The sound was much too loud but no one bothered to turn down the volume. Rebecca, who until now had steadfastly ignored all her husband's summonses, finally ventured it out of the kitchen in an attempt to lower the decibels, but Eddie glared at her and she retreated, merely glancing at Melvyn and murmuring under her breath that Eddie showed no consideration for the neighbours and that she was the one who would have to face them the next day.

Charley was asleep before the record ended, his loud snores cutting into Miles Davis's trumpet solo.

"Have you seen Fellini's latest film, *La Notta*?" David asked Melvyn.

"Yes."

"What do you think of it?"

Melvyn was at a loss. "I couldn't quite follow it," he admitted. "Nothing seems to happen. And it ends on such an inconclusive note."

"That's the beauty of it. We're so accustomed to following a linear plot that we don't know what to make of something without one. That's why a picture like *La Notta* catches you unprepared. It's a wonderful picture, even though our censors have probably shredded it with their misplaced morality. It's literature brought to the screen. I've never before seen stream-of-consciousness translated into film so well. Françoise Sagan's *Aimes-vous Brahms*, which I read the other day, is written almost in the same style. The American and English writers I've read haven't even attempted that style yet."

David's remarks left Melvyn speechless, but after the third drink, he was completely at ease. Their talk, flippant at times, never dwelled on the rape-and-robbery cases which filled pages of the *Post*; they never concerned themselves with the sports round-up his rugby-playing friends so loved, or lapsed into the inane politeness that often passed as conversation.

"David," he said, when he deemed the time right, "I've brought a bottle." He removed the bottle from the canvas bag. "It's Harvey's Cream Sherry."

Charley opened his eyes at the crackling of paper.

"Welcome to the club," he said and reached for the bottle.

Melvyn reluctantly released the bottle.

"It's a nice wine," Eddie grudgingly admitted.

David did not comment. I wonder what makes Melvyn so eager to impress us? I told him that we'd be sitting around talking and drinking, and he comes here all togged-up as if he been invited to a debutantes' ball. And if he has to buy sherry and not ordinary sweet wine, why not Old Brown Sherry? Why Harvey's Cream?

Melvyn was disappointed at David's silence. He had thought that David would approve of his choice of wine. He had made a careful study of the book on wine he had borrowed from the library, marking the various kinds.

"These fancy wines are all right, but it costs too much and certainly hasn't got the kick of the people's wine!" Charley announced after finishing his glass of the cream sherry with one long swallow.

David saw the crestfallen look on Melvyn's face. Lesson one, he thought. Let's hope he learns from it.

"You should get used to drinking good wine," Terence reprimanded Charley.

"In that case, pour me another," and Charley pushed his glass forward.

"Pour for all of us," David added.

Melvyn had drunk more than he had intended by the time he was ready to leave. Earlier on he had loosened his tie. Now he draped his jacket across his shoulder and bid them good night.

"Thank you, I have enjoyed myself. If I may, I'd like to repeat my visit, Mr Patterson," he said unsteadily from the door.

Terence decided to accompay Melvyn, while David, looking at the recumbent Charley, decided that he would leave later.

4

The children were in bed, asleep. Yvonne was closing the curtains when she saw Melvyn Francis walking up the lane. It was Friday evening, six days since she had taken him to Eddie's place. Hastily she withdrew her head from the window to peep at him from behind the curtains.

Her pulse was racing by the time he had opened the gate and knocked at the door.

She took a deep breath before opening the door.

"Good evening, Mrs Patterson."

"Good evening. Come inside, Mr Francis."

"I was walking past and I thought I'd drop in. I hope you don't mind."

"No, not at all," she assured him. "David's gone to work but he say you welcome any time."

For once she felt no annoyance at David's custom of inviting everyone he met to their house.

"Sit down. You like a cup of cocoa?"

"Please. That's if it's not too much bother."

"It won't be. I was just going to make some for myself." She had actually intended to make a pot of tea after she had had a bath.

She went to the kitchen and put a heaped spoon of cocoa in the mugs, topping them up with hot milk. Normally, she would haave used water with just a splash of milk to whiten it. She placed the mugs with a sugar bowl on a tray and returned to the front room.

He got up from his chair. Sugar spoon in hand, she asked, "How many?"

"Three, please. I like it sweet."

"Do you like everything sweet?" she said, tilting her head and adding, "Women as well?" She ended with a sharp girlish laugh.

Melvyn bowed his head over his mug in an effort to conceal his consternation. He was attracted to Yvonne. It had happened almost at first sight. Without wanting to admit it to himself, he had half wished that David would not be here tonight.

"Where's your girl, a smart young man like you?"

No, he would not tell her of Vera who was becoming a drag with her clinging and her demands. Or of the easy conquests he had among the girls in his set. Girls as insipid as their chatter, whom he bedded and afterwards discarded because they were of no concequence to him. But he wasn't comfortable with intellectual women either. They made him feel inadequate, their conversation revealed his limitations, made him read books with repressed fury later to broaden his knowledge.

"Don't you like girls?" Yvonne asked when he did not answer, alarmed at the sudden thought that he might share Terence's sexual preferences.

"Yes, I like girls," he answered, his eyes involuntarily flitting from her face to her breasts.

Yvonne responded by pulling in her stomach so that her breasts lifted.

The effect was as she had expected. He nervously crossed his legs and looked away. I shouldn't tease him like this, she thought.

"Would you care for a cigarette?" Melvyn asked, reaching for his case.

It was a silver one. She took a cigarette and waited for him to produce a light. The lighter matched the case. She put her hand around his knuckles as he held the little flame in front of her, her index finger resting on the soft flesh between his thumb and the rest of his hand. Was she imagining it or could she feel a vein throbbing beneath her finger? She let her hand linger longer than necessary.

What's she up to? Melvyn was bewildered. He was not used to such boldness.

Yvonne removed her hand and blew out a cloud of smoke, creating a screen between them. All I have to do now is make him forget his high regard for David and he is mine. She shivered sensuously.

"May I please play a record?"

Yvonne nodded her head.

As he reached down to put a record on the player, Yvonne took stock of the taut fit of his jacket. The jacket moved up and she noticed how tightly his trousers fitted over his buttocks.

It's a pity he didn't put on a blues number, Yvonne thought as the notes of some Spanish tune filled the room and he turned down the volume. Then he wouldn't be able to say no if I asked him to dance with me.

The urge to have him embrace her suddenly overwhelmed her. To have him kiss her. To feel his hands on her body. Damn David! Does he hold back when he gets the chance to run his hands over the body of some little bitch? While I have to pretend that it doesn't bother me and ignore the dirt Rebecca scatters. If I could take off the record without offending him, I would, she thought, just as the record ended.

"I like the Habenera, it's one of Bizet's best compositions," Melvyn said.

"So do I. It's from the set of Readers' Digest records David got. It's one of my favourites," Yvonne lied with a smile.

Silence settled between them. Then Melvyn suddenly stammered, "I don't know how to say it, but I feel very much at home here, Mrs Patterson. The way David has accepted me, introducing me to his friends, telling me that I'm free to visit any time, even if he's not home. The way you let me play your record. There's always an argument between my father and I when I play music in my room. I have to play it softly when he's around."

"You be much more at home if you call me Yvonne," she said, looking him straight in the eye.

"All right ... Yvonne."

"Now that you've chosen a record, can I do the same?"

She selected Billy Vaughan's *For Lovers*.

When the music entered a dreamy phase, she switched off the outside light as well as the one in the front room. She waited for the first cut to end before she asked Melvyn to dance with her.

He held her as if she were made of porcelain and took great care not to step on her toes. He hardly dared to breathe.

At the end of the cut she remained in his arms, waiting for the music to resume.

Bit by bit, Melvyn's tenseness disappeared as they swayed to the music, Yvonne resting her head on his chest, tightening her arms around his neck and not once moving away from him in between cuts on the record. He could feel her warmth. He was intoxicated by her female smell.

He recalled the image of her walking in front of him, the sway of her body, the joggle of her hips underneath her dress, the odd shadow cast by the street lamp. He sighed. No matter how much he reproached himself, he could not get past the fact that he desired her.

He knew that Yvonne was aware of his raised manhood pressing against her thigh. I should stop this, he decided. She's David's wife. I really didn't come here with this in mind.

Neither of them noticed that the front door had opened.

Eddie had to wait for his eyes to adjust to the gloom in the room.

The bastard certainly didn't waste his time! he thought as he made out Melvyn's tall frame moving slowly from side to side and a pair of hands clasping around his neck.

"Well, well! What a cuddlesome twosome you are," he said, taking care not to let his resentment spill over in his speech. "I'm almost sorry that I came over."

Guiltily, they broke apart. Yvonne strolled over and switched on the light.

Eddie searched their faces. Yvonne stared straight back at him, challenging him to put his accusations into words. Melvyn, on the other hand, displayed his contrition like a badge.

Eddie moved over to the record player. "Good old Billy Vaughan," he laughed. "There's nothing like his trumpet to make you aware of a special woman. What do you say, Melvyn?"

Melvyn did not reply, instead he slumped down in a chair and busied himself with a record cover.

What are you up to, Eddie? Yvonne thought as she looked at Eddie. Of course! The realisation suddenly struck her: He's jealous of Melvyn! He thought I'd be here alone and he could try his act with me.

"You should know, Eddie," she mocked. "A blues, a room with the lights off, a woman that move you. What more do you want?" She put her head back and laughed.

Melvyn could not take his eyes off Yvonne. The bold glint in her eyes; the slow, deep breaths that pushed her breasts ever higher; the animal grace of her body as she eased herself into the chair next to his.

He switched his gaze to Eddie's face and recognised the same hunger Yvonne had aroused in him.

Then Eddie's features became as noncommittal as his speech. "It all depends on the woman."

"Do you think I'm that sort of a woman?" Yvonne taunted.

"It's not for me to say."

"I think you know me by now."

Melvyn listened and looked on uneasily. He was lost in the conversation so full of innuendo and shared understanding.

Eddie eyed the two mugs, dried cocoa lining their insides. "Any more left?" he asked.

When Yvonne silently gathered the tray, Eddie knew that he had been replaced. Earlier, he would never have had to ask for something to drink.

"Smoke?" Melvyn offered, producing his cigarette case and matching lighter.

"Thanks."

Swanky bastard! Eddie could feel a chill of hostility coming from Yvonne. She clearly wanted him to feel unwelcome.

"You don't have to worry about cocoa in the future," Melvyn said, happy to find a neutral topic. "I'll bring a large tin when I come next time. For that matter, you should buy all your groceries through me. You'd get it at wholesale prices."

"Thank you, Melvyn. I tell David about your kind offer." After a few seconds Yvonne added: "I pay you for the cocoa."

"Don't worry about that. It'll be my contribution for these winter nights."

"I still have to check with David," she said, thinking: He'll just have to accept it. If we take stuff from that Paula bitch then I can take whatever Melvyn brings along.

"The boss is very pleased with the way I'm running things. He says if he gets shifted to manage the new branch we're opening there's a chance that I'd be put in charge of the supermarket in Klipfontein Road."

Eddie's cocoa had turned to gall, yet he could not bring himself to leave.

5

The work-week had come to an end and the Beverley Street off-sales, two blocks from Athlone Station, was overflowing with Friday after-work customers eager to embark on the first stage of release. Street sweepers, forestry workers and linesmen – their muddy-brown uniforms identifying

109

them as City Council workers; teachers in sober, grey suits, housewives buying weekend supplies for their husbands, down-and-outs who scavenged drinking money from people passing street-corners they proclaimed as their domain, their faces showing the ravages of over-consumption.

David savoured the anticipation as he waited outside the entrance for Melvyn. During the last few weekends, Melvyn had gradually been accepted as one of the group, and David was amused by the newcomer's growing attraction towards Yvonne. When he slyly suggested the previous Saturday evening that Yvonne had found in him another man to add to her string of admirers, Melvyn had blushed and stammered in a most ridiculous way, saying that he had meant no disrespect. That was when David said that he would have to pay for the liquor the next weekend.

An old man, shoes soiled with red clay, paused next to him to thrust a demijohn of semi-sweet wine in his haversack.

"That's the right stuff after a hard day's work," David said, smiling at the tanned face.

"Feel like a dop?" the old man offered generously, patting his pocket where another bottle bulged. "We can have a quick one in the lane."

"Save it for next time, grandpa. I'm waiting for my chummy."

Every face held a smile except those in grey suits who just stared straight ahead and passed by. At last Melvyn appeared.

"I bought two bottles of madeira and a bottle of Frotinac – after consulting Yvonne."

David's smile concealed his thoughts. Hell, he knew the guy was trapped in Yvonne's snare but did he have to act like an idiot by asking her what drink to buy?

They stopped at a bakery where Melvyn bought a loaf of rye bread.

David looked at the stack of french loaves and urged him to buy one. Not allowing the assistent to wrap it, he took the loaf, and to Melvyn's shock broke off a piece and stuffed it into his mouth. He made further onslaughts on the bread as they walked towards the bus stop. He giggled to himself, thinking that Melvyn was probably hoping that they would not meet anyone he knew. Then a malicious thought flitted through him mind.

"Let's dip in here," he said, pointing to a public convenience.

Melvyn obediently complied.

David took one of the bottles of madeira and twisted off the top. He raised the bottle to his mouth and swallowed deeply.

"Here," he said, passing the bottle to Melvyn.

Melvyn was not altogether certain that he should comply with David's latest request. He looked at the bottle and then at David.

110

"Come'n," David urged, shaking the bottle.

Melvyn reached for the bottle, took a tentative sip and passed it back to David.

David grinned. "Hell, that's not the way to drink."

With horrified fascination Melvyn watched as David tilted the bottle and swallowed, a trickle of wine running down his chin.

David's roguish smile confirmed to Melvyn that he was putting him through a test. He took the bottle, titled it like David had done and swallowed. The bottle was halfed when he passed it back to David.

"That's better, docco man," David said approvingly. "Now let's finish it off."

A few more gulps between the two of them and the bottle was empty. David stood the bottle against the wall, Melvyn belched loudly. "Pardon me," he said, his voice as proper as that of a dowager.

"Of course," David responded, his manner matching Melvyn's.

The rushed drinking was taking its toll on Melvyn. The white tiles on the wall of the public convenience were dissolving into one another right in front of his eyes and taking on the shape of a crazy mirror at a fairground, transforming every shape into an oddity. He felt like resting his fevered head on the cool tiles.

David reached out for the second bottle of madeira.

"Let's see if we can start on this one."

Melvyn blinked at him owlishly.

David, head aslant like a bantam cock, looked at Melvyn's condition. Hell, the guy was pissed!

His earlier feeling of irritation disappeared. I'd better pull him together, he thought. And keep the second madeira for home. "Hey, Melvyn. There's a basin. Wash your face," he urged.

When Melvyn did not respond, he led him to the basin and splashed water on his face. Melvyn yielded to his ministrations.

"Do you feel all right?" David asked, patting him on the back like a big brother. He dabbed at Melvyn's face with a soaked handkerchief. "Drink some water and rinse your gut."

A spasm of nausea shook Melvyn. He just had time to crouch over the basin before his shoulders wrenched and sour-smelling wine poured from his mouth.

"I'll ask Yvonne for some mince curry when we get home, now that your insides are clear. The fish oil will line your stomach and you'd be able to drink from now until tomorrow."

The prospect of curry and more wine made Melvyn retch all over again.

On unsteady feet he got onto the bus and followed David to the rear and sat down. The slightest swaying movement brought on fresh waves of nausea. Melvyn silently prayed that he would keep down whatever was still left inside him.

David was conversing with the passenger sitting next to him on the back seat. Melvyn shuddered when he saw the man take out a bottle of wine and pass it to David.

The bottle was passed up and down the line. When the bottle paused in front of him, David declined on his behalf. Gratefully he rested his cheek against the cool window.

When the bus finally stopped he lurched to his feet and stumbled after David.

Yvonne stared at Melvyn with alarm. She turned to David.

"There's nothing wrong with him," he said good-humouredly. "He just had a few drinks on an empty stomach. I told him that you'll give him some mince curry, and that that should pull him straight."

Melvyn grinned weakly at Yvonne. She glared at David. "And where were you drinking?" she charged, for she knew this was all David's doing.

"We dipped in at the piss-house opposite the Kismet and finished off a bottle of madeira."

"You mean to tell me that you take Melvyn to a lavatory to drink out a bottle of wine? Have you no shame? Is is too much to wait till you get home? What if there was somebody there that know Melvyn?" She visualised the many people entering the public convenience while David and Melvyn stood there consuming the wine.

When David did not answer, Yvonne turned and suggested to Melvyn that he should lie down while she prepared some coffee.

"Stop treating him like an over-grown baby," David growled. "Getting him to lie down will only make him drunker."

As Yvonne retreated to the kitchen, Shirley walked into the front room. She stared curiously at Melvyn who had sat down at the table. His head rested heavily on his cupped hands, a vacant look in his eyes. His neatly combed hair was in disarray and a film of sweat glistened on his face.

"What's wrong with him, Daddy?" she asked, her voice consumed with worry.

"There's nothing wrong with him, darling. He's just had a bit too much to drink."

"Shirley!" Yvonne shouted from the kitchen. "Go to your room and leave Mr Francis alone."

David could hear the anger in Yvonne's voice. It did not disturb him. "Give me a kiss, darling," he said.

Shirley put her hands around her father's neck and pulled him towards her. The short bristles on his jaw prickled her skin; his breath was warm on her face and smelled of wine. "Now, do what your mummy told you to do," he said. "Go to your room and look at your books."

David was sipping from the second bottle of madeira when Yvonne returned with the coffee. "You want coffee?" she asked him curtly.

"No, I'll stick to the same brand."

Melvyn sipped his coffee with downcast eyes. He only lifted his head once the cup was empty. "I'm terribly sorry," he apologised meekly.

"There's nothing to be sorry about," David soothed him. "Getting drunk is a good thing. It knocks all the pretentiousness out of a man, makes him realise that a human being shouldn't be bolstered by pomposity and false pride."

"It also make him a fool and a weakling!" Yvonne snapped.

David raised the glass of wine in front of his eyes and squinted at Yvonne through it before taking another sip and saying, "You're right, my darling. But is it because I'm a fool that I do this weak thing, or because I'm a weakling that I can't rid myself of my foolishness? I don't always drink for the same reasons. There are times when I take to wine for the pleasant feeling. There are times when I drink to forget pain. And, then there are times when I must drink to hide my many weaknesses. Now, may I eat?"

The food, a hearty stew, had a settling effect on Melvyn and he did not demur when David filled his glass.

"I bought some Frontinac," he said to Yvonne. "Would you like some?"

Because it was Melvyn, she nodded her head.

"And now to sleep," David announced, stretching himself out on the mat. As Melvyn got up to take his plate to the kitchen, he pointed to the mat on the other side of the table. "Leave that to Yvonne. You get yourself to that mat. We'll leave the bottle in the middle. Whoever feels thirsty can pour himself a shot."

Yvonne hid her disappointment. She had thought that David meant to go to sleep, which would have left Melvyn free to join her in the kitchen.

"Don't you think we should leave the bottle for later?" Melvyn said apprehensively.

"Why wait for later?"

Late afternoon drifted into evening. And still David would stretch out his hand for the bottle and fill his glass each time it seemed that he had fallen asleep. Yvonne, disappointed, bathed Thelma and prepared her for bed, urging Cynthia and Shirley to do the same.

After prayers, Thelma called to her father.

Yvonne nudged David's shoulder. "There, your daughter's calling." David sauntered off.

He stood in the door and looked at Thelma, blanket tucked in under her chin. Yvonne's outlines were traced upon her face. He smiled at the long plait so like that of her mother's and thought of the strong love Yvonne had awakened in him the first moment he had seen her, a love that had now been transmitted to the daughters she had borne him.

He sat down on the bed, took Thelma in his arms and kissed her on the cheek, his fingertips caressing her smooth black hair.

He had an overwhelming desire to weep and struggled to get rid of the lump in his throat.

"What's the matter, Daddy?"

He could not immediately speak. She had been so small at birth – just a tiny little body in a bundle of soft blanket, the eyes narrow little glinting slits, crowned by an unusual profusion of hair for a new-born baby.

"Nothing, darling. It's just that I love you so much. All of you."

Cynthia and Shirley, faces shiny and hair brushed, joined them and got into bed.

"Daddy must tell us a story," Thelma demanded.

"Would you like to listen to Cindy-Ella?" he asked.

"Yes, yes, Daddy," they choroused.

Back in the lounge some minutes later, David discovered that Eddie had joined Yvonne and Melvyn.

"I see they're looking after you."

"Yes," Eddie answered, raising his glass towards Melvyn. "Thanks to the acting host. I was just telling Yvonne that it's a pleasure seeing so much of Melvyn. I found him and Yvonne having a cozy scene when I came over a couple of weeks ago."

David did not respond to Eddie's probing.

"I take it that he's now a member of the club?"

Yvonne anxiously searched David's face, while he rested his eyes on Melvyn's face. Melvyn shifted uneasily in his chair.

Then David switched his gaze to Eddie. With a smile he said, "Yes, Melvyn is a member of the club. I don't know how you feel about it. If you think that he won't fit in, and the others agree, then he'd still be welcome in my house. And if he feels that way inclined, he could even take Yvonne to a show. It's not often she gets a chance to go places."

Eddie, to hide his confusion, hastily agreed.

"You want a drink, David?" Melvyn asked to indicate his gratitude.

"Why not?"

Their glasses filled, David related Melvyn's drinking escapade earlier the day to Eddie.

"He matched me swallow for swallow."

Melvyn basked in David's praise, and Eddie did not miss the look in Yvonne's eyes. David's a damn fool in his trust, he decided. Only a cretin wouldn't see that there's something brewing between Yvonne and that shit-arse Melvyn!

6

The small panel van careened around the corner and they were all flung off their seats in the back.

David hugged the bottle to his waist with one hand, the other hand coming to rest on Hester's breast.

What would her reaction be if he squeezed it? A snort of laughter ripped through him. Maybe she'd make a sound like a truck's hooter – honk! honk! His fingers clenched in anticipation, but another jerk rolled them apart. They were a mass of limbs seeking support in the plunging van.

"We should've taken a bus." Hester sounded vexed. "I don't know why you insisted that he bring us through. We'll end up in hospital or the morgue the way he's driving."

"Now, now," David said soothingly. "Don't you worry. Tommy's a good driver, an old friend of mine. He's a mechanic at a garage in Salt River, so the van comes with him. And Terence is keeping an eye on him in the front. Take a little sip. It will settle your nerves."

Hester shook her head very firmly.

"Anyone for a drink?"

"I'll have one," Melvyn said.

Hester tucked the hem of her dress in under her knees and leaned against Steward for support. She would have prefered to come to Arnold's birthday party with only him as company, but Steward had stated that Arnold had invited David and Terence, as well, and would not object to the others accompanying them.

She looked at Melvyn drinking directly from the bottle, amused that he copied David so apishly. Her lips curled in dislike. His display of manners didn't fool her, she had noticed his sly attentions towards Yvonne. And his pretence at erudition was so tiresome, right from the start. Like a school-boy showing off how much he knew. The more she saw of him, the more he revealed that he had a good memory but not much intellect. Poor Yvonne.

David was watching Hester. Now why the hell can't Yvonne be like her? What difference does it make if there are people around that she doesn't know? Here he was by himself going to a party: Yvonne and the girls visiting her sister in Salt River, Dawn probably on her way to a film with some upper-class Coloured bore, Paula god-knows-where.

"What's the hold-up with the bottle?" he demanded of Eddie.

"Every man gets a turn!"

David, after a deep swallow, flung the empty bottle out the window. It exploded in the gutter.

"Are you sure it's all right taking us along?" Eddie asked.

"What the hell do you mean 'are you sure it's all right'?" David exploded. "Of course it's all right! Arnold invited us, didn't he?"

"Not all of us, he didn't. He invited you and Steward and Terence. He didn't say anything about us. How do you know he'd put up with uninvited guests?"

"Would you stop acting the bitch, Eddie? You always carp when Steward visits his whites friends. Now we take you along to Arnold, who is one of us, and still you come up with crap!"

In the uneasy silence that followed, Steward trained his eyes on his shoes and Hester found time to adjust her dress. Melvyn looked from David to Eddie and back to David.

Eddie braved David's searing stare for a while but then shifted his gaze to Charley, who suddenly let out a long, drawn-out snore.

David banged his fist against the side of the van. "You can fuck off home if you want to get out."

The van slithered to a halt at the pavement.

Terence jumped out and rushed to peer into the back of the van. "What's wrong? What's the banging in aid of?"

"Ask him." David jerked his head at Eddie.

"There's nothing wrong." Eddie's words were controlled, unlike the fury raging in his head. "All I wanted to know is whether it would be all right for me to go along with all of you. After all, Arnold didn't invite me."

Terence hesitated before replying, "I don't think Arnold would mind. Could we move on now?"

As he walked back to the front of the van, Terence told himself not to worry. Another bottle of wine would wash away any problem between David and Eddie long before they reached the party.

Melvyn took out his cigarette case and offered it around. First to Eddie, then to Hester and Steward. Eddie struck a match before Melvyn could reach for his lighter and held it out to David.

116

David's anger swirled away like the smoke streaming from his nostrils. He looked at Eddie and rested his hand on his thigh, shaking it.

"I'll leave with you if Arnold should come up shit, okay?" he reassured him.

Eddie's face relaxed into a grin. "Just as you say, doc."

"That's better. Now you're mit it."

All acrimony forgotten, talk swung to parties they had had among themselves and outside parties to which they had been invited. Melvyn sat quietly regretting the wasted time before he met David.

"I still think that the Easter party last year was the best we've had," Eddie said. "It started on Good Friday and ended on Easter Monday afternoon, moving from David's place to mine."

"What you mean is that we went to your place once or twice," David remarked dryly. "But it certainly was a son-of-a-bitch of a party, that one," he agreed. "Remember, at one stage, it seemed we were going to run out of money, but trust old money-bags Steward to have had the spare rands. The only thing that brought the party to a bit of a halt was when someone passed out. But luckily everyone didn't pass out at the same time. Yes, that was one hell of a party. And that's what I like about our parties – no planning, just two guys get together with a jug of wine, and it's party time. As long as you're mit it, docco man."

"It reminds me of the Friday and Saturday evenings I've spent at the Naaz in Woodstock," Melvyn said, not to be left out of the conversation. "It's the in place. You have to book a table for the night. All of us would be wearing paper hats and masks and ..."

"That's the problem with some of us Coloureds," David interrupted him. "They must be as bourgeois as the whites to show how they enjoy themselves. I went there once. It was pathetic! Tables crowded with people and bottles. Everyone singing and drinking, desperate to show they're with it. Bewildered Coloureds making whoopee in a restaurant the owner tries to pass off as a nightclub. What ridiculous decor – badly painted and out of proportion minarets with crescents on top. And fucked-up Coloureds gladly emptying their purse so that they can go back to work on Monday morning and boast about the fabulous weekend they had. Honest to God, I pitied the miserable sods!"

"I think you're mistaken," Melvyn protested meekly. "It's quite a nice place. You can't get in there on weekends."

"Have you ever had a good look at what you booked? The decor is an insult to one's sensibilities. The food's not bad, I grant you, especially the curry, but the price! Almost what whites pay at the Grand Hotel where no

Black bastard is even allowed to buy himself a cup of coffee. No, the Naaz is all right if you're a damn tourist. But I hope that by now you're no longer one of them."

Melvyn dropped his gaze to avoid David's challenging stare and withdrew into silence.

The van stopped in front of an imposing double-storeyed white house with light-green shutters in Bree Street, on the same side as St Paul's Church. Two smaller houses, less grand, huddled on either side.

"Now this is what I call a house!" David said and whistled appreciatively.

Everybody tumbled out of the van and waited on the pavement.

David noticed five strangers getting out of a car parked on the other side of the street. When they reached the gate leading to the door he attached himself to them and followed them up the steps onto the veranda.

On either side of the door stood a wooden tub with a brass rim and small palm tree. Above the door hung a cab's lantern.

While they were waiting for someone to answer the door bell, David tapped a girl on the shoulder. She swung round, took one look at his flushed face and disarranged clothing and hurriedly shifted away from him. At that moment, the door opened and the group entered. David pushed his way forward. "What's your hurry, docco man?" he asked the tall white man who was about to close the door. "Wait for me!"

The tall man peered down at him through a monocle. "I think you're at the wrong address," he said haughtily.

"This is 40 Kloof Street, isn't it?"

"Yes, that's right."

"Then this is where the party is for dear old Arnold. Right?"

The tall man's monocle just about dropped from his eye when he noticed the rest of the group, led by Hester, walking up the pathway. As if seeking help, he turned his head and looked down the dark passage behind him.

David shoved him aside. "Arnold, you bastard!" he shouted into the darkness beyond the brightly lit entrance. "We're here."

The tall man was completely shaken. "Would you wait here for moment while I get Arnold?" he asked, trying to sound in control.

David's response was a mischievous smile and a loud "Shit!"

Hester moved away as if to detach herself from David's outburst. Steward had turned around and was looking down the deserted street. Only Terence tried to hush David with a reminder that they were, after all, strangers to what seemed to be Arnold's host.

Arnold Barker, accompanied by the tall gentleman with the monocle

118

now neatly back in place, emerged from the dark. "I thought you weren't coming any more," he said.

"Ag, you know how it is," David smilingly replied. "We sat around with a few bottles we had to finish. We were lucky we ran into him," and he pointed at Tommy, who was swaying on his heels in front of one of the elegant veranda poles. "He brought us through."

He did not bother to introduce the driver to Arnold.

"This is Laurence van Dyk who has arranged the party for me," Arnold said, inclining his head towards the tall man who was nervously polishing his monocle, not looking at them.

Arnold rattled off their names: David Patterson, Eddie Williams, Terence Voight, Steward Thompson, Hester Loubster, Melvyn Francis. The driver he ignored.

From behind the gloom someone called for Arnold, and he vanished into the shadows.

"This is my house," Laurence van Dyk said, his voice suddenly deep and booming as if he was addressing an audience. "I bid you welcome. In my house we are all equal. A man's colour is of no importance. Merit is what counts. Anyone who is a friend of Arnold's is a friend of mine."

"Shit! Not another one!" David snorted. "Would you please spare us all that crap? Next thing you're going to tell me how much you love Coloured people and how you admire their sense of humour, in the face of everything the whites have done to them."

Laurence van Dyk was still at a loss for words when Arnold returned from the shadows.

"Do you think I could go to the toilet?" Hester asked.

"Certainly, my dear," Laurence van Dyk said. "Come this way."

He peered over his shoulder as they walked down the passage. "What makes him so aggressive towards people?"

Hester did not attempt to enlighten him.

David glared after the retreating couple, then turned his attention towards Arnold. "What about a drink?"

"It's about time," Charley mumbled.

They followed Arnold into the patch of gloom. "Shit!" David swore as he stumbled over someone's feet. "Why don't they switch on some lights?"

The lights came on as they were halfway across the hallway. A hush fell as everybody blinked in the sudden glare.

The guests were as startled as Laurence van Dyk was on first seeing the new arrivals, and their eyes reflected puzzlement, even shock. But then the buzz of conversation resumed.

"This is cosy," David said to Arnold, relishing the fact that the women present outnumbered the men. But a closer inspection evoked a burst of laughter: some of the females were in fact males dressed in what looked like ballet tights and blouses, their hair hanging loose to their shoulders. Their eyeshadow matched that of the women and it seemed that there had been a sharing of lipstick as well.

"Will you sort us out or do we go by touch in the dark?"

Arnold smiled and moved to the sideboard with the drinks and filled a paper cup for each of them.

"You're among equals," Eddie said, nudging Terence.

"They're most probably more intelligent than you," Terence lashed back.

Ignoring Terence's remark, Eddie leered over the rim of the paper cup and said, "Arnold, how should we term them – a harem of homos, a frolic of fairies, or a quarter of queers?" He looked at David and added: "This is how David would like to describe them if he had the style."

In the spasm of laughter that shook him, Charley crushed his paper cup and the wine squirted in his face.

"Please, everyone here is my guest," Arnold replied, his eyes narrowing slightly. "I don't go around insulting people at your place."

"Bear that in mind, Eddie," David cautioned. "Eat, drink and be merry. We are here to celebrate Arnold's nativity."

"Thanks, David," and Arnold extended his hand.

Drink in hand, Melvyn looked around the room. Terence had moved off and was chatting to one of the males in tights. Steward had seated himself at the bottom of the three steps leading from the hall to the back of the house, obviously waiting for Hester. The driver and Charley were pouring themselves another drink, thirstily eyeing the array of bottles.

Melvyn did not know whether to remain with David and Eddie or join one of the others. He watched Terence and the ballet clan. Peals of giggling punctuated their talk. No, the profusion of homosexuals unnerved him. But not as much as they did Hester, for when she entered the hall shortly afterwards and observed the group of young men in tights flocking around Terence, she stopped in her tracks, distaste written all over her face. He gave her an amused smile when she looked around the room and caught his eye, and turned to join Charley and the driver.

"Olé,!" Laurence van Dyk shouted as the first notes of a José Greco record were heard, and immediately more "olés" reverberated as a troop of males in tights stormed the floor with a clicking of heels and a spirited tossing of manes.

The music was far too infectious for Terence to remain aloof. He snaked out of his coat and with one slick movement hooked it onto his thumb and slung it across his shoulders. With hand aloft he glided onto the middle of the floor and stomped a staccato beat with his heels.

The dancers formed a circle around him, clapping their hands in time with the music, and Terence, like a toreador, advanced then retreated from one to the other. When the music reached its climax, he dropped his coat on the floor and used his heels like castanets.

"Olé!" A chorus of "olés" followed and one of the admirers pulled three long-stemmed roses from a side-table and threw them at his feet.

Terence bowed, retrieved his coat and the roses, and said, "Mucho graçias, senors and senoritas."

While everyone's attention was centred on Terence, Melvyn noticed Charley take a bottle from the sideboard and motion to the driver to follow him to the courtyard, where they settled themselves on a bench. In the meantime, one of the dancers had approached Terence and they took to the floor with slow, measured steps. The intensity of their movements increased as the rhythm of the next piece of music mounted. Terence's face was a mask of pain and pleasure. After a while, his partner moved aside and was replaced by another, and another, in an obvious act of initiation.

When the music ended, the first partner took Terence into the courtyard.

"As I said earlier, Terence is among friends," Eddie said and winked at David.

"I can understand why Terence might prefer them."

Eddie, rebuffed by David's reply, asked a newly arrived girl to dance. She gingerly moved into his arms and as they passed David, Eddie said, "I don't see you dancing, old chap."

"Shit!"

On his way to the courtyard, David passed Steward and Hester.

He stood with his back to the wall. The air outside was heavy with the scent of blooming flowers. He looked up. A host of sparkling attendants indicated the Milky Way. A scimitar moon hung above Lion's Head.

"Hey, David, come over here. See what we've got," Charley called, waving the bottle in the air.

"Where the hell did you get that from?"

"Inside."

"What's happened to Terence?"

"He went up there," Charley said, pointing to a wooden staircase that led to some rooms at the back of the house. "With one of his new-found friends."

"I'll go and see what's he up to."

"Have a swallow before you go."

David lifted the bottle to his mouth and swallowed deeply.

There were four doors on the landing. In which room would Terence be? A soft murmur of voices drew him towards the second door. He could make out Terence's voice.

Without bothering to knock, he opened the door.

They turned around.

Terence and his new friend were seated on a low couch. Rows of books lined one wall. A second wall was adorned with photographs of dancers. An African drum stood in a corner.

"Nice place you've got here," David said.

He inspected the photographs. They were all of the same person. The face looked familiar. Then he recognised the person: Ram Gopal, the Indian classical dancer.

Some magazines on top of the bookshelf caught his attention and he paged through one. Pictures of body-builders posturing and training with weights greeted him.

"Who's into building muscles?"

The stranger remained silent for a moment, then said in soft, melodious tones, "I am."

David looked at him. The skin on his roly-poly body stretched tight and did not show a bulge of muscle.

"David," Terence said, "meet Vernon."

David clasped a soft, pudgy hand.

"I'm awfully thrilled to meet you," Vernon said. "Terence and I were having a nice chat. He's made me feel quite envious."

Terence smiled at David.

"Do you think I could come out to your place one weekend?"

What the hell has he been spreading about me? David thought as he looked into Vernon's anxious eyes. I don't know whether Yvonne would like me inviting him. She can take Terence, but this one is white and more way-out. Inviting him could start something which she might not be able to handle …

"You don't have to decide now. Let me know via Terence when you feel that you'd be able to arrange it. Is that all right with you, Terence?"

"Of course. It just depends on David."

"How's your writing getting on?" Vernon asked David.

"Who told you I write?" he snapped.

"I did," Terence said, still smiling.

"I'd like to read some of your stories. That is if you don't mind."

The words reassured David somewhat. Vernon was not trying to patronise him like some of the whites did when first they met him.

"Let's just say that it's not moving at present." David shrugged his shoulders apologetically. "Weekends seem to come and go, and no weekend is a weekend without a booze session."

"I would very much like to share a drink with you," Vernon said.

"Why not? It is weekend, isn't it?"

Vernon took out a bottle of Créme de Menthe. "This is my special stock."

"It looks lovely," Terence rhapsodised.

"It tastes as heavenly as its appearance," Vernon confirmed with a smile.

He left the room and returned with a beaker of crushed ice and three glasses. He lined the glasses with ice and filled them with Créme de Menthe.

Terence gave a tentative sip. "You're right," he agreed. "It tastes divine."

David sat down on the bed, Vernon reclined next to Terence on the couch. "Have you read any of Genet's plays?" he eagerly asked David. "Saint Genet, Sartre calls him."

David admitted that he was not altogether familiar with Genet.

"Have you perhaps come across an early novel by Gore Vidal, *The City and the Pillar*?"

"Yes, I read that one a long time ago.."

"What about Baldwin's *A Far Country*?"

So there's more to you than just your interest in the shape of the male body, David speculated, eyeing the bookshelf. "Yes," he replied. "I've read that, as well as *Giovanni's Room*, his previous novel."

Vernon looked at David speculatively. "What did you think of it?"

"I found both first class. But the early one, good as it is, seems to me like a preparatory piece for the later one. The love scene between the two homosexuals ..."

David glanced at Vernon to see if he was offended by the term.

"Go on."

"Those scenes were extremely well done and moving."

"Have you any copies of these books, Vernon?" Terence asked.

"I'll let you have the Vidal one before you leave but let me have it back. You won't get it at any of the bookshops. It's banned."

Terence filled their glasses, pleased at the conversation between David and Vernon.

It was quiet in the room until Vernon suddenly very seriously said, "You should write a novel about homosexuals, David."

123

David looked at the two figures on the couch. Vernon, he thought, I wish I had your faith in my writing ability. How could I write a novel about your anguish if I can't even put my own into words? My pain is different, but it matches yours.

Laurence van Dyk took up a position in the centre of the hall. "Friends, one and all," he started, his voice theatrical. "Gather around with drink in hand so that I can laud one who has become more than a mere friend to me. A kindred spirit whose desire matches mine, who uses words to mould an art adorned with beauty. The forms we use may differ, but the pursuit is the same. For the man of letters, the search for perfection goes on. Who cares whether the tale has been twice-told or a thousand times read? It could still be garbed afresh."

He placed an affectionate hand on Arnold's shoulder. "We shall not go into the number of birthdays celebrated. But today gives us cause to celebrate an anniversary of a light destined to illuminate our hearts with the power of his pen. Hail, dear friend, Arnold."

Hester looked around at Charley and the driver who had fallen asleep in the courtyard, their backs to the wall, heads drooping on their chest, and at the approaching David. "I hope he's not going to upset things," she whispered to Steward.

"I agree," David said loudly, his voice mimicking that of Laurence van Dyk. "Arnold is a sweet-arsed son-of-a-bitch! And so say all of us."

A deadly silence followed.

With stricken face, Laurence van Dyk fled from the hall with Arnold in pursuit.

"I knew something like this would happen before the night's over." Hester reached for Steward's hand.

Arnold returned and with measured steps strode up to David. "I'm afraid you'll have to leave. Laurence is terribly upset. This isn't my place. I'm his guest, as are the people I've invited."

"I don't suppose you'd allow a condemned man a slice of bread and a cup of wine for the road?"

The smile on David's face crumpled as Arnold snapped, "Certainly not!"

At that moment, Charley and the driver tottered into the hall rubbing their eyes. Someone had clearly just woken them up. Charley lumbered towards David. "What's up?"

"I've done it again, Charley," David said, his voice contrite. "We're leaving. I've over-taxed the hospitality."

124

Nobody saw them to the door.

As he was getting into the van, the driver handed David a bottle of wine. "I took one for the road as we passed the drinks table," he explained.

7

David looked at his own dispirited face in the mirror. All of his free time the previous evening at the *Cape Times* had been spent staring at the sheet of white paper in the typewriter. Words would not come. He had returned home in the small hours of the morning, heavy with dejection. His despair had only intensified when he woke Yvonne and had been greeted with irritation. For hours he had lain next to her, staring into the darknesss. The mood was still pressing him when he woke up. He tried to ring Dawn from Wilton's Corner Café, but she was out.

He was tucking his shirt into his trousers and tightening his belt when Yvonne entered their bedroom.

"I'm going through to town. I'll be back later."

"You don't mind if I go to the Kismet with Melvyn? After all, it is Saturday. He went up to Athlone to check what's on."

David turned and looked at her. "You better pretty up for him."

Yvonne looked at his face searchingly. "You not worried?"

"Should I be? I trust you. Besides, he's too much of a kid still. A woman like you would be wasted on him."

Yvonne smiled quietly as she looked at David.

"I'll push off."

"What about your coat?" she asked him.

"I'm taking my jersey, the light one. I won't stay very long. Margo said she's going out so I should be back before you."

He embraced Yvonne and kissed her. "Tell Cynthia I don't want them outside the gate when I get home."

David thought briefly of Melvyn and Yvonne as he sat in the bus, secure in the knowledge that the relationship between them would go no further than the bond of friendship. He hoped that Melvyn would have the sense to take Yvonne to see a movie they could discuss on his return.

When he phoned Margo Pearce from the telephone booth at the Post Office in Darling Street, she said she was home and invited him over.

"Come inside." She smiled and led him into the lounge of her flat in Three Anchor Bay. "Sit down. I'm preparing lunch. I've been in town this morning and I've just come back so you'll have to be satisfied with what you get."

"That's all right with me."

She excused herself and went back to the kitchen.

David smiled, remembering how shy he had felt the first time he had come here for one of Margo's famous dinner parties. How tense he had been, how ready for feeling patronised and losing his temper. Edward Blakely, the politician, had been one of the guests, he remembered. He had never seen the man since then, but Margo had become a true friend, and the book-lined room had become familiar territory.

He got up and reached for two books on top of a bookshelf. Carson McCullers' *The Heart is a Lonely Hunter*. The other, *Meet my Maker, the Mad Molecule*, by J P Donleavy. Donleavy was new to him and he opened the collection of short stories, settling on a story with a writer as the protagonist. A line hooked him: "There is no romance, no glory that you as a writer sat down and bravely sweated on the white sheets. Of paper. To create something."

It shunted him in the direction of his own inadequacy with words. He pushed the book aside with a grimace of pain. Dejection was descending on him again.

"Here we are," Margo said cheerfully, placing a tray on the coffee table. "Let's eat."

Her poked listlessly at a tomato filled with cream cheese. He wanted to be polite, but the food stuck in his throat. "Could I have a drink?" he finally blurted out.

Margo looked at him anxiously. "Of course."

She got up and returned with a bottle of chianti and two glasses.

"It's wine for struggling artists," she said in a light tone.

He filled his glass and looked at her. "Not too much for me," she smiled.

He finished his wine in almost one gulp and refilled his glass.

"Is anything wrong?" Margo sounded genuinely concerned.

"I don't know what's happening to me," David said, rubbing his hand across his brow. "My head is filled with scenes, but when I sit at my typewriter nothing happens. And it's becoming more frequent. It's frightening me."

Margo placed her knife and fork on her plate and reached for his hand.

"I haven't been able to work on my novel for more than a month now. Yesterday I sit down and put words on paper. When I later look at what I've written, it's just a jumble of letters making meaningless words. Words that have no life or relation to what I really wanted to say. My mind becomes a morass in which my thoughts flounder and are sucked down, leaving not even a trace of the corpses." He gave a bitter laugh. "I feel that I'm never going to complete my novel! You know what, Margo? One more year and I'm thirty-six. Half of my life is gone, done, frittered away. And on what?"

"What about the story in the anthology and the stories published in the weekend papers?"

"Fifteen stories that whisper about things that I want to shout about! Fifteen stories for my thirty-five years. What does it add up to? Nothing! You read it in the toilet and flush it down and it's gone. Who remembers stories published in weekend papers?"

"That's not true. I still clearly remember most of them."

David raised his head. He looked less tense. "You're right, Margo. Perhaps the stories are not that bad. Only they're supposed to be the appetisers before the big feast. And what happens? I'm hungry, and it's only words that can feed me. There are so many things that I want to write about. I sit in a bus or train and observe a scene or overhear a phrase and a story starts forming in my head. But the moment I sit down in front of my typewriter, my mind becomes a blank! It's pure torture to be pent up with images and yet unable to put them into words."

"It will pass. I know it must be very painful for you, but look, your first story has been selected for an overseas anthology. More will follow."

David shook his head and placed his glass on the table. "I don't think so, Margo."

"What's really the matter, David? Look, you know that story is far superior to what you've written in the past. It shows development in your political awareness ..."

David closed his eyes and tried to answered her question.

"That's it, Margo! The story expresses strong political concepts. That's why I've sent it outside to be published. The theme of the novel is political as well, and I don't seem to be able to handle it. I want to write the truth! Where are Alex la Guma and the rest of the Black writers who have written social and political stories?" He gave the answer himself: "House arrest. Stories banned. And then exile."

"Could it be that what has happened to other Black writers brought on a fear that prevents you from writing what you would want to write?"

Margo was expressing a possibility he had never thought of before.

"I don't know any more, Margo," he said after a while.

Yvonne looked at herself in the mirror. She had swept her hair up onto her head, a Spanish comb holding it in place. A set of small coins dangled from each ear and a ring that could have passed as a brooch adorned the ring finger on her right hand – all things that David did not approve of. She had decided on her black court shoes with the tall, slender heels; shoes she only wore when she was going out on her own because of David's sensitivity about his height.

She quickly dabbed some Goya behind her ears and gave her image another critical look in the mirror, then walked through to the front room.

Melvyn could not take his eyes off her favourite red dress with its tight fit and low-cut neckline.

She purposely took a deep breath. "Like it?"

"Yes, very much! All you need is a mantilla and a red rose in your hair. There's an air about you that I can't explain."

"Wickedness?" she teased.

To hide his confusion, Melvyn looked at his watch. "There should be another a bus a few minutes from now."

"I'm ready."

Yvonne stopped to warn Cynthia that they were to remain inside the fence until their father came home. Rebecca was taking washing from the line on the other side of the lane. She stopped to stare at Yvonne and Melvyn.

This should give you something to chew on, bitch! The thought delighted Yvonne.

The way the men glanced at Yvonne as they walked to the bus stop tempted Melvyn to put a possessive arm across her shoulders, but he did not dare. His chance only came when the bus pulled away with a jerk and Yvonne was jolted against him.

He alighted from the bus first when it stopped at the Mowbray terminus, and with an outstretched hand waited to assist Yvonne. He did not want her to trip when she stepped down onto the pavement in her high heels.

Before entering the cinema, he stopped at a café, and bought a small box of chocolates.

"Thanks," Yvonne said when they were shown to their seats, and snuggled close. How different he was from David. The chocolates were the perfect gift. She didn't really want to compare the two, but on one of her birthdays David had turned up with a huge bunch of red roses and a poem, not with the pair of stylish shoes she had hinted she liked so much.

With a shake of her head, Yvonne banished the memory from her mind.

Their hands touched as she offered Melvyn a chocolate in the darkness.

128

She pressed the palm of his hand. After a moment the pressure was returned. They sat rubbing each other's palms like two adolescents.

Yvonne placed her hands demurely over the box of chocolates on her lap when the lights came on. Melvyn found it difficult to appear calm. Her earlier touch had awakened wild fantasies in his mind and swept all his apprehension away. He impatiently waited for the lights to be dimmed again.

The concealing dimness emboldened Yvonne as well. She hiked up her dress a few inches, guided his hand above her knee, gently rested her left hand on top of his, and then put her right hand with the chocolate box on top. I don't care how far this goes. I'm going to make him care for me, she thought.

Melvyn swallowed deeply as her hand pressed his onto her thigh. He recalled her body as she had pressed it against his when they had danced in the darkened front room. How could he have stayed away from her presence for so long?

They were oblivious to what was happening on the screen.

David found the girls dutifully playing in front of the door. The sound of a Strauss waltz welcomed him through the open window. He tugged at Thelma's braid before kissing her.

"What have you been up to?"

"Nothing, Daddy. I was going to to play with Maureen but Cynthia say no."

"That's right. I told your mother I would expect to find all of you here when I get home." He dipped into his pocket for thirty cents. "Here," he said, giving the money to Cynthia. "Go and buy each of you an ice cream."

"Can I go with?" Thelma pleaded.

"Yes. Shirley, you also go along, and Cynthia, watch out for cars and come straight home."

David found Eddie seated at the table in the front room, nursing a half-full glass and staring at a bottle of sweet wine in front of him.

"Hope you don't mind?" he said, pointing at the record player. "I got here and only the children were home."

"I went to town, and Melvyn took Yvonne to the movies."

"I know. Cynthia told me." Unable to conceal his irritation, he said, "You should've let me know. I could've gone with them. I didn't have anything on this afternoon. That's why I brought a bottle over." He looked at David. "I wonder if Yvonne has found another worshipper in Melvyn?"

David grinned. "It happens every time."

8

Yvonne hastily herded the children to bed, then washed and dressed, taking particular care with her toilet. She had been wondering whether Melvyn would pursue his covert courting after what had taken place between them in the Kismet. He had finally phoned to invite her to go with him to the Naaz. A woman living in the circle at the back of their lane had sent one of her children to call Yvonne to the phone earlier. When she had lifted the receiver and heard it was Melvyn, her breath had caught in her throat. She had softly agreed to meet him at Mowbray Station. She had told David that her sister in Salt River had rung and invited her over for the evening. He had readily agreed that she make the visit alone as his relationship with her sister was not always altogether cordial.

Yvonne sat in the bus, impatiently looking out of the window. Her flesh tingled at the memory of the first time Melvyn had held her in his arms. She still couldn't quite forgive Eddie for arriving just when the dancing was promising to blossom into something else.

Before the bus pulled to a halt at the Mowbray terminus, Yvonne rose fom her seat. She quickly walked past the straggly lines of commuters waiting for transport back to the townships. As she turned into Main Road, a car hooted at the traffic lights. She turned and saw Melvyn opening the back door.

He eased her onto the back seat and settled next to her.

"Yvonne, meet Wallace and Ann."

She murmured politely to the couple in the front, pleased that Melvyn did not mention her surname or that she was married.

She could tell that he had been drinking when he handed her a cigarette and leaned over to light it for her. Next he took a hip flask from the inside pocket of his jacket, unscrewed the top and passed the flask to her.

The car's tyres were humming softly as they sped along Main Road in the direction of the city centre.

She took a tentative sip, tasted it was brandy and Coke, and shifted so that her thigh pressed against Melvyn's. She slipped her hand in his.

"This is it," Melvyn said as the car came to a halt across from the double-storey with the illuminated sign NAAZ. Cars were already lining both sides of Albert Road.

"I've booked us a table," he informed her as he ushered them upstairs. His voice was thick with anticipation.

Yvonne's eyes darted from wall to wall. She loved the cute minarets lit up by the soft, coloured bulbs and the seductive dance music coming from speakers she could not see.

Most of the tables were occupied, some crowded with bottles and glasses.

A waitress escorted them to a table near the centre of the room. "Would you care to order now, sir?" she asked Melvyn.

"Check with the manager, please. My name is Melvyn Francis. I phoned this afternoon."

"I'm sorry, sir. I'll do that."

"Quite all right," Melvyn smiled. Then to Wallace: "I think we could do with a pre-dinner drink."

Yvonne was dazzled by the ease with which Melvyn handled the situation. Imagine David walking in here!

Wallace produced a bottle of marsala from a leather bag. He waved to a passing waitress and asked for four glasses.

"This is just an appetiser until the meal arrives," Melvyn explained, straightening his legs under the table and leaning back on his chair. "I've got some Liebfraumilch to go with the food. And for later some gin and lime – to finish off the evening."

Yvonne glimpsed the attentive look on Ann's face while Melvyn spoke. She took a closer look at the girl's features. She may be younger than me, but I got what Melvyn wants, she decided.

"I feel like a cigarette, Melvyn," she said and leaned over to him, closer than necessary.

"Certainly, Yvonne."

He produced his silver case and offered it to her, then in turn to Ann and Wallace. She sat with head held imperiously, assured of the light that was to follow. She inhaled, then blew out the flickering flame before he could pass the lighter to Ann.

"I'm sorry," she drawled, her eyes holding Ann's, her hand resting on Melvyn's arm to signify her claim.

The waitress approached with a huge tray. A bowl of steaming rice was placed in the centre of the table and small bowls of sambal were arranged around it. Next to the empty plate in front of everybody she put a small bowl of chicken curry.

"The chicken curry is absolutely marvellous," Melvyn enthused. "They've got a chef from Bombay. Be careful, though," he warned Yvonne. "The curry here is really hot. Not like the curry you get at most restaurants."

Melvyn rested the mouth of the bottle of Liebfraumlich on each glass in turn, pouring ever so gently so that every glass held exactly the same volume of wine, without a drop being spilt in the process. He basked in the look of approval from Yvonne when they all raised their glasses. "To new friendship," he said.

The curry was indeed fiery. Yvonne had to admit that the food came up to Melvyn's recommendation. Not even she could have bettered it.

After the meal Melvyn signalled the waitress to clear the table.

"Could you please show me where the cloakroom is?" Yvonne asked Ann. The younger woman escorted her there, and as she dabbed at her make-up in the mirror, Yvonne casually asked her whether Melvyn often accompanied her and Wallace to the Naaz.

"Yes, and every time he brings a different girl along," Ann replied.

"We're just good friends."

"I can see that," Ann said with an envious laugh.

What would you say if you knew that a married woman is accompanying him this time? thought Yvonne.

The Naaz had filled up completely by the time the women returned to the table. Couples were dancing to music that was now provided by a quartet that had taken the stand in their absence.

"Dance?" Melvyn asked, his voice husky.

Yvonne rested her head on his chest as they circled the floor. She shivered voluptuously as his hands spanned first her hips and then moved down to her buttocks. "No one's going to dance with you like this tonight," he whispered in her ear.

Only once did he allow Wallace to dance with her – when the band presented its version of the twist. Ann tried to switch his attention from Yvonne to herself, but he fidgeted impatiently as he watched Yvonne move to the beat of the music, and at the end of the dance he boldly walked over to the bandstand. He clinched the deal with the bandleader by slipping a bank note, into his hand.

"We will now play _Tammy_ for the many young lovers in the room," the bandleader announced. The announcement was greeted by enthusiatic clapping.

Yvonne's eyes twinkled as Melvyn took her in his arms. He manoeuvered her into a corner where they would not obstruct dancers circling past. There he lowered his head, his mouth covering hers. Their tongues touched like embracing lovers.

Yvonne closed her eyes to quieten the quivering of her body. But her trembling was infecting Melvyn and his hand moved up and down her thigh.

Neither of them spoke as they clung to each other, aware that they had broken some final barrier. After this there could no longer be any restraint between them. When the music ended, they returned to their table hand-in-hand.

132

Terence recognised the couple at the table at once. He had decided to come to the Naaz on the spur of the moment and was pleased to see someone he knew. He was going over to greet them when the intimacy of Melvyn's actions suddenly struck him. Melvyn's hand was resting possessively on Yvonne's thigh as he filled her glass!

The band resumed playing. Terence looked on as Melvyn and Yvonne took to the floor again, closed in each other's arms, Melvyn kissing her and she avidly responding.

Terence moved away so that he could watch unobtrusively. He was perplexed by Yvonne's behaviour, Melvyn's he found simply disgusting.

Terence had often danced with Yvonne himself. And she had always teased him by pressing her body closer to him. But from her actions he could see that it was no tease this time. But why would she be doing this to David? It couldn't be just for the sake of dancing, because David had never objected to anyone dancing with her. Then it occurred to him that Yvonne was flattered by Melvyn's attention and was probably only playing with him. But still he felt sick at her betrayal of David's trust. Melvyn could not altogether be blamed. Most men were aroused by Yvonne's sensuality. David often joked about it, laughingly taking a head-count of men drinking in Yvonne's tantalising form as they went out together. He should leave before they saw him.

Terence glanced at his watch: there was still time to catch the last bus home.

The band had reverted to twist numbers and Ann and Wallace were cavorting a few paces from where Melvyn and Yvonne sat at their table.

"What time does David come home?" Melvyn asked nervously.

Yvonne smiled and raised his hand to her lips. "Don't worry! About two-thirty. No one's going to check. I say to Cora and Christine I go to see my sister. The children are all right. Shirley see they go to bed."

"I wish the band would stop this crap," Melvyn said, petulantly pouring himself another drink.

They had consumed the last of the gin and lime when Wallace announced it was time to go.

They passed their waitress at the door. Melvyn stopped her, and to impress Yvonne took a coin from his pocket and handed it to her. "Thank you, sir," the waitress said with a servile smile.

Melvyn arranged himself in the back of the car so that Yvonne could recline in his arms. She removed his hands from her waist, and leaned forward indicating that he should unzip her dress and unfasten her brassiere. She stuffed the bra in her coat pocket as Melvyn put his hands inside the front of her dress, cradling her breasts in his palms.

133

His fingers gently caressed the swell of her breasts. Her nipples stiffened at his touch. Earlier, her breasts had a softnesss that invited him to lay his head upon them. Now they had a tautness that awakened an unfamiliar desire in him.

Yvonne arched her body back and her legs spread apart. Her breath came in short, sharp gasps.

Melvyn's breath was as laboured as hers. Her breasts beneath his hands had aroused him to an extent that could only be stilled by taking possession of her. The image of her arched underneath him produced a grunt of pleasure.

"Yvonne," he whispered. "Couldn't we stop off somewhere?"

She lowered her hand to his crotch and cupped it over the raised cloth. "I'm sorry, Melvyn," she whispered back. "There be another time, and I promise you it be different." She lifted her head. "Kiss me."

Melvyn eased himself forward and touched Wallace's shoulder.

"You could put us off, here."

The car glided to a halt at the entrance of the lane leading to the house, and they exchanged goodbyes.

"Sleep tight," Wallace said, winking at Melvyn.

They watched the car turn the corner, then the street was deserted and they were alone.

They held hands as they walked up the lane. Melvyn opened the gate and Yvonne led him to the side of the house that could not be seen from the lane. She stood with her back to the wall. Melvyn leaned heavily against her.

"Kiss me before you go."

Each kiss increased the torment, his lips demanding what his flesh craved. She raised her dress, took his hand and placed it inside her panties. He felt her pubic hair curling around his fingers. She pressed her thighs together, holding his hand hostage.

"Yvonne," he murmured brokenly. But she pushed him away, fearful suddenly that she would give in to the desire that threatened to overwhelm her.

Melvyn stood staring at her as she fled into the dark house.

Yvonne, hands tightly clenched together, stood in the darkened front room. The click of the gate announced that Melvyn had gone.

She was still awake when David arrived back from work. He undressed and got into bed and bit playfully at her ear, his hand reaching underneath her nightdress.

She flinched at his touch. "Don't," she said. "I got a headache."

"I'm sorry. I'll make you some hot milk."

He watched as she sipped the milk. So like a kitten, he thought. "Here, you'd better take two asprins with it," he said.

9

It was Saturday afternoon. The rain had eased off, and clouds were breaking apart and letting the sun send down welcome rays of warmth. David had phoned Paula from the *Cape Times* on Wednesday evening, arranging to meet her in Mowbray. She had immediately cancelled all other plans so that she would be free, as she had always done on the few occasions he had phoned her, sensing that he needed to see her.

They were waiting for a bus. Paula watched David shift his weight from one foot to the other. Earlier she had waited outside the Thistle Bar while he had a drink inside. "David, you so selfish," she had teased him on his return. "You know I can't go with you!"

"It's the bloody Government," he had countered, "who doesn't allow Coloured females to sit in a bar with their men. Not me!"

Mowbray's Main Road was almost deserted of traffic. What people there were, were mainly Coloured males, all heading in the direction of the bar. A few scroungers hung around the entrance.

"I wish the bloody bus would show up," David complained, and as the bus jerked to a halt in front of them a few minutes later: "It's about time."

"Come along, move it up!" the conductor shouted from the back of the bus.

David ignored the conductor's strident voice, walked past the seats marked *Whites Only* and seated himself on the back seat that ran the width of the bus. He joggled his buttocks to make a place for Paula.

"Two to Claremont," he grunted at the conductor.

He sat absorbed in his thoughts as the bus rolled along. Paula glanced anxiously at his face. She knew that he had not told Yvonnne that he was taking her out.

"We get out at the next stop."

Paula followed him down the aisle. "Where we going?" she asked.

"To Arnold."

"Does he know we coming?"

David shook his head, a broad smile on his face.

"My house is his house, and I take it his house is my house. Since when should friends first inform each other of a visit?"

She knew David regarded his own as an open house for everybody – to her knowledge only 'tourists' were not welcome – but she was not so sure that all his friends shared his sentiment.

They turned into Selous Road and David opened a gate leading to a double-storied block of flats. Paula followed David up the stairs.

The door was not locked, and David did not bother to knock. He walked straight into Arnold's lounge, with Paula in his wake.

Arnold was seated at the desk, typing, a pile of sheets next to the typewriter.

"Don't tell me you work on Saturdays?" David said by way of greeting.

"I've just finished the draft of a story. Unlike you, I have to keep my hand at it. We're not all as gifted as you."

"You're damn right," David laughed. "A genius like myself doesn't have to produce on Saturdays. Saturdays are for drinking!"

"You should watch your drinking," Arnold said.

"Are you going to give me a drink or a lecture?"

Arnold shrugged his shoulders and looked at Paula, before kissing her on the cheek. He got up, took a bottle of cream sherry and glasses from a drinks cabinet and poured three drinks. He passed the first to Paula.

David measured the dark golden liquid in his glass with his eyes.

"Hell, I don't want such a pissing little drink! Fill it up!"

Arnold's restraint was wearing thin. "Cream sherry isn't Lieberstein, one doesn't drink by the mug – unless one has no sense of propriety."

David got up. "Arnold," he said, tilting the bottle to fill his glass, "you know I haven't any use for fancy manners, so you don't mind if I ..."

"Is it really necessary?" Arnold asked.

David took another deep swallow. "Yes, it is." He walked over to the window and stood staring down into the street.

"I wonder what makes you behave like this, David? You're setting everybody against you. You seem to derive a perverse satisfaction from proving just how uncouth you can be, from antagonising people."

"Who needs them? I can get along without them!"

"Can you? Then why do you come here?"

David swung round and looked at Arnold. "To see you, of course."

"I thought you could do without people?"

"You're different. You're my friend. You're not one of those bastards!"

"So everybody else are bastards. Except *your* friends. What about the people you insulted at my party? They are *my* friends. I suppose they also fall under the 'bastard' category. It didn't strike you that you offended me as much as you offended them, did it? Everybody must pay for the neurosis of David Patterson – who doesn't care a fuck, as you call it, for social conventions."

136

Paula's alarmed eyes shifted from Arnold to David. Didn't Arnold understand? David wasn't really like that.

The indifferent look on David's face did not reveal his inner unhappiness.

Arnold's pent up fury burst out in a torrent of angry words: "What made you come here? I would've told you to stay away if you had phoned. I prefer you to keep to your jungle! To put it bluntly: I suggest that you leave now as I wouldn't like my friends to find you here when they arrive."

He turned towards Paula. "I'm awfully sorry, my dear. It must be terribly distressing for you. Under different circumstances, your presence here would always be welcome."

David smarted from Arnold's words. But he would not show it. "Bang goes another friendship," he said, trying to put a lightness in the words.

"Friendship!" Arnold exploded. "You've convinced me you don't need people. Friendship is a foreign emotion to you!"

David turned the glass in his hands, studying the dark golden liquid as if he had not seen it before.

"You're wrong, Arnold," he said. "I do need the few friends that I have. But I don't need people in the sense that I want them around all the time." He would have liked to tell Arnold how much he valued his friendship, but his tirade had made it impossible.

"Finish that drink," Arnold prompted. "I've got another appointment."

David emptied his glass in a leisurely manner, got up and walked over to the drinks cabinet. Paula's chest tightened as she watched him take the bottle of cream sherry and fill his glass to the brim.

Arnold was white around his mouth. He clenched and unclenched his fists. "Do excuse me," he said to Paula. "I have to go to the bathroom. Would you please close the door behind you when you leave?"

David looked at Arnold's retreating back.

"Hurry up so that we can go," Paula urged.

"I'm not in a hurry."

He sat down in Arnold's chair, slowly sipping the sherry. The minutes ticked away. Paula glanced at the bathroom door, praying that nothing would happen, praying that David would finish his drink and go.

"Don't you want anything to drink?"

She shook her head.

David put his empty glass down next to the typewriter. "I wonder if I should take the bottle with me?"

Paula shrugged her shoulders as if she did not care.

"No, better leave it," he said. "Let's blow, seeing dear old Arnold's not going to see us off."

As they stepped from the foyer onto the pavement, David turned and looked back. Arnold stood at the window, watching them. Then he turned and disappeared from their sight.

"I would never have believed the day would come that I'm kicked out by Arnold." David's voice was thick with regret. "I'm really going to miss seeing him around. You know, I always felt free to discuss things with him."

Paula touched him lightly on his shoulder. "I don't think he really mean it. It's just that he's angry. Next time, you see, he make a big joke of it."

David was not inclined to agree. He had often in the past baited Arnold with his words and actions, but this time he wasn't sure that their friendship would survive. This time, he feared, he might have gone too far.

Deep in thought he waited with Paula at the bus stop and did not immediately notice the two youths who had stopped a few yards away. He was also not aware of the remarks they were broadcasting about Paula until one said, "I like to fuck her!"

David looked up into two pairs of dark-brown eyes that contemptuously returned his glare.

One youth turned away, sending his eyes slowly from Paula's breasts to her thighs. "Yah, she got a fat pussy," he slurred.

"What was that?" David demanded.

"I like to fuck her!" the youth repeated arrogantly, pointing at Paula.

"Don't," Paula said as David moved towards them.

"Why worry, cherrikkee!" the other youth chimed in. "No problem!"

David struck the nearest youth a blow in the face. He grabbed hold of his shirtfront, but before he could deliver a second blow, he felt a sharp pain at the back of his head. He turned to see the second youth swinging a buckled belt twisted around his wrist.

"Omo, old man!" the youth yelled derisively, shaking the belt at David.

David lunged at the belt and got his hand entangled in it. They stood tugging at either end.

Paula's scream warned him that the other youth was moving in. It was too late. He was swept off his feet but managed to drag one of them to the ground with him. A kick in the ribs released his hold. He covered his face to protect it from their boots. When he managed to get to his knees, the belt caught him across the cheek. Then both were upon him. He swung wildly. A grunt came from one of the youths.

David found it difficult to see, and more blows smashed into his face. He tasted the warm, salty blood streaming from his nose into his mouth and down his chin.

138

Paula was screaming and tearing at the shoulders of the youths. One of them turned, grabbed her around the waist and flung her to the ground.

A white man appeared as if from nowhere. With a backhand slap he sent one of the youths staggering.

"White bastard!" they spat as they fled.

They only stopped when they reached the corner of Station Road. There they straightened up as if nothing had happened, and with a swaggering strut slowly ambled away.

"Are you all right?" the white man asked with concern. He had the build of a rugby player.

David laughed wryly. Would I be all right with my face bashed in? he thought. He grinned at Paula as she dabbed at his face with a sweet-smelling lady's handkerchief.

David hadn't noticed that the bus had arrived and that the conductor was an interested spectator. "Are you getting in?" he asked. "I can't keep the bus waiting forever."

"Hold on," the white rugby player said to him, then to David: "Are you taking the bus?"

"Yes. Thanks for stopping the massacre."

"Watch out for those skollies," the rugby player warned. "They should be locked up!"

David dropped onto the first empty seat, despite the conductor's protestations that it was designated for whites.

Paula sank down next to him. She ignored the other passengers and continued her ministrations.

After one horrified look at David's face, the whites, as they boarded the bus, hastily moved on and seated themselves as far away as possible.

By the time they reached Mowbray, David couldn't see properly through his left eye. "It's all right," he told Paula. "You don't have to worry about me. You go straight through."

"I'm not going to Sea Point," she insisted, close to tears. "I'm going home with you first."

The following morning, their offspring at school and their washing on the line, Christine, Cora and Rebecca were having tea with Yvonne in her kitchen.

"David is just mad," Yvonne said to Cora, pretending that she found his strange behaviour amusing. "When he's got a drink in, he's another man."

"I don't think it's very funny," Rebecca said tartly. "Don't he care what people say when he come home with his face smashed in and another woman hanging on his arm?"

"No, he don't care a damn! Why should he? He always say that he don't got to impress people."

"And what about you?"

"I agree with him. We not bothered what you, or anybody else, think of us. If I feel like doing a thing, I do it and everybody else can go to hell!"

"I think you very foolish to let David take Paula out alone."

Yvonne measured Rebecca with her eyes. "You know why I let David take Paula out? Because I trust him, that's why!"

"Not me! I know men! Let them take out another woman and it don't take long for them to climb into her bed."

Yvonne had often wondered if David had not already done just that, climbed into Paula's bed. But her pride had always made her push the idea of sharing her man with another woman out of her head.

"That's the trouble with you, Rebecca," she said. "You know men. Tell me, how many men you know, or are you talking about Eddie?"

Rebecca gave a sharp sniff.

"We not brought up like that! My mother learn me to respect my body. Eddie's the only man I know that way. The first time he touch me was after we married. My mother learn us the right way."

Yvonne laughed condescendingly. "Your mother forget to teach you the pleasure you get when you do it!"

Rebecca's mouth tightened into a prune.

"The water's boiling," Christine said.

Rebecca's prudishness and malicious tongue had often irked her, but she could not bring herself to attacking Rebecca in turn. "Rebecca," she added teasingly, "I think both of you are right. But a change now and then is nice. What do you think, Cora?"

Cora gave an embarrassed laugh and reached for the tea pot to fill their cups. Their talk drifted round to the day's work and children.

10

"How are you making out?" David asked Charley.

They were sharing a bottle of Old Brown Sherry which Charley had brought in the front room, waiting for the others to properly start their Saturday night drinking session.

"I've completed another verse. It won't be long before I finish the poem."

David wondered whether it was the wine he had drank earlier that was talking or whether Charley was really almost finished. He gazed affectionately at him. "I hope it's near the end. You've suffered enough getting it down."

The door opened and Paula stood in the doorway.

"Hello," David said, and Charley grinned his welcome.

"Where are the children?" Paula said. "I've brought some stuff for them."

"They in town with their grandmother. Yvonne's in the kitchen. Do you want a drink?"

"Yes," Paula replied. "But let me first greet Yvonne and give her the stuff for the children." She reached into her bag and put a bottle of brandy next to the Old Brown on the table. "I also got a bottle of muscadel I bring from work."

"Let's try your muscadel," David said when she returned.

Paula traced her fingertips across his cheek, the two-week-old scars had healed into uneven white lines on his brown skin.

"Your knight in tarnished armour," he said.

She kissed David.

"If ever I should want a girl," Charley said, "it will have to be someone like you, Paula. You're a right one."

Paula acknowledged his compliment with a kiss on his forehead.

"I can get you a girl from where I work, Charley."

"No, thanks. I've got two women and they're more than I can handle: a book of verse and a bottle of wine are my only mistresses. When my muse forsakes me, I seek solace in wine."

"Don't you ever want a woman?" David asked.

"If the need crops up, I find myself a woman who'll give me a meal. I don't want her around all the time. An occasional meal, that's all I want. I ..."

"Look who's here," David cut the discussion short.

Hester and Steward walked in.

"Are you two going steady?" David asked.

A pleased smile appeared on Hester's face.

"I met Hester at Mowbray terminus on my way here from home," Steward explained.

Hester mockingly asked Charley, "Drinking again?"

"That's right, teacher. Drinking again."

"Is that the only thing you do?"

"It's not the only thing in my favour, Hester." Charley's eyelids dropped as he squinted at her. "Have you ever listed my virtues? I don't steal. I don't have a hankering for another man's piece of meat. I support my mother with the money I earn as a packer at OK Bazaars. I don't measure myself against my neighbour's material wealth. All I do is get drunk. Now what do you want me to do? Start doing what every hypocritical bastard is doing, or stay with the bottle? What do you tell the youngsters you teach?"

Hester gave an embarrassed laugh.

To steer the the conversation in a different direction, David said, "You know there's a story that I want to write that's been inside me for a long time. When I was still a youngster, my father was away one night, working night-shift at the docks. All my brothers and sisters were asleep. It was only my mother and I who were awake. It must have been chilly, because I was sitting on a chair covered with my father's heavy army coat. I was reading a comic book, and my mother was nursing the baby. She had been to the clinic several times with little Anna who was suffering from gastro-enteritis, and she was making soothing sounds to the baby. Suddenly she stopped. I looked up. She was staring at the baby's face. Then she shrieked: 'Anna is dead!' I looked at my mother's contorted face. I wasn't terrified or sad at the death of my baby sister, but I was quivering with the grief etched on my mother's face. If I could only today describe the way she felt when she realised that the baby had died."

Paula moved to David and squeezed his arm. He smiled back at her.

"I know what you're saying," Steward said. "Sometimes in the afternoon, on my way to Wynberg, the light catches Devil's Peak and transforms it into a composition of grey and black and green. A marvellous image that I'd like to put down on canvas. All art, even if one can't recognise it straight away, seems to me inspired by one's observation of reality."

"You're right," David said. "Sometimes, I'd even provoke scenes just to see how people react."

Hester thought back to the scene David had provoked at Laurence van Dyk's place and its disastrous results.

"But is that fair?" Melvyn asked, who had joined them. "Doesn't it make an artist an eavesdropper and Peeping Tom, a parasite that lives off others?" "Dead right! Every writer is parasitical in what he does."

"David, are you telling us that you could write a story based on the talk we're having now?" Hester asked.

"I don't see why not, because characters reveal themselves in what they say." Suddenly he laughed sheepishly. "It's just that I don't always pull it off. In fact, mostly not."

"That's the truth of it!" Charley burst out. "I also just can't seem to dredge up words from my muddy mind that ..."

"Anyone for a dance?" Terence asked, bursting in through the front door, a shiny new record in his hand. He put the new LP on the turn-table and the enticing Latin-American sound of George Shearing filled the room.

"About time someone put on a record!" Yvonne shouted from the kitchen. "Else we be in for a night of talks."

Melvyn went to the kitchen to see if he could help her, and Charley retired to the children's bedroom at the back.

Hester was waiting for Steward to ask her for a dance when Terence swayed to a standstill before her. "May I have a dance, madame?" he asked with an elegant bow.

Before she could refuse, he put his hands on her hips and started to move her around. But Hester could not cope with the intricate steps and pulled herself free.

"What's the matter?" he asked.

"I prefer to dance, not perform!" she snapped.

"Performing is beyond your capabilities, madame. That goes for dancing as well, but I'm prepared to teach you."

"Go to hell, you bloody moffie!"

Terence looked as if she had slapped him. He pulled in his breath and wailed, "Bitch!" his nostrils flaring.

"Moffie!" Hester flung back at him and stomped from the room.

Terence shrugged off David's hand and rushed after her. In the kitchen he grabbed her under the armpits and tried to lift her off the floor. Unable to do this, he pushed her away. She staggered against the stove and then fled from the kitchen through the back door. Terence followed her outside.

"I'd better go and see what's happened to him."

David found Terence huddled against the back wall, shoulders shaking up and down. He sank to his knees next to him and put his arm around his shoulders. "It's all right, Terence," he said soothingly. He looked around. Hester was nowhere to be seen, so unable to control his curiosity, he asked, "What were you going to do when you grabbed hold of Hester?"

"I was going to put her arse-first on the stove."

The thought of Hester wriggling her posterior on a hot plate set David into a paroxysm of laughter. Terence followed suit, and the two of them sat supporting each other as their mirth shook them.

"How do you feel?"

"All right."

"Let's go back inside then."

Melvyn was studying the inside of his glass and avoided looking at Terence as he and David entered the lounge.

"What's happened to Hester?" David asked. "I never suspected she feels this way about homosexuals."

143

"She left with Steward," Yvonne replied.

"Does that mean our little party is over?"

She gave him a calculating look. "Probably not while you still got Paula as partner."

"Then let's get mit it."

Terence could feel the tension in the kitchen when he returned the next morning.

"Where's Paula?" he asked.

"Ask David," Yvonne replied, her back to Terence, and slammed down a plate in front of David. "He's so cunt-struck that he can't wait to be alone with his bitch before running his hand up her arse!"

Terence was speechless. David's stare was fixed on the food on his plate.

"It's a wonder he still eat with those hands," Yvonne stormed on, staring pointedly at David.

David, his head lowered, did not reply.

"Won't be long before he pay jintoes for a piece of pussy!"

Suddenly, David threw his fork on the table. "What are you getting at?"

"You know!"

"I don't know!"

"Ah! You don't remember what you do with Paula on the bed in the children's room last night?"

"So I sat next to her on the bed. So what?"

"So, siss, you pig!" Yvonne's voice had turned into a screech. "What your hands doing running up her cunt?"

Terence's eys flittered from face to face, then darted away.

"Hell, Yvonne. It wasn't like that at all."

"You think I'm blind not to see the way you two carry on last night?"

"Look, it was no different from the way you and Melvyn were dancing. You don't hear me complaining about that, do you?"

"No!" Yvonne's screamed. "But bed's not on my mind with Melvyn like that bitch Paula and you!"

Unease about what he had witnessed in the Naaz filled Terence, but he dared not open his mouth.

"I tell you again," David said. "I didn't mean anything by it. Alright, so my hand was on her leg but I swear I had no intention of climbing into bed with her."

"It was in your eyes and she waiting for it like the bitch she is!"

"Why didn't you start this morning before Paula left?"

Yvonne's eyes were daggers slashing at him.

"And let her think I fight over you?"

"At least, she would've had a chance to defend herself."

"What for? You her pimp! You speak up for her. You want to dirty the children's bed whoring with her."

David pushed his chair back. "Now you are going too far. Paula would never do a thing like that!"

"That's right! Speak up for your bitch!" Yvonne screamed. In her rage she reached for Terence's plate. "You bastard!"

She threw the plate at David. He warded it off and it smashed into the wall. David cleared the space on the table between Yvonne and himself and raised his arm.

"Go on, do it!" she ranted. "Hit me, you bastard! I stand by every fucking thing you do. And this is how you pay me back, carrying on with that whore!"

Her hair had got untied and hung lose around her shoulders, her face wet with tears. "Why don't you fuck off and go to her before she drag another man into her bed? You know servant bitches!"

David could take it no longer. "I will!" he said, shoved Yvonne aside and walked out of the kitchen.

"And don't come back because if you do, I walk out and you get the bitch to feed your children!"

He slammed the front door behind him and ploughed his way through the sandy pathway to the gate.

Terence picked up the broken pieces of the plate and went outside to drop them into the bin in the yard.

Yvonne was still seated at the table when he returned, tears running down her cheeks. As he offered her his handkerchief, the intimate scene in the Naaz flashed into his mind. What was he to do? He couldn't tell David, and to tell *her* that he had seen them would only worsen matters. And when he tried to ask Steward's advice the Sunday after it had happened, Steward had said, "I don't want to hear about this. And I'm not going to say a word. I'm not going to take sides. Whatever happens, I'm going to keep out of it. Yvonne is being silly, but she could have her reasons for doing what she is doing."

David waited impatiently for his telephone call from Wilton's Corner Café, to be answered. Eventually someone picked up.

"Hello, Gwen." – "David." – "Could I come through to you? It's important." – "No, I can't tell you over the phone." – "All right, I'm taking the bus. I should be there about half-hour from now. So long."

He was relieved that Gwen did not object to his request. On the few occasions he had been in Dawn's company, she had taken him to Gwen's place two or three times. Despite the second bizarre visit, and Dawn's fear that he would upset Gwen again when he had had a little too much to drink, a good relationship had developed between Gwen and himself.

All the way to Elsies River his mind seethed with anger and the industrial area slipped past the window unnoticed. Yvonne was right to a certain extent. He did caress Paula's thigh in the back room, but Charley was asleep on the opposite bunk and he never dreamt of bedding Paula under his own roof.

It was only when the bus slowed down as it entered the residential section of Elsies River that David looked to see where he should alight.

He side-stepped the noisy hawkers vying for his attention, ignoring their humorous comments on the fruit and toys displayed on the pavement. He strode past them and down the main street until he found himself at the steps leading to Gwen's flat.

Gwen opened the door at the angry rattle of his knuckles.

"Come in," she said, scanning his scowling face.

She followed him to the lounge where he flung himself down onto the couch. "Listen, David, you didn't give me a chance to tell you that Dawn is here – one of her two-day visits. She's in the kitchen, making some coffee." She laughed nervously. "I thought you might need some. What happened? What's so important that you couldn't tell me over the phone?"

Dawn entered before he could speak. "Hello," she said as she put the tray down on the low table in front of him.

He grunted a greeting, not at all pleased at her presence. She would certainly not approve of what he had to say.

"I need a place to stay," he blurted out. The announcement was met with bewilderment. "Yvonne and myself had a helluva row and I need somewhere to rest."

Dawn replaced her mug on the table. "What was the disagreement about?" she asked quietly.

He repeated every angry word that had passed between Yvonne and himself and concluded, "That's why I need a place to stay."

"Can you honestly blame Yvonne for reacting that way?" Dawn asked. "Didn't you bring it upon yourself with your behaviour?"

"Dawn, look. I'm not in the mood for a lecture. I can push off if Gwen doesn't like the idea of having me around."

"How long do you intend to stay?" asked Gwen.

"Only tonight." He rubbed his eyes. "I'll go through tomorrow and pick up some of my stuff."

"Fine. We can risk tonight without the neighbours having too many doubts about our morals."

"Thanks, Gwen. I don't suppose there's anything to drink?"

"No. I've taken Dawn's advice. I don't want a repeat performance of the last time you were here."

"That's right! Miss Morals will always see the dark side. I simply don't know what I'd do without her."

From the way she pushed her hair away from her face, David knew that he had annoyed her. "I'm sorry, Dawn," he immediately apologised. "I don't really mean it. I'm very grateful for your friendship."

To prevent David becoming sentimental, Dawn quickly changed the subject and asked, "Tell me, how are things with Steward?"

"He's busy with a new painting. He started last week."

"That's good. What about you?"

"As you see. I don't do anything except get into trouble."

11

The loneliness of the night in Gwen's flat was more than David could bear, so as soon as the two women were awake, he thanked Gwen and said goodbye to her and Dawn. He didn't want to stay for breakfast, even though they insisted.

He glanced impatiently at the buildings gliding past the bus. Dawn's parting advice was that the only way for him to make amends was to go back and apologise. He had listened in silence. Dawn had squeezed his arm when he left. It was the first time ever she had showed any affection towards him.

David gave a relieved sigh when the bus neared his stop.

It was about eleven and Rebecca was hanging washing on the line as he walked up the lane. He waved to her. She stared at him with open curiosity, almost forgetting to return his greeting.

He paused in front of the gate, bracing himself before opening it. "Daddy!" Thelma shouted and tumbled from the doorway and ran towards him. She flung her arms around his neck as he bent down to embrace her.

There was a tightening in his chest and he buried his head in her hair.

"I was looking for Daddy all day yesterday. And when I get up this morning, I don't see Daddy. Where did Daddy go to?"

David swallowed before answering, "Didn't Mummy tell you?"

"No, Mummy didn't tell me nothing."

His heart raced. She must've known that he would be coming back!

"I had to go out yesterday and then I worked all night. Is Mummy inside?"

"Mummy's in the kitchen."

"I better go in and say hello."

Thelma held onto his hand as they entered the house. He could hear the clump-clump of the iron. Yvonne must be busy ironing clothes.

"I'm back," David said nervously from the kitchen door.

Yvonne's lips disappeared into a thin line and her eyes narrowed. "So? What do I do, clap my hands and sing a song?"

Thelma's hand tightened in his.

He turned his eyes away from Yvonne's flinty face and took a two-cent piece from his pocket. He placed it in Thelma's hand and kissed her on the cheek, saying softly, "Go buy a toffee-apple for yourself."

He waited until she had left the house before he said, "I came back because I missed you and the children. I'm very sorry for what I've done. I'm to blame altogether."

Yvonne's eyes were two piercing stilettos.

"You think your plea will change things? No matter what you say, I know that whore of yours want you in her bed, and you willing to crawl in there. You don't give a damn who is there to see it. David I-don't-care-a-damn Patterson! Well, I'll show you. I also don't care a damn any more! If you didn't come today, me and the children will be long gone to my sister tomorrow. You and your whore can take the house, furniture and all. I got my fill of you!"

He held out his hands. "Yvonne, you have all the right to feel the way you do." He pleaded with his eyes and with his voice. "I've told Paula that there can never be anything between her and myself, that always there will be just one woman for me. She won't be coming here anymore and I promise I will not see her either."

That was the part that had caused him the most distress, meeting Paula. He had phoned her from Gwen's place as soon as he had got up – her madam was clearly not properly awake yet when he asked to talk to her, and had been rather abrupt, but she had had the decency to call Paula to the phone – and arranged to meet her at the entrance to Government Avenue at the top end of Adderley Street.

She stood there next to the cathedral with large, worried eyes. Must have suspected that something was wrong. He had led her to a bench under some trees and told her that she was no longer welcome in Bridgetown, that everything was over between them.

First there had been a look of incredulity on her face, and then her face crumbled in anguish. He did not have it in his heart to walk her back to the bus stop, so he left her weeping on the bench.

"I don't care what you tell your bitch! You can keep on whoring with her – if she's not too busy with the half-dozen others she sleep with."

The unjustness of the accusation stung David, but he dared not provoke Yvonne further by defending Paula. When he did not reply, Yvonne ignored him and focused her attention on the pile of damp clothes in front of her on the table. She responded to his efforts at friendly conversation with monosyllabic grunts as he followed her from room to room. Finally Cynthia and Shirley came home from school and he went and sat with them while they did their homework.

At supper that evening Yvonne informed him that she had phoned her sister and that she was going to town. He nodded his head in assent. They finished the meal in silence, the children aware of their mother's grim face and their father's downcast head. A glare from Yvonne put an end to Thelma's prattle when she suddenly started telling them about some new puppy up the lane.

While Yvonne changed her clothes, David bathed Thelma and afterwards tucked her into bed. Cynthia and Shirley were already waiting for the bedtime story, so he started to read them a story from Hans Christian Anderson.

Without waiting for a break in the story or for him even to finish a sentence, Yvonne came in and kissed the children good night. David put the book aside and reached to embrace her, but she pulled away from him and strode from the room. The front door slammed behind her.

The girls sat looking at him with huge, questioning eyes. He pretended not to notice and continued reading in a quavering voice.

After a few minutes he could no longer keep up the pretence. He handed the book to Shirley and walked from the bedroom to the bathroom, where he blindly grabbed at the towel hanging from the rail on the wall, and stuffed it into his mouth to stifle his sobbing.

Melvyn was waiting for Yvonne in Klipfontein Road.

"Who is looking after the children?"

"David came back and he's with them."

"Oh."

"I'm free tonight."

She pushed her hand into his pocket and touched him. His breath quickened.

"Where's the car?"

"It's around the corner, at the Athlone Hotel."

Yvonne withdrew her hand and boldly hooked her arm in his as they walked towards the car, where she noticed Wallace was waiting.

After exchanging a few sentences with Melvyn, he disappeared into the hotel and after a short interval returned with a brown paper parcel.

"The wine steward gave me two half-jacks of gin mixed with lime," he announced.

"Why don't we go to Second Beach at Clifton?" Yvonne suggested. "Its a nice night for the beach."

Melvyn readily agreed.

"Suits me," Wallace said. "I'll pick up Ann."

He stopped in front of a house in Lawrence Road, a few blocks from the hotel, and hooted. The front curtain was raised and dropped, and after a moment the door opened and Ann came walking towards the car.

"Get in," Wallace said. "We're going to the beach."

"Please stop at the next shop," Melvyn said. "We need some paper cups."

Wallace parked the car in an open area off Victoria Road above Clifton. "Ann and me, we'll stay in the car," he told Melvyn, who happily accepted.

He opened the door on Yvonne's side and helped her out. Yvonne hastily slipped off her shoes and stockings, and walked down to Second Beach two, three steep steps at a time. Hand in hand they struggled through the dry sand high up and away from the water, looking for a sheltered spot.

They sat down behind some milkwood trees. The beautiful bikini girls and blond hunks that sunbathed here during the day had all left. As if to give himself courage, Melvyn finished his drink in swift swallows. Yvonne sipped sedately and carefully placed her cup next to the bottle when she had finished and turned towards him.

Her kisses were demanding, lips parted and tongue darting to touch his. Then she sat back, took off her blouse and with the same movement turned on her side so that Melvyn could unhook her brassiere. She twisted her breasts free and lay facing him. Melvyn sat as if bewitched. She guided his hands to her breasts and placed her arms around his neck, pulling him towards her.

The summer air was warm on her body as she slipped out of her skirt and slip. Melvyn threw his clothing in a heap on top of hers. Then he was above her. She opened her arms and thighs. Together they whirled away in a storm of their own making.

Yvonne, for a moment forgetting that it was David's attempted intimacy with Paula that had caused her to leave home tonight, was filled with maternal tenderness towards Melvyn's sudden clumsiness.

"Pour me a drink," she said.

Melvyn filled her cup, then his own.

She smeared her nipples with the last of the wine in her cup, lay back and pulled his head down. His tongue was thirsty for the wine on her breasts. With patient care, she taught him the intimacies she had shared with David.

Sated, Yvonne did not demur when Melvyn, in answer to the hooting from the car, suggested that they get dressed. With half-lame legs she struggled up the steps after him. During the ride home, she lay contented in his arms, her body pleasantly tired.

"You can drop us here," Melvyn said as the car turned into Klipfontein Road.

Yvonne did not offer any resistance when he stopped in the shadow of a hedge in the lane and raised the hem of her skirt to touch her, but she firmly refused his offer to walk her to the gate.

The light in the bedroom was still on. David was reading in bed. Yvonne took off her clothes and scattered them on the floor, purposely not putting on her nightdress as she got into bed.

David tossed his book aside and kissed her. She lay unresponsive. He could smell the alcohol on her breath and he kissed her again, forcing her lips apart, his hand covering her breast. This time she pushed him aside, her hand brushing at her lips as if to erase his kisses.

"I'm not your Paula bitch!" She turned her back on him.

He stared at the nape of her neck, a wave of impotent sadness washing over him.

12

Friday night. David's eyes swept with disgust over the four walls of the room that housed the *Cape Times* switchboard. Its isolation from the editorial offices made it a place of imprisonment for him.

His hand hovered over the dial to ring Dawn's number. He hadn't spoken to her since Gwen's place two weeks before.

The switchboard sounded its sharp demand and he took a call. "Good evening," he said dispiritedly.

"Relax," the voice at the other end said. "No murders, no rapes to report."

He was speechless with surprise.

"Hello? I'll have to report you to the management. We can't have a mute operating the switchboard."

"Hello, Arnold," David said awkwardly.

"I don't suppose you've seen the *New Statesman*, the latest one. It carries a review of the anthology. You are among illustrious people – Doris Lessing, Nadine Gordimer. The reviewer comments on your story in particular, praising its sensitivity."

David swallowed deeply. He blinked his eyes to focus. His troubles with Yvonne evaporated.

"Well, haven't you anything to say?"

"I don't know what to say, Arnold. I didn't think that it would draw much attention. But to appear in an anthology with Nadine Gordimer … "

He could burst with excitement. Appearing in print alongside those big names, and other famous writers he most probably did not even know of, was too much to comprehend.

"Your modesty doesn't become you."

"Honestly … I … " David stuttered.

Arnold burst out laughing. "I believe you."

In his mind's eye David saw bookshop windows arrayed with copies of the anthology. Copies on the shelves of libraries. Readers taking it out and reading his story. And a copy of the book in his possession. When will it arrive? "Jesus! Jesus!" he whispered. "I am a writer. Goddamnit, I am." All that struggling to put down words that would be appropriate and pleasing. And now *his* story, next to Gordimer and Lessing …

"Where can I get a copy of the *New Statesman*?" He almost tripped over his words.

"Court Agency at the top of Adderley Street should have a copy."

There was a brief silence before David said hesitantly, "Arnold, may I ask you a favour?"

"What is it? I hope you haven't got a repeat performance of what you did at Laurence's place in mind? Or the last time at my place. If I were not so excited about the review, I would not have phoned -"

"No, no," David said hastily. "I've got some new stories that I'd like you to go through. I've shown them to Margo and Dawn."

"Who is Dawn? If she is a new woman in your life, I hope you're not inflicting your anger and frustration on her as well!"

David had to swallow a sudden annoyance. "Not to worry," he said.

152

"She is a very good friend. Has been for a long time." He did not mention Dawn's reprimands when he got out of line. "Both liked them but I want you to read them and tell me honestly what you think. I finally wrote the one about the exhibition. It is included."

Arnold coughed on the other end. "David, I don't know if I'll have the time to do it. I'm pretty busy with my own writing."

"I'm not in a great rush, Arnold. You can take your time."

"All right. Send the lot to me next week. My novel's shaping up nicely. I should finish it soon if all goes well. How's your one doing?"

"I've shelved it."

Arnold was quiet for a few seconds.

"Probably the best thing to do. For the time being. Have you got anything in mind with the stories?" The old familiar sympathetic tone was back in his voice.

"That's something else I'd like to discuss with you. I hope to bring out a collection of stories, social and political but ... "

Arnold waited for David to continue, but he did not. After an uncomfortable silence, he gently prompted, "But what, David?".

"I'll talk about it when I see you."

"Give me a ring before you come so that I can clear the decks."

"Thanks, Arnold."

"So long."

13

It appeared a normal evening to start with. They all sat in the lounge, drinking. But gradually, each of them became aware of the tension between David and Yvonne. Early on, Eddie tried to draw David out of his morose state with sharp little barbs, but when it seemed only to drive Dave to drink more desperately, he gave up.

Steward, afraid that David's drinking would end in another violent outburst, was the first to leave.

Terence, taking one last look at Melvyn, who had been nervously glancing at David and Yvonne all evening, followed him with a few hasty good nights.

Eddie lingered on, hoping that David would let on what it was that caused him to be so silent. Then finally he, too, left.

David sat brooding behind a refilled glass, unaware of Melvyn's restlessness. A few minutes earlier, Yvonne, with a sign to Melvyn, had left on the pretext of going to Cora to fetch some magazines.

153

When David at last lifted his eyes from the glass in his hand, he caught Melvyn furtively glancing at his watch.

"What is bothering you?" David barked.

"I have to check some books for the supermarket. I think I'll leave," Melvyn said. "See you tomorrow."

"Yah," David grunted.

He finished the wine, carried the glasses to the kitchen, placed them in the sink, checked that the children were asleep, took a book from the bookshelf and without even looking at the title lay down on the bed and opened it. He scanned the pages disinterestedly, trying to concentrate, but the words refused to make sense. When he could no longer fool himself, he threw the book aside and glanced at the clock on the dressing table.

Fifteen minutes had passed since Yvonne had left.

Hell, she said she was just going to pick up her picture love-stories, he thought. His unease increased as another fifteen minutes passed. What the shit's keeping her?

His anxiety became unbearable. He checked on the children again, then locked the front door behind him. He could see Cora's house from where he stood in the lane. The kitchen and back bedroom windows were dark.

A worm of worry fretted him. He looked across to Eddie's place. The lights were off. Most of the houses were in darkness.

David slowly walked up the lane. His curiosity was aroused by the shape of a couple huddling in the shadows of a row of shrubs. The couple burst apart when he drew nearer and the tall figure of a man hastily walked away towards Klipfontein Road. The lamplight caught him as he turned the corner. It was Melvyn.

Quite oblivious of what just about everybody else knew, David could not understand why Melvyn would run away from him. And who was the other figure pressed against the fence?

He was almost on top of her before he realised that it was Yvonne.

The shock paralysed him. He stared at her, unable to move or speak. The buttons at the top of her blouse were unfastened and in the semi-darkness he could see her breasts were free of a halter.

"How long have you been out here with him?" he finally managed to ask. He was not aware that he was shouting.

"If you got anything to say, then say it at home," she said as she strutted past him. "Don't shout at me so that everybody hear!"

David grabbed at her shoulder. With a vicious shrug she pulled free and continued down the lane, head high and looking neither left nor right.

He followed her on limbs that seemed to lack volition, his mind a cauldron of boiling questions.

Yvonne stood waiting for him to unlock the door. David fumbled at the keyhole. He could not get his hand to do his bidding.

She waited in silence as he struggled with the key. At last the door swung open. She pushed past him and walked to their bedroom.

He locked the door and followed her.

The Drift Road,
Teslaarsdal
France:
nov. 1956

BOOK
THREE

1

When he got to the bedroom, only the top of her head was visible as she lay curled up underneath the blankets, her back to him. He raised his hand. It was trembling. He brought it down gently and rested it on her hair. He let his fingers sink into the silkiness. Her hair fascinated him. Heavy, black and glossy, it seemed to give off sparks when she brushed it. His fingers tightened their hold and he breathed deeply. With a small jerk she pulled her head free and brought her knees up to her chin.

Her body was a barrier shutting him out.

David covered his face with his hands and his body shook with long, shuddering sobs. Words milled around in his mind – angry, searing words, the kind they had so often hurled at one another in the past. He bit the palm of his hand in an attempt to control his sobbing, his eyes searching the familiar walls for some kind of assurance. For a brief moment his gaze rested on the small Peter Clarke pencil sketch of a country lane. It had always filled him with a feeling of peace. He sat down on the bed.

"Yvonne . . ." He faltered.

She lay motionless. He pretended to himself that she was listening.

"I will never forget the first time I saw you. I was twelve. It was a summer's day. I went to the kraal to play marbles, and there you were, leaning with your back against the wall."

He could still see the graffiti scrawled all over the wall: CLUSTER-BUSTER TERRITORY. SEXY BOYS ARE HEAVY FUCKERS. JOU MOER. SALLY IS A JINTOE. FUCK YOU TOO.

Why it was called the kraal he could never understand. It was no enclosure for sheep or cattle, just a sandy track between two crumbling houses in Chiappini Street that led into a little valley at the foot of Signal Hill. Entering the little valley was like being transported to the countryside. A stone's throw from the narrow plantless lanes there were trees – two fig trees and three towering giants, the names of which he never discovered, and, what he had always found strange and intriguing, an imposing palm gracing a large white house with ten cement steps leading to the front door.

"You were the funniest thing one could imagine. Skinny, all legs, light-

159

brown face with large black eyes, and breasts of a girl two or three years your senior. Your hair was plaited into two thick braids that leapt over your shoulders when you moved your head."

His fingers crawled across the blanket to touch her hair, but stopped short. "Every time I looked at you I wanted to shout, to jump into the air or turn a somersault, anything to get you to look at me. You made something happen inside me. I couldn't then explain it, but I now know: I'd found the girl that had featured in all my storybooks."

He gave a sharp, bitter laugh.

"I didn't dare speak to you because I was afraid, afraid that you'd laugh at me. I've always been sensitive, especially then, about people laughing at me because I'm so short." He snorted. "That's probably why I always have to do things to prove that my lack of height doesn't mean that I'm less of a man."

Yvonne's breathing had become shallow, her body less rigid, and with half an eye on her, David continued, "After that first day I kept going back to the kraal, hoping to see you again. And each time you were there and smiled at a boy, I felt like rushing up to him and knocking him flat. Then you became friendly with the girls in Shortmarket Street and joined them sitting on the corner. I used to chase all of you away from the corner, saying that the corner wasn't a place for you girls. But it was just an excuse to touch you, to touch your hair. I always made sure that you were my partner when we boys played with the girls. If I couldn't, then I dropped out.

"I was fourteen, almost fifteen when I sent you a note with one of the girls. Don't even remember her name anymore. I wrote because I was too shy to ask you to be my girl. I prayed so hard that you would say yes! And you wrote back. I could almost not read your reply, my heart was thumping so unbearably. Then I had to fight the impulse to run down the stairs and rush up to your place. I don't know how I managed to finish supper and help with the dishes. Afterwards I ran all the way to Maxwell Lane where you promised to meet me. A whole ten minutes early. You were five minutes late. It didn't matter. Time didn't matter. For the first time I would have you all to myself. When you appeared, I couldn't utter a word, only speak to you with my eyes. When I finally did say your name, it came out in a rush. Then I dared what I had always been dying to do: I took you in my arms and kissed you."

David lay back against his pillow. From the way Yvonne had moved her head, he could see she was listening.

"I suppose now it wouldn't rate as a kiss. But it was the first time that I had kissed a girl. I can still feel it. Your lips were soft and slightly parted. I couldn't breathe. A ringing noise filled my ears. When you pulled away, my body seemed to be weightless – I could have floated. I didn't even mind when you said you had to go home. We held hands as I walked you back. Every now and again, I'd sneak a look at your face. Your name chimed inside my head. I was whispering it softly. You insisted that when we came to Hout Street, I should go up Rose Street. You said we'd meet on the next corner. I could die because you weren't there. I could hardly sleep that night for thinking of you."

Suddenly, Yvonne pulled the blankets over her head, covering herself from his gaze, blocking out his words. David gave another bitter laugh.

"I can remember everything, no matter how long ago it happened, everything that has linked us together. I've known you now for twenty-three years. Twenty-three years is a long time. Almost forever, and for twenty-three years, I've loved you! Can you remember the first time I said that I was going to marry you? We were sitting at the back of Mrs William's house. I held your hand and whispered in your ear that I intended to marry you and that we would have four sons. We'd live in Alicedale, out in Athlone, almost the countryside for us at that time. Only Alicedale was good enough, because there families didn't live dozen to a room like in the Bo-Kaap.

"Well, nothing turned out the way we imagined it would be. Our four sons were going to live a better life, you were going to be a school teacher and I a writer. Well, we have three daughters, and they *are* living a better life. You are not a teacher, but I believe that I'm a writer. And we live in Bridgetown, not Alicedale. Some of the dreams, at least, have not been kicked in the guts."

Yvonne stirred beneath the blankets and sat up. The blankets piled in her lap. He could see her breasts pressing against her nightdress.

"Why you telling me all this?" She looked at him and he tried to hold her gaze but could not.

"Because I love you."

"Love me? Huh! Well, perhaps you love me, but let me tell you, Mr Patterson, I got nothing in my heart for you!"

She stared past him. He could feel her withdrawing into herself. Her words were like whips. Suddenly, he was terribly frightened. His trembling returned.

"Get me the cigarettes."

He got up and walked to the dressing table. Reflected in the mirror, he glimpsed his naked body. He automatically tensed his muscles and pulled in his stomach.

He lit the cigarette, feeling like a primate performing a trick for a master who had rejected it, and knelt at the side of the bed, ashtray in his hand.

"Get into bed."

"May I?" He immediately regretted the sarcastic tone of his voice.

She clucked her tongue in annoyance and the abrupt movement of her hand made the ash fall on the blanket.

"I'm sorry," he said. "Let me wipe it off."

She kept the ashtray between them, forcing him to stay on his side of the bed.

"Yvonne, why do you do this to me? Was the first time not enough? But that I could somehow understand. How was I to know that you'd become a woman long before I saw myself as a man? I was still filled with the things of a boy when you had already tired of what I could teach you. You wanted the world of broad-shouldered men and their ways, while it was enough for me to read about them in books. I was bewildered by your moods. I knew that I was losing you but I didn't know what to do about it.

"I became accustomed to hearing that Yvonne had been seen with this and that one, and always I could hear your wild laughter. But I was happy in the belief that it didn't matter, that I was the one that you truly loved, and that you'd always come back to me."

Yvonne was lying on her back, eyes closed, twin streams of smoke coming from her nostrils.

"I turned to books to get away from the taunts of the girls on the corner. I've always loved reading. Remember what they used to call me? Mr Know-all! If there's anything you want to know, just ask Mr Know-all, he'll get the answer from a book. I even fooled myself.

"But no book prepared me for what I was told later. Despite all the dirty things that happened around us, you were still the beautiful princess of my storybooks. Then they told me that you were going to have a baby, you who had just turned fifteen."

"I'm not the first girl there to get a baby when she's fifteen," Yvonne said drily.

"That day I was home, reading. My mother sent me to the shop. As usual, Tommy, Boet and George were holding up the outside wall of the shop with their backs. Tommy called me. I was reluctant to go over. I had long ago stopped hanging out with them because whenever I was around, they'd go into detail about what they would do to you if they got hold of you alone in a lane at night. Their talk sickened me and in the beginning I rushed at them with fists flailing. After the first six beatings, I had to tell myself that my small size was no asset."

David laughed bitterly. "But that day their attitude made me realise that their invitation involved you. Something nasty. Tommy straight away asked me if I've heard the news. He looked at Boet and George, then sniggered. He feigned surprise at my blank stare and said that he would've thought that I'd be the first to get the news."

Yvonne took a last, long draw and crushed the cigarette butt in the ashtray.

"I told him to get on with it before he threw a fit. He sniggered again, saying that *he* wouldn't be the one to throw a fit. Then he said that you were going to have a baby. That you were carrying a bundle. That that Johnson boy had been giving it to you good and solid. That they all were of the opinion that I was too slow, that I didn't know how to go about it.

"I shouted that it wasn't true, that he was making it up, that you weren't like that."

Yvonne looked at him steadily. That's the trouble with you, she thought, you always was stupid with things like that. Then she turned on her side, facing away from him, and covered her head with the bed sheet.

"I was ready to fight all three of them when Boet told me to stop being so stupid, that it had to happen. That you'd been taking me for the horse's arse all the time. Why do you always want to defend her and get hurt in the process? he asked me.

"I walked away, their jeers following me back home. Then that evening when I met you face to face, even I could see the bulge your belly made under the coat you were wearing. My eyes couldn't hold yours and my throat was too tight to talk. I walked away from you. I never knew that there could be so much weeping inside me.

"Inside me a voice shrieked that you were indeed the bitch they had said, that I was a fool who preferred to walk with veiled eyes and wax-stuffed ears. No matter how many times I screamed Bitch! Bitch! Bitch! it gave me no solace."

"Yes, you walked away, and that night I need your help." Yvonne's voice came as if from very far away. "If you'd had any guts, I was yours. I was looking for help and you always help me. But that evening when your eyes look on my body, I see no help coming from you and I was too proud to ask. You had to make the first move. And you fail me!"

She pulled the sheet off her head and sat up.

"I was no bitch then. I loved Derick Johnson. I don't think I ever was a bitch! I always went around with one man at a time and Derick Johnson was the first one to make a woman of me. I never lay with any of the others. I know what people say about me but piss on them!" She shook her free of the sheet and her hair fell back like a mare's mane. "The filth they spit cannot touch me!"

"You tell me that you loved Derick Johnson. Then why didn't you marry him?"

She smoothed the blankets with her hands before answering, "That's my secret, but love him I did." It was her turn to give a bitter laugh. "It's true what they say. A woman never forget the man who had her first."

She looked at David and saw the anguish her words caused. She stifled the words of comfort she for a brief moment was tempted to offer.

"Yes, you very much would like to know why I didn't marry Derick, why I let the child I carried be born a bastard and adopted? You can fry in hell, first! I've never told anyone, not even my mother, who know Derick make me pregnant."

David reached out his hand, but Yvonne pushed it aside.

Her gesture filled his mind with memories. He so badly wanted to help her then, protect her, but he didn't know how to approach her. He could also not bear being near her, her body an ever-constant reminder of what she'd done, a barrier between them. Yet he would have given his life to restore her to the princess in his storybooks.

A smile flitted across his face: the day he had proposed and she had accepted, all the pain had been cancelled out by the happiness her answer had given him. It had been some months after the baby had been born and Yvonne had been back to her precocious self.

"Can you still remember when I asked you to marry me? It was the day of the picnic. At first I didn't want to go but you kept on urging me and I was afraid that should I refuse, you'd go on your own. You were still in bed when I arrived at your place that morning. The door was locked and your mother had to let me in."

Yvonne leaned across the bed and reached for the packet of cigarettes. She lit one.

"You shouted to me to wait in the passage. When you appeared, you looked like a schoolgirl at first, your hair plaited into two pigtails, complete with two tiny bows. But the way you were dressed – clinging tights and sweater – showed that schoolrooms could no longer contain you.

"On our way to where the lorries were waiting on Riebeek Square, the sway of your hips drew the eyes of every passing man. I could tell that you found the bold stares pleasing. That was when the thought came to me that I should ask you to marry me or else I might lose you again.

"I was irritated by the crush of people in the lorry, but at the same time I wished the trip to Houwhoek would never end because we were squeezed together and you had fallen asleep in my arms. As soon as we arrived, you rushed off to where the hired band had set up their instruments. I asked a little boy to look after our blanket and food and went for a swim in the river. When I came back I found you dancing."

"I was already sick then of the way you check on me," Yvonne sighed.

He continued as if he had not heard her. "The band was beating out a kwela. I watched you: plaits banging across your forehead, mouth open and face wet with sweat, your hands caressing the air in front of you, your body gyrating to the strain of the music. A man danced towards you, and the two of you danced together for a while, then you split apart again. A strange gleam in your eyes had me transfixed. I couldn't look away."

David recalled the almost unbearable pitch of the note with which the saxophonist brought the number to a shrieking halt, Yvonne's quivering body, and the heat patch in the region of his crotch. When the music had died down, she had started to walk across the clearing in a cloud of dust, away from him.

"Afterwards you walked away in the direction of the forest and I had to run after you. When I asked you where you were going, you looked at me with that wild gleam still in your eyes and said: to our things. The strong smell of your sweat stirred my senses and I took your hand and led you into the plantation. I found it odd when you docilely followed me."

"It was the woman in me. That's why I let you take me into the bush."

"Later you made no objection when I pulled you to the ground next to me. Your breasts were two birds fluttering in my hands."

"You always was a fool. Fancy talk and nothing to follow. I was waiting for you to take me, and all you can do is fondle my breasts and think up different ways of telling me how much you love me. It must be all that sweet talk that made me soft in the head and I agree to marry you."

Yvonne lit another cigarette. "I was so foolish that I let you keep me prisoner for the rest of the day," she said with an irritated shake of her hair. "Afterwards I say to myself I never again go on a picnic with you. You don't understand I must be free. You want to keep me in in glass cabinet for yourself."

"I didn't force you to marry me. Why did you agree?"

She raised her shoulders and lifted her hands, palms up.

"I suppose I was fond of you, and marrying you was one way of getting the hell out our place and away from my mother."

The morning of the wedding, David thought that she had changed her mind. He waited with Martin on Riebeek Square, at the public toilets. When it came to half past eight he became panicky and was about to ask

Martin to go up to her place when her noticed her and Gertie coming round the corner.

She was wearing her yellow dress, and he noticed, as they walked, that her heels were higher than usual. But he couldn't be bothered. She could've been walking on stilts and it wouldn't have mattered. It was their wedding day, the day on which he would be entitled to call her wife. Everyone who passed could've guessed it. He could hardly stop talking, but she was quiet, never saying a word while they walked to court.

With the barely audible sound of Yvonne pulling the cigarette smoke deep into her lungs and then exhaling it slowly, David thought back to how he had told her over and over how beautiful she looked as they sat on the bench outside the magistrate's office. On the other bench, a yard away from them, a white groom had been waiting, even more nervous. The man couldn't sit still, got up every few minutes to stride up and down the passage. David had whispered to Yvonne that perhaps his bride had run out on him. He'd tried to picture what sort of woman would be marrying him. When she'd finally arrived, it turned out that he had been completely wrong. She'd towered above him, thin as a pole in her pink dress, her hair dyed a hideous red. His heart had gone out to her groom.

Wasted sympathy, David thought, the man was probably much happier than him – at least at the present moment.

They had been taken to an office, in the front of which stood a chair and a table covered with a lace cloth. Printed forms, two ballpoint pens and a vase with artificial flowers were stiffly arranged on the table. The magistrate's chair looked more comfortable than the office chairs on which he and Yvonne were sitting. Gertie and Martin had sat a few rows back, trying to be as inconspicuous as possible.

When it was their turn, the magistrate had asked some questions and filled in the forms. He and Yvonne had mumbled the marriage vows read to them. Then it was over. They were man and wife.

"Do you remember how you objected to having rice strewn over our heads when we came out of the magistrate's court?" David said when Yvonne stirred as if she was about to get up. "I had read somewhere that rice was a symbol of fertility, and the previous evening I had carefully put some in a fancy little bag I had asked my mother to sew. Anyway, then Gertie and Martin went back to work and we on our honeymoon."

"Is that what it was?" Yvonne asked sarcastically.

"Well, how many people can say that they spent the first phase of their honeymoon in a cinema? We went all the way to Athlone for that morning show. It cost me forty cents for the fare and another rand for the tickets. And

166

there in the darkness of the cinema, with a hundred unsuspecting people around us, we started our honeymoon."

"Yes, harp on how much it cost you to get married to me in court. Why not mention the ten rand as well? I wonder why you didn't take the church, or better still, the poor man's way in court with our names on the notice board for every curious bastard to read."

"You know I'm only joking when I mention the money I paid. I would've gladly paid ten times ten rand."

"The ten rand you pay, you got more than your money out of me!"

"Don't talk that way, Yvonne. I didn't marry you for that!"

"I wonder? It was certainly a wedding night to remember."

Yvonne had come to his place, as usual. But he had specially prepared it: the lamp low, a blanket on the couch. He'd even bought a bottle of milk and two avocados. He'd been impatient. He'd kept on telling himself that it was true, that she was his, belonged to him. He could no longer restrain himself when she'd come into the room. All the years of waiting finally at an end. All the years of torment had fallen away when he took her. He'd feasted on her flesh, drunk with the delight of it.

A sharp laugh came from her. "I had to tell you to call a halt to it."

"But it wasn't just a case of flesh. Why do you refuse to believe that I love you for yourself? You and the children are the most important things in my life. So is my writing. But from the day you saw my first story published in the *Argus*, you were only interested in how much I got paid for it."

"And why not?" Yvonne asked defiantly. "A writer, huh! You not a writer's arsehole. When you finish that book you been working on for the last two years? The book that will knock out everybody? The book suppose to get us out of this dump? The only knock-out is me, and it's not the book that do it. I just get tired of waiting for you to finish that book. All you got to show is a story in a book in England and you don't even got the book to show!"

"I tried writing poetry as well," David said, ignoring her remark about the novel that he had just about abandoned, and the anthology of short stories of which he still had not received a copy. "But I never got further than the few pieces I wrote for you. Have you still got the one about the moth and the flame?"

He silently repeated the words to himself:

To you I am drawn unresistingly
A moth fascinated by the flame
Until it is too late, and I ...

"Why don't you can it?" she interrupted his thoughts. "You beginning to sound like a gramophone record. So you write me some poetry. So what it make you, and what it give me? Sweet fuck-all! It's only more fancy crap!"

"It seems you'll never forget where you come from. I hoped that as you grew older, and with new faces around, you'd drop the habits of the past. But habits with you seem to be life-long things."

"Why must I change? Did I ask you to bring me to this damn rat-trap?" She pointed to the cracked paint on a wall. "What the hell's there for me to do here? When night come, I'm a prisoner. When daylight break, I go through the same drag of washing up and feeding. In the Bo-Kaap, nights don't mean going in a prison cage. There was always something to do."

"You didn't call this a rat-trap when we moved in. I could see how proud you were of the furniture and that we had a house to ourselves. And it didn't take you long to make friends with the neighbourhood wives ..."

She gave a disparaging look at the four walls of the room. "And this is the grand house you going to build for me? It's just like that trip to Beira we going to take. A second honeymoon, it was going to be. And what happen? I'm damn lucky you take me to Simonstown. And that's only a hour's ride from here. You all words and wind. You just a phoney! All of you – Eddie, Terence. Charley's the worst. All of you except Steward. When you full of wine then you big with words as to what great things you will do. If your work is judged by the wine you drink, the bookshelf be filled with your books."

A tightness in his chest made it difficult for David to speak. He did not intend the conversation to take this turn. But he needed to know: "Is that what you really think of me? I've heard you boast to the other women about how good a husband I am, how much trust you have in me."

"That was before you start drinking so much. And that was before your whore Paula come on the scene."

"You were delighted when I started drinking. You said it made me more convivial."

"I never say you must drink and turn into a drunk pig!"

"You've never liked the discussions we have. My idea was to turn our house into a place where people who are interested in the creative arts could meet and exchange ideas and discuss their work."

"And what happen? It end up in drunk parties!"

"But it didn't start out that way. We did have a number of serious discussions. Remember, Peter Clarke came over once. He gave us that drawing. And so did Richard Rive. He has had a collection of short stories and a novel published, and he has edited an anthology of stories. Both of them have gone to Europe. Those are the people I wish to associate with."

168

"You never make it. You don't move around with them because they write and paint and not just talk about it. You not even seeing Steward as much as before. You stick to drinking. Booze sessions more your line."

"Yes. Boozing seems to be more my line, and for which you're partly to blame. No serious talk. Always ready for a dash of vino because that's the way you like it. You've become the hostess who's always on the ball."

"It's a bit late in the day for you to complain. You have as big a ball as the next sonnuva bitch! With the second glass in you, you rattle-and-roll with the best of them. I know very well what you do when there's a blues number on the gram. And always with the youngest one present. Christ alone know what you want to prove."

"I'm not trying to prove anything. It's an act of desperation," he said sadly. "If you'd only feel the pain it brings on when you go into your dance routine, with that bitch-gleam lighting up your face. Dancing is like a sex act to you. Love-making without the necessity of stripping and going to bed!"

"That's another thing that make me sick! You don't like what I read. You don't like the music I listen to. You don't like the way I dance. You even want to think for me, tell me what I got to say. Well, you go take a long walk because you never get me the way you want me to be! I do what I want to do and when I feel like it!"

"You're right. No, not any more. I don't have to tell you which music to listen to. You've got someone else now. You're even reading decent literature. In the twelve years that we've been married, I couldn't get you started on a collection of stories. Soon you'd be reading Dostoevski. Charley would like that. You must love Melvyn very much."

"I do! I never met anyone like him. I fall in love with him the first time he come looking for you. I tremble at the sound of his voice. If he touch me at that moment, I be his to do with as he please."

"I never thought I'd hear you say those words about another man." David didn't care if she could hear the hurt in his voice. "All the time that we've been married, apart from the last few weeks, you've been faithful to me. No man could've asked more of his wife. I would've bet my life that you'd never play me false for another man. That's why I wasn't worried with your behaviour towards Eddie. It certainly took me all this time to realise that everything was not as it should be in my little garden of Eden."

"Things go wrong in your garden of Eden for a long, long time but you too busy getting drunk and squeezing the tits of the little hot bitches to catch on. You take me for granted, part of the furniture. Something that's always around. Something you reach out for in the middle of the night after the bitches leave. With Melvyn it's different."

169

"I knew that he had become something special to you but I looked upon him as a younger brother. I didn't mind when he started turning up with blankets and a change of clothing and staying over Saturday nights. Not to forget the wine he so generously offered me.

"I was so trusting and he so honourable. That was your hymn of praise. How honourable a young man he was. He was so honourable that I encouraged him to take you out while I was working. What harm could come from it? I should have caught on earlier, but I was too flattered. Flattered by the way he followed my lead. He started asking the children about their homework, he read stories to them. He helped you with the dishes. Sunday mornings, while I was still in bed, he was up and doing in the kitchen, you busy at the stove and him peeling potatoes.

"I was fool. Only to discover last night that I've been done in by a man of honour!"

"I was going to tell you this morning when the children go to school. But look how you act last night. You grab me by the shoulder and start shouting so the whole lane can hear. You'd send me to the morgue if it's not for the children in the back room."

"I'm sorry, I wasn't going to hurt you."

"I don't see why it upset you that much. How many times you tell me, when tight with wine, that you had your fill of me and that I was no help to you? Well, here's your chance. I don't want any part of you. I don't love you. I stop loving you a long time ago. I lose all respect for you. It's Melvyn I love."

"Please, Yvonne. You don't know what you're saying. I can only reject you when I'm drunk. I love you and can never love another woman. Melvyn's not for you. Behind that façade of attentiveness there's a little boy in search of a mother. That's what he really sees in you."

"This thing is of your own making!" Yvonne snapped back. "Who invite him to the house? It was you who say he can take me out, and who remind me on rainy nights to keep a plate of hot soup ready for him." She sat up. "What's the time? I can hear the buses."

"It's six o'clock."

"I think I get up now."

"It's early. Why do you want to get up now?"

"No point to stay in bed."

David looked at her as she got dressed. "Yvonne, what about us?"

"My loving Jesus! You nag all night. Don't tell me I got to listen to you all morning as well. What more is there to say?"

"Nag, you call it? What a hard-hearted bitch you are!"

170

"Yes, why don't you? Go on. Hit me! Show your children what a coward their father is. They awake and listening to everything we say. Come'n, let go of me!"

"I won't let go of you. Not before you tell me that it's all foolishness, this nonsense between Melvyn and you."

With a forceful movement Yvonne shook his hands from her shoulders and stalked towards the door. "I show you how much nonsense this is. When the children go to school, I tell Cynthia to go to Melvyn and say he must come here. Then you see how much nonsense this is!"

2

Melvyn searched Yvonne's face as she and David sat on opposite sides of the table in the lounge.

"What's wrong? Cynthia said that I had to come straight away, that it was very important." He looked questioningly from Yvonne to David.

Before Yvonne could answer, David spoke. "Yes, Melvyn. It's very important. Sit down. Yvonne says that she's going to leave me, that she doesn't love me any more, that you're the one she loves. Do *you* love *her*?"

Melvyn's eyes flickered to Yvonne's tense face and back to David's.

"Yes, I love her."

"Melvyn ..."

"Wait, Yvonne. You stay out of this. This is between Melvyn and myself. Melvyn, you say that you love Yvonne. Do you love her strongly enough to take her away from me, right now? If you do, then tell her to leave with you, now. She can take her stuff and I won't do a thing to stop you two. Don't hesitate. Make up your mind now. All you have to say is yes and she's yours."

"Look, David. I do love Yvonne but I've never told her that I love her the same way you do. I love her, but it's a different kind of love. You've known Yvonne all your life. I've only got to know you people since July, and that's only four months ago. You can't expect there to be the same feeling between Yvonne and myself."

"But you could enter a room and meet a woman for the first time and fall in love and know in your heart that there would never be another love for you."

"Yes. That's what has happened to me. I was drawn to Yvonne the very first night I came looking for you, and my love has grown stronger day by day."

"But it's not strong enough for you to take her right now? That's the difference between us. Yvonne is my life. If she leaves me, I die. All night I trembled at the thought of losing her. You once told me that all the girls come a running after you, that your big cock draws them like a wino to wine. Is Yvonne also cock-struck?"

The challenging look and blunt question made Melvyn lower his gaze. "I never meant it to refer to Yvonne."

"It's not that easy after all, is it? It's no boy's game taking a woman from her man. You're not quite prepared to tackle the task, are you? What are you waiting for? Yvonne is prepared to throw everything overboard and go off with you. All you have to do is reach out and take her. It's as easy as all that!"

To cover his agitation, Melvyn got up, tugged at the back of his blazer and said, "I have to leave. I have to be at the shop." At the door, he turned. "I'll come and see you tonight, Yvonne."

"Do that, Melvyn. I'll also be here," David said. "Or have you forgotten that I'll be home every night for the next three weeks? I started my leave yesterday."

Yvonne waited for the door to close behind Melvyn before she allowed her composure to crack. She lowered her head to the table and her body shook with sobs.

David rose from his chair on the other side of the table and moved to her side. He rested his hand gently on her shoulder. "Don't cry, Yvonne. Don't feel bad about it. Melvyn couldn't help himself. After all, he's only a youngster compared to us. He's way out of his depth. This is something he can't cope with."

She shrugged off his hand and raised her tear-streaked face. "You must think you damn smart when you ask him to make up his mind the moment he come into the room. You know he's not able to drop everything and go off with me. Who going to look after the shop if he leave with me?"

"I had to do it. I had to take the gamble. I had to show him up in front of you. Melvyn's not important. I've met so many Melvyns before. They are all half-baked potatoes. On his own, he could never bother me. It is the status you give him with your love that makes him important. If you persist in carrying on with him, we'll end up hurting each other and he'll walk away. You'll see. He's got nothing to lose. We two will be the losers. The children will suffer as well."

"David, it don't matter how many ways you find to tell me, nothing going to change my mind. I still go on loving Melvyn. The children don't matter. They grow up. Nothing's important, only Melvyn! If you think so much about your children then you can leave the house. I will stay and you can support the children. You don't have to worry about me."

"You must've given this thing a lot of thought. You've worked out everything: I leave and he takes over. I brought him here in the name of friendship and now, because of him, I must leave my house. His suits are to hang on my hangers. His shoes under my bed. His body in my bed."

David sat down on the chair again in an effort to calm the shaking of his body. "Now you break down in tears over another man. Have you ever cried over me?"

"Yes, I cry. But my tears are for what you do to me!"

"Your tears turn him into a god. And me? I become a lump of shit. No matter what success I achieve, if he comes up to me and says, 'I own your wife', my triumph becomes a pot of ashes!"

"Leave me alone! Shut up! Your nagging give me a headache. I want to get on with my work!"

In silence David watched her stomp off into the kitchen and grab the broom from behind the door.

3

How the hell am I going to get through to her? She's still got her arse up in the air because Melvyn didn't turn up last night. She doesn't believe that I meant it when I said that what had happened did not mean that Melvyn's visits should stop. All I want is a chance to win her back.

David had made several half-hearted attempts at conversation, all ending in an uneasy silence. Yvonne refused to respond to his overtures. It had been the same all morning. He tried to be helpful, but she snatched the broom from his hands as he clumsily swept the kitchen.

He stood looking at her for a while. She maintained the same forbidding silence. He could feel the confidence of the previous day drain away, leaving him empty and cold.

Not to aggravate the situation, he sat down on a chair, out of her way, and watched her prepare their lunch. When she had finished, she lay a dish cloth on one side of the table and slammed a plate with two slices of bread and a huge helping of tomato pilchards down on it. She put a cup of coffee next to it and left the kitchen with the children's food.

The time signal chimed from the small radio on the window sill.

David placed his plate and the empty cup in the sink and walked to the children's bedroom.

Thelma was seated on the mat, her plate of food between her short little legs. Yvonne was stretched out on the one bunk bed reading a picture love-story. She made no sign to acknowledge his presence, studiously flicking the pages of the magazine.

"I think I'll go to the cinema. They've got a Gary Cooper picture that I missed the first time round."

His proposal was received in silence.

He walked out of the house and closed the gate behind him. A bus pulled away just as he turned the corner, and he decided to walk to the Empire Cinema in Athlone.

David scarcely bothered to look at the garish posters and bought a ticket to get him inside. He stumbled to his seat and sat through the cartoons without bothering to distinguish one mayhem-inflicting character from another.

When the lights came on for the intermission, he felt the need for wine. Looking listlessly at the stills in the foyer, he decided against it and went back inside.

He tried to work up interest for the main feature. He remembered telling Eddie and Steward that the studio had paid Hemmingway enough money for the film rights to *For Whom The Bell Tolls* for him to take it easy for quite some time before having to write another novel. They compared the amount of money to what the weekend papers normally paid for a story and laughed because in a life-time of writing short stories he would not come to earning a tenth of what Hemmingway got for the film rights of one single novel.

David forced himself to look at the screen, but Ingrid Bergman and Gary Cooper could not keep his mind from wandering back to Yvonne and Melvyn.

Yvonne sat looking moodily through her picture love-story, comparing the heroine's plight with her own.

At the crunch of shoes on the pathway, she peered through the window. Melvyn's tall frame was almost at the door. She hastily pushed the magazine in a drawer and at his knock opened the door, a relieved smile on her face. "What happened to you?" she asked.

He looked at her, then lowered his face.

"I didn't come back because I first wanted a chance to think the whole matter over carefully, to consider every facet of the situation." Looking into her eyes, he said, "I do love you but I must also admit what David said was very true. How's his behaviour towards you?"

174

"I don't speak to him if I can help it. He sit here watching me with eyes ready to drown me in. Everywhere I move, I can feel his eyes on me. If I step outside, he's there with 'Yvonne, where you going?' If he can go to the toilet with me, he do that! Then he try his sweet talk. But it's not going to make me change my mind. I mean every word I say."

"I feel so guilty about the whole thing. I think so highly of David. I've learnt a lot from him in the short time I've known him."

She pushed aside his apologetic words with a wave of her hand. "You don't have to feel guilty about anything. You don't really know David. You got to live with him for that, and I live with him far too long and with all his shit! He and his great plans! He made even me believe it. He was the one who say we must leave town, that we must come to stay in this miserable place."

He reached out his hand then stopped. "Where is Thelma?"

"Out in the park, playing."

He caressed her cheek.

"He was going to write such big things. The money we going to have, the things we going to do and the places we travel to. And what happen? I get three kids and I do all my travel to town. And that's my week. Six nights I look at the walls and the seventh night I look at David on the floor."

"Where's David?"

"Thank God I'm rid of him for a few hours. He went to the bioscope."

She returned Melvyn's gaze, then went to lock the front door. "Lock the kitchen door," she said.

David sank down lower in his seat and closed his eyes. The voices from the screen didn't make sense any longer. Ingrid Bergman had assumed Yvonne's face and the scorn she poured on Gary Cooper was all too familiar. He rubbed his eyes, got up and stumbled out of the darkened cinema.

The sight of a young couple walking hand-in-hand as they passed him in the street intensified his pain. He had to stop himself from running all the way home.

The door refused to yield when he turned the knob. He tried again, using the palm of his hand as a lever. "Damn it!"

He walked to the back of the house. The kitchen door was also locked. His impatience gave way to anger. He walked back to the front door and hammered on it with his fist.

Yvonne opened the door.

"What's the matter with you?"

"Why the hell are the doors locked?"

"No need to swear at me," she said cooly. "We listen to some music and I don't want Thelma to bother us with her marching in and out."

"We?"

"Yes. Melvyn and me." She waved to where Melvyn was sitting at the table.

The now familiar unease swept through him. His eyes flitted over her face, hair and clothing, searching for signs of disarrangement. Neither her answer or the orderly state of her clothing satisfied him. He dared not question her further, fearing a straight answer to the gnawing suspicions in his mind.

Yvonne left him and Melvyn sitting on opposite sides of the table.

To David, Melvyn appeared as flustered as himself, and when Melvyn spoke his voice was huskier than usual: "Yvonne was kind enough to let me listen to some of your Readers' Digest classics. I enjoyed the music, especialy Rossini's William Tell Overture."

What sort of a fool they think I am? Since when have the children become a nuisance when a record is playing? David did not reply.

After a few uncomfortable seconds, Melvyn asked, "How was the film?"

"I had a headache and that putrid sound system of the Empire worsened it. I stopped at a bar for relief."

Their conversation petered out and Melvyn sought refuge behind a screen of cigarette smoke. David's mind kept darting back to the locked doors.

Yvonne returned with two mugs of coffee. The first she placed in front of Melvyn, the second next to David's elbow. He pushed his aside and some of the coffee spilt onto the table.

Impassively, Yvonne looked at Melvyn, who turned his gaze away from her. David got up and slammed the front door behind him.

Why the hell don't I just tell the bastard to leave my house?

Thelma, coming round the corner from the park, ran up to him and tugged at his sleeve. He walked on. "Daddy, daddy," she piped after him. He hardened his heart and ignored her call.

It was dark by the time he returned. He stumbled up the lane and leaned over the gate before pushing it open with his body. His feet were unsteady as he walked towards the door. It was not locked.

The front room was in darkness and he shoved a chair out of his way.

The children were asleep and Yvonne was propped up in bed, surrounded by picture magazines. A slab of chocolate lay on his pillow.

He swayed in front of her.

"Your food's in the oven."

"Where's your lover boy?" He had difficulty pronouncing the words.

176

She turned her back on him.

He lurched forwards and fell against the side of the bed and slid onto the floor.

Yvonne looked at him for an instant as he lay with eyes closed, a silver ribbon of saliva running from his mouth. Then she turned back to her magazine.

4

It was the only house with a tree, a giant oak standing tall and free in a ridiculously small patch of paved earth. David stared at the tree and in his inebriated state wondered who could have spent countless years nursing a solitary tree in a field of cement slabs. Could it have been someone whose soul was not completely crushed by life's heavy blows, someone who still had time to reflect on the beauty nature produced?

"Is this the dump?"

Steward confirmed his suspicion. The wife of a couple whom he had known for quite some time had bought a painting from him a week ago. She and her husband had subsequently written him a letter and invited him to a party. He had phoned them the previous day and asked if he and Hester could bring a friend along.

"You and Hester better go ahead and I'll sort of stumble after you," David suggested.

They skirted the tree, walked through an open front door and up a steep flight of stairs.

David had glimpses of flesh winking at him from above stocking tops. Hester was wearing an uncharacteristically short mini. He looked at her posterior in a disinterested manner. Flesh belonging to a soul sister could not stir him. Eddie would of course not believe him when he said it and maintained that it would be a long day dawning when David could look at a woman and not think of bedding her. Even Steward, at first, was doubtful whether David could keep his hands off Hester. She was prim and proper, but she was equally pretty. Only recently had Steward started to believe him when he said that he did not eat his brother's meat.

David touched Hester lightly on the buttocks and as she turned, he said, "Fuck them all, catto! You are my sister. Truly you are!"

She gave a weak grin, full of apprehension.

The first chime of the bell had hardly settled when the door to the flat was opened by a short, busty blonde in black tights and a sweater.

"Hello, Steward, Hester. Glad you could come. Go through. Lester's in the kitchen preparing a bottle for the baby. He won't go to bed without it." Then she saw David. With eyebrows raised, she turned to Hester and Steward.

"Brenda, this is David," Steward said.

"The one who writes?" She held out her hand.

David watched the changing expression on her face as she took a closer look at his clothes.

Steward and Hester had come around to Bridgetown earlier in the day to discuss the party. In order to stop his brooding and solitary boozing, Steward had insisted that he accompany them. He had agreed on condition that he could remain in the same clothes he had slept in after passing out from a drinking session earlier in the day.

"Come in, the air is rather chilly outside." Brenda's invitation was followed by a sharp whinny of a laugh.

"It is, isn't it?" David replied, matching her laugh with a hoarser neigh.

The three of them stared at him for a moment, the hostess clearly not knowing how to take David. A nervous tic David had never noticed before started in Hester's cheek. Steward had the look of a man who wished to be a thousand miles away.

The passage was not much wider than the stairway. Their footsteps were muffled by the thick runner, but the baby must have sensed their approach, because a soft cry came from a room they were passing.

"Daddy will be with you in a minute, Sean," Brenda cooed as she closed the door.

She ushered them into a large room. "Find some seats, you're the first to arrive."

David sank into a low sofa. An equally low coffee table separated him from Steward and Hester, who had sat down on the opposite side. Brenda remained standing. He took in the three huge plates with biscuits, avocado pear and pieces of cheese on the table in front of him.

"Have some biscuits," Brenda suggested.

"You think I could have some wine?" David said. "I'd rather drink than eat."

"Of course. There's some white as well as red wine. Which do you prefer?"

"I'll take both. I'll start off with the white, then see how the red works out."

With a rather cool, "Help yourself, it's on the table behind you", she made her exit from the room.

178

David poured some wine from a carafe and peered over the rim of his glass at Hester and Steward who were having a hushed conference. He could guess the trend of their conversation. But how did they expect him to behave?

Music was filtering through from another room. He took a closer look around. Persian rugs were scattered on the floor and a large kelim hung on the wall facing him. The other walls held paintings. There was no need to scrutinise them. He knew they would be originals. It was a room that oozed warmth and gracious living.

David swallowed his wine with a defiant gesture and refilled his glass, switching from white to red. He put the carafe next to his seat.

"Hello, Hester, Steward," a male voice boomed. The owner of the voice materialised next to David and a pudgy hand reached out. "I'm the lord of the manor."

David looked up. The lord of the manor was as tall as his wife and had the same colouring. They could have been cut from the same cloth, David thought and waved his glass at him.

The sound of the doorbell reverberated down the passage.

"Lester, be a dear," Brenda called from the kitchen. "See who's at the door."

Two couples entered the room, and before they could be introduced, another couple followed.

David did not attempt to remember any of the names, content to wave his half-full glass at them. It slowly dawned on him that he was the object of everyone's attention. He gave a lopsided smile.

After putting a record on the player, Lester returned to the kitchen. Conversation resumed.

The voices, backed by township jazz, became a lullaby and David drifted away in a state between sleep and wakefulness. He was roused by the sharp shriek of penny whistles. A deep thirst made him grope for the carafe of wine at his side. It was not there. He turned his head and saw a youngish woman seated on the floor near him, her fingers curved around the neck of the carafe.

"Is this what you're looking for?" The voice was teasing.

"Are you reading my mind, catto?"

Some wine spilled when he filled his glass and he raised his wrist to his mouth and licked the liquid from his skin.

The woman did not comment, just looked on.

"How long have you been here?" he asked. "And why didn't you wake me?"

"It must've been all of three minutes. I didn't want to wake you as your face had such a peaceful expression."

"Don't let it fool you. I always look like that when I'm thinking up ways of doing people in. Most people give me the shits."

"Do I give you the shits?" she asked, her voice still teasing.

David searched her face, taking in the smooth, fair skin faintly sprinkled with freckles, grey-green eyes under thick, dark eyebrows. Her lips were bare of lipstick. He was conscious of her perfume. It was exhilaratingly disturbing.

"No, catto. You affect me differently. What's your name?"

"Jeanette."

"No, can't be Jeanette. Jeanette's far too prissy for you."

"Then what's my name?"

"Sheila."

"No, I don't like Sheila."

"Norma-Louisa-Thelma-Margo-Julia-Francis-Gwen-Velda. I'm running out of names. Take your pick."

"No. I don't like any of them. I'll stick to Jeanette."

"I've got it. I should've known from the start. You're a woman of light." He waved a deprecatory finger at the other women in the room. "With you in the room, they're all dead. There's only you, Lilah. I'm your Samson for the slaying."

"Lilah? Yes, I suppose that would do. And what's your name?"

"Should I have a name? Would a name make me less of a bastard than I am? Speak not to me of names but take me as you find me. Will we make out, catto, sweet catto?"

"I don't know."

"See, it's as I said. The world's a shit house and people stink it up."

"You shouldn't speak like that. You're too cynical for your years. How old are you? Thirty-four, thirty-six?"

"Does the number of years matter? I've seen many years and they've all played me dirty. Inside my mother's womb there was safety, then I was spewed out and ever since then my spirit has slowly but surely been castrated."

She looked at him without replying.

Testing her, he said:

"You play it cool
your grab a chick
and make a scene
the chick don't dig

180

A freeze sets in
Is it for real
or for the birds?"

"I'm not sure if it could pass as poetry, but it certainly reflects your cynicism. Brenda tells me that you write short stories. I write poetry, but it's mainly pastoral."

"No, I don't really make out with poetry. I don't figure the technical side of it. Metre and all that crap."

"I'm particularly fond of Shakespeare's sonnets. Do you know them?"

"Shakespeare's a scorcher! He's got it made. He burns real bright. It's as the man said: the world's a stage. But I think we stink up the scene with our performance. I want to write but most times I'm a spoiler mutilating a fine piece of ivory with a hacksaw and the words produced are jagged slivers, sharp and ugly, sticking in my throat."

Someone touched his shoulder lightly. He shook off the hand. "Drop dead!" he said. "Can't you see I'm communing with my new-found soul mate?"

"Let's go and listen to Bach, everybody," Brenda announced shrilly.

"Yah, go and listen to Bach, and leave me be!"

The room emptied of people except for him and Jeanette, who had remained silent during his outburst.

They were still sitting in the same position when Steward and Hester returned a few minutes later. David was pouring out words like an uncorked cask of wine.

"David, I think you'd better get ready," Hester interrupted him. "We're leaving."

David swung around to peer belligerently at her.

"What the hell do you mean we're leaving? We just got here. I thought you said that they going to feed us? If you want to go, then clear off. Me, I'm staying. I think I can make out with this catto. Some cats I've met are for eating, some are for show, and a few can speak. Here I find a sweet catto who's everything wrapped up in one, and you want me to leave. What the hell's wrong with you?"

"I'm afraid you'll have to leave," Lester boomed. "I want you to leave my house this very moment!"

"Please, David. No trouble."

"Listen, Hester. You're a sister for me but don't stretch it. No rules! No rules for me!"

"I don't care about your no rules." Lester's bellow threatened to turn into a shriek. "I don't want you in my house any longer."

David looked around. Lester was shouting at him from halfway across the room. Steward, hands thrust into his pockets, head bowed stood next to the lord of the manor. Hester faced him and stared at Jeanette from the other side of the coffee table. The other guests cluttered around the doorway.

David turned his back on them and spoke to Jeanette in a whisper that did not carry beyond them: "This is what I mean. People always ready to kick you in the face. Just when you think you've got it made, there's a son of a bitch ever ready to shovel you shit!" He turned to Lester: "Lord and master of the manor, you desire I should make like piss and flow?"

"David, please. After all, it's Steward's friends. Let's leave," Hester urged.

"I'm not going to tell you again, sister mine. You and Steward leave. I'll leave but I'm not going along with you. I'll find a place to suit me."

David, with a last look at Jeanette, lurched from the room and pushed his way through the throng around the door. He was joined by Hester and Steward before he had reached the door. Brenda brought up the rear.

"Don't forget to give me a ring," Brenda reminded Hester.

"Your night's not altogether a flop!" David retorted. "You've got something to talk about now. Having two blacks at your dinner party shows how liberal you are. A pity about the extra nigger in the woodpile that created chaos. It just goes to show, one can't trust these darkies. Accept them in your company, and they lose all sense of respect."

"I'm sorry, Brenda," Steward apologised.

"Shit!" David ejaculated.

David toddled off ahead of Hester and Steward and at the first corner changed direction.

"David!" Steward called hesitantly.

He did not reply. He walked on, shoulders hunched and hands thrust into his pockets.

"Leave him alone," Hester said. "Let him go!"

5

David's mind raced home as the three of them got out of the bus, filled with the ever-constant fear: He's with her. I know he is.

He could see them – Melvyn and Yvonne – sitting or standing within touching distance, speaking softly about things he preferred not to hear of for it held no comfort for him.

He quickened his footsteps.

"Hey, David. What the hell's the rush? Hang on. We're going to my place for a drink!" Eddie called after him.

"I just want to drop these parcels with Yvonne. We've got the rest of the afternoon, and there's the party tonight," he shouted back.

"Aw, come'n, David. First drop in for a shot. Yvonne won't run away." A snort of laughter erupted from him before he added: "Or would she, David?"

David could imagine the sly look he exchanged with Steward.

"All afternoon you've acted like a man who expects his house to be burnt down on his return. After all, you've no cause for concern. Didn't you tell me that you and Yvonne have solved your problems? Hey, I hope Melvyn's coming to the party."

That's right, you bastard! Dig in a little deeper. Extract the last drop of blood. You've waited a long time for this. Go ahead, rejoice! You were never man enough to try it yourself. Always had to get your thrills second-hand. How much more pleasure it would've given you if you were the cause of my suffering. A friend indeed! My personal Iago!

David slowed down. He had to swallow before he could say: "Okay. Come in with me so I can drop the parcels. Then we'll go over with you."

"That's fair enough," Steward agreed.

"Oh, well," Eddie reluctantly consented. "We'll go with you, but then don't tell me that you've changed your mind and that you're going to stay put. You hardly have time for us anymore. Looks like you're avoiding us the last couple of weeks. Remember us? We're your friends. There's nothing like old friends."

They turned up the lane. Cora, who was cleaning her front yard, greeted them, but David did not notice. He wanted to get home ahead of the others.

He heaved a loud sigh of relief at the open front door with no sign of Melvyn lounging in the entrance. Eddie and Steward followed him through the gate.

Thelonious Monk was plonking his way through one of his ponderous compositions. Their footsteps were drowned out by the loud music.

Eddie and Steward slumped onto the sofa in the front room as he continued towards the kitchen. He had earlier run into them in Cape Town by accident. He had steered clear of Eddie as much as possible lately, and Steward he had last seen on the disastrous visit to Lester and Brenda. He had known that they were going to town to get some things for Hester's party, but he had left before Eddie could send over a message to tell him exactly when. He could not take much more of Eddie's sly insinuations that he was all washed-up, finished as far as Yvonne was concerned, that

Melvyn was now more man about the house than he was. So when Yvonne agreed to accept the perfume he had offered to buy her for the party, he had left immediately, pathetically grateful.

He entered the kitchen with the wrapped bottle of perfume held aloft like a banner of peace.

The words he had rehearsed expired on his lips. Melvyn was towering over the refrigerator, staring into Yvonne's eyes on the other side.

They were not immediately aware of his presence. Yvonne's gaze was one of adoration – a look that he had not had the privilege of seeing on her face for a long time.

In the instant before he spoke, the familiar pangs of pain and desolation shot through him. His hand tightened on the package as he blurted out: "I've brought you the perfume."

He waited, expecting some sort of answer, but they seemed unwilling to break the intimacy of their interrupted conversation.

Finally Melvyn turned towards him. Of late Melvyn had been looking at him with a cool assurance which David found as disconcerting as the unspoken insult it implied, an assurance bordering on arrogance. It made him feel like a stranger in his own house, as if his presence was a cause of irritation for the true inhabitants. Yvonne's glare reinforced his discomfort.

He put the perfume on top of the refrigerator and left the kitchen.

"I couldn't wait," Eddie said, pointing to the three glasses on the table.

David reached for a glass, trying to catch a word from the kitchen. He emptied his glass in one gulp and refilled it. "This one's for Melvyn," he said.

In the kitchen he passed the wine to Melvyn. "I brought you a drink. Yvonne, you want one?"

"No. I got work to do. There's washing on the line that must come off. I don't want to be bothered with things later. There's a lot to do before the party."

Yvonne squeezed her way through between the refrigerator and Melvyn. She deliberately brushed against him as she passed.

Pain seared through David, leaving his throat dry. He followed her to the yard. "Yvonne," he stammered, "do you have to rub against him like that? Couldn't you ask him to move?"

She did not bother to answer, just continued to take the washing from the line and dumping it in the clothes basket.

David opened his mouth to speak, then noticed Melvyn watching them through the window. Impotent rage flared up in him. Hell! Can't he even speak to Yvonne without the man's shadow looming over them?

The kitchen was deserted when he went back inside.

"Ready to push?" Eddie asked as he entered the front room. "We've had a second round while we waited for you. What's the hold-up? Where's Yvonne? How is she?" His eyes shifted to Melvyn.

David mumbled an indistinct reply and poured himself wine in an empty, used glass. He sipped slowly, lengthening the moment of departure.

"Come'n, hurry it up, will you?" Eddie urged.

"Wine and women are two things which should never be rushed," he replied in an attempt at joviality. "Both should be savoured slowly."

"I've heard that line before, and my advice to you is to change your technique."

David was thankful for the admonishing look Steward gave Eddie: it stopped him from embroidering forth on his favourite theme. "Are you coming with us, Melvyn?" David asked, trying to keep a pleading tone out of his voice.

As if Melvyn's response was of no interest to him, Steward stared out through the window at some children playing in the lane. Eddie watched Melvyn and David with a sardonic smile on his face.

David waited like a little child who was not sure whether he was going to be treated with a smile or rejected with a curse.

"Why not?" Melvyn drawled after a few seconds. "I might as well get myself in the party mood."

David relaxed. His head seemed to lose its feeling of tightness.

"Yes, why not?" Eddie cheerfully added. "After all, we're buddies. What's David's is Melvyn's, and what's Melvyn's is mine. Isn't that right, Steward, old horse?"

"Are we going or not?" Steward demanded, hoping to spare David further jibes from Eddie.

David sipped the last of his wine, collected the empty glasses and before joining the others at the gate went and placed them in the kitchen sink.

Yvonne watched the men walk up the lane. David, a good head shorter than any of the others, lagged behind. She watched them climb over the low wire fence into Eddie's yard. As he turned, David looked over his shoulder at her. They stared at each other for a moment before she reached for his shirt above her head.

Eddie made a big show of flopping down on their studio couch with its tired springs. "Ease your bunnions, we're here," he invited. "Steward, would you call one of the kids and ask him where my old cow is?"

Steward's face contorted into a look of long suffering. "Andrew, your father wants you," he called from the front door.

A short, sturdy youngster detached himself from the group kicking a rugby ball and ambled reluctantly towards the house. Steward winced inwardly. Andrew's shirt tail was hanging out and any disorder, whether in behaviour or manner of dress, offended him. He shuddered as the boy lumbered past, pushing a chair aside. Irritated, he carefully replaced the chair in its former position.

"Where's your mother?" Eddie asked.

"I dunno, Daddy."

"What do you mean, you don't know? Has she gone out?"

"No, Daddy. I mean, yes, Daddy, she over at Mrs Walker."

"Go and tell her I'm home. But first get us some glasses. Four."

"We only got three glasses. Stevey break a glass this morning."

"Clumsy little sod! I'll break his backside for him. All right, don't just stand there! Bring a cup."

"And the glasses, Daddy?"

"Of course, you idiot! And hurry before I brain you."

The exchange between father and son changed David's mood. "Eddie, Andrew isn't quite the buffoon he acts," he said. "I've watched him closely. You keep on calling him an idiot, and he uses that as a excuse, getting away with a lot of things. He most probably will end up smarter than his old man."

"I think you're right," Melvyn joined in. "Why don't you use him in a story? I'm sure Eddie won't mind. Would you, Eddie?"

"Of course not. But remember, I get half of the sale."

"Who's all coming tonight?" Steward changed the topic. "I know that Terence will be there because Hester apologised to him for upsetting him the other time, and he said he was sorry too."

A glint of amusement lit up David's face as he recalled Terence's outburst when Hester called him a moffie. "Well," he said, suddenly in a good mood. "Hester asked Yvonne if she could invite a few of her friends over. She asked me to contribute two bottles of wine, which I bought yesterday."

"She also asked me to buy some wine," Eddie said, "but I feel like finishing off the one I bought. What about you," he prompted Melvyn, "what are you bringing?"

"Myself."

"I never thought you were hot for Hester?"

"No, I'm not. With all due respect to Steward, she doesn't appeal to me. She can't ever forget that she's a school teacher."

"So who appeals to you?"

"Certainly not Hester."

With lowered head David swallowed his wine and refilled his glass. His brief good humour had evaporated and his resentment was back.

Yes, you bastard! Hester doesn't appeal to you because she sees through your fancy manners and sweet talk. Yvonne's easy meat for you. Her you've got in a daze with your playing the big innocent young man, grateful for a woman's attentions.

His suppressed anger almost exploded in words as he remembered the previous Saturday. Yvonne and Melvyn were sitting next to each other on the doorstep in the sun, Hester standing facing them. From inside he could hear the conversation. Hester was telling them about the cockroach plague in Durban. Yvonne, not to be outdone, cut in with Cape Town's problem. "Where we stay in town, it was terrible summer nights," she said. "Cockroaches crawl out of the drains and cover the lamp lights. The heat burn them and they drop on the heads of the children playing under the lights. They really big ones."

"Do you mean to tell me that they can fly?" Melvyn asked, his voice full of wonder.

"Don't you know?" Yvonne asked, thrilled that she had told him something he did not know.

The mere thought of it! What a put-on. Melvyn knew as well as everyone else who grew up on the streets of Cape Town that cockroaches can fly!

"No, not Hester. My wife appeals to you!" he burst out.

Melvyn's gaze shifted to David and came to rest on the empty glass he clutched in his hand.

"And where the hell have you been gossiping?" Eddie greeted Rebecca, who had come in from the kitchen unseen.

"Good afternoon, David, Steward. Good afternoon, Mr Francis." She turned to face Eddie. "Have you got no manners? Is that the way to greet a person?"

"All right! All right! Now that you've shown us how polite you can be, would you stir youself and make us something to eat? Mr Moneybags Steward has bought some sausage."

"Steward, will you speak to that man? He think a person got nothing to do but jump to his orders. I still have to clean the place."

"You were going to clean the place this morning when we left. What the hell have you been doing? Where are the kids? They could've cleaned up."

"I talk to them over and over to do things in the house, but it's the way you treat me. You don't care what you say in front of them."

Eddie leaned across the couch and opened the window and shouted, "Andrew! Timothy! Steven! Come'n in, at once!"

They made their entry like three stampeding horses.

"Why the hell don't you boys help your mother clean up the place?"

"I help Mummy this morning but Timmy and Stevey they just wait for Daddy to go, then they run out to play football."

"I suppose you joined them ten minutes later," Eddie said, aiming a slap at Andrew's head. But the boy ducked with the ease of a boxer side-stepping a blow. "Not one of you will go to cinema if you don't get on with what you have to do."

Rebecca retreated to the kitchen, and the boys, with much gusto, tackled their task. Andrew selected the front room. Every floor rug was picked up and given a violent shake on the front stoep. In the kitchen Rebecca could be heard lamenting the rough treatment of her pots.

Eddie settled himself for serious drinking, loudly complaining that he would starve to death before his wife got around to feeding him and his friends.

"I don't think I'll wait for food," Melvyn said. "I'll push off after finishing this drink."

"Are you missing Yvonne?" David tried to make the words sound casual.

"I'm going home. I want to take a shower and change into something more comfortable for tonight."

David sat brooding as they drank. The drinking had done nothing to allay his fears or douse the fire of his rage. As Melvyn started towards the door, he put his glass on the table and got up.

"Are you also going?" Eddie's voice stopped him at the door.

He did not respond.

He greeted Melvyn's parents with a handshake. Before the old man could trap him into listening to a discourse on the merits and demerits of the white rugby teams playing at Newlands that afternoon, Melvyn told him to follow him to his room.

He opened his wardrobe and took out a bottle of Frontinac. David smiled bitterly as he poured two glasses: Yvonne's favourite. He sipped slowly, enjoying the sweetness tinged with fire, while Melvyn showered.

David ran his hand over the smooth wooden frame of the long, low bed he had made himself comfortable on. Ah, he thought, this must be the bed Melvyn had made. Early on, Melvyn had told him and Yvonne how difficult it was for him to sleep in a bed of normal length, and how, in desperation, he had built one for himself. Yvonne had been greatly impressed by yet another manifestation of Melvyn's many talents. David, totally inept at carpentry, had watched ruefully as Melvyn basked in her praise.

Now it struck him for the first time that the length of the bunk bed in the children's room never discouraged Melvyn from wanting to stay over at their place. With unseeing eyes he looked at the framed reproductions of paintings by Degas, Rembrandt and Van Gogh on loan from the Kewtown library hanging on the walls.

Half automatically, David took a book from the pile on the table next to the bed. He almost choked on his wine – *How to Mould Your Character*. He tossed the book aside and picked up another. The books were all more of the same: books on character-building and self-improvement. He gave a mirthless laugh when he read the title of the last one: *Happiness in Ten Easy Lessons*.

The old feeling of superiority surged up. That's the trouble with the idiot. Like most young men with a smattering of intellect, he has not discovered a thing for himself. Whatever he thinks he knows comes from what he has read in a book. And then they think they know everything there is to know about life!

Melvyn's eyes widened when he returned and found David with his books strewn all over on the floor. But he kept quiet.

"I bet you've also read Carnegie's guide on *How to Make Friends and Influence People*," David said in mock seriousness, pointing at the books.

Melvyn nodded his head and grinned self-consciously. "You'd be surprised at how well it works, especially with women."

"Sit down," David said, wishing to ignore the unintended irony of the last remark. "But first fill our glasses. There's a few things I need to tell you."

Melvyn sank down onto the other end of the bed, clearly very uneasy.

"I know I've made a fool of myself in this affair," David began, slowly. "I should never have lost my head. After all, I know Yvonne and all her moods. I should've handled it differently. You're really nothing. Just an instrument of torture. If it weren't you, it would've been someone else, equally young. Sure, Yvonne's loves her ability to get someone as young as you to trot after her with dove eyes. It satisfies her vanity."

Melvyn searched David's face for signs that it was the liquor talking, but apart from a slight thickening of speech, David seemed sober.

"Do you really know what it is to love a woman? How it feels to have her in your blood like a sickness, a fever that you do not want to be cured of? That's how it is with me. Do you know how long I've had this sickness? Twenty-three years. Since I first met her, I've been in love with Yvonne. That was before you started school. That is two-thirds of my thirty-five years. And for the past twelve years I've been married to her. I'm not going to allow you to take her from me!"

David's voice was free of rancour now and for a moment Melvyn was shaken by the fervour of his words.

"I'm done with crawling. It's time that I regain my self-respect and face my children without a feeling of shame. We could've been very good friends. In the beginning, I looked upon you as a younger brother. A St Bernard."

He ignored the frown on Melvyn's face. "But I had to change my mind. I saw this coming. Yet I did not interfere. Do you know why? Because I was too sure of myself. I would never have believed that Yvonne would trade me for someone like you."

Melvyn could keep quiet no longer. "Haven't you been asking for it? Look how you treat her when you're drunk. It is now that you know that you can lose her that you're full of this great love you have for her. When we first got to know each other, you told me a few times that if Yvonne should find someone else there'd be no regrets on your part, even if the marriage fell apart."

"Yes," David said, putting his glass down on the bedside table. "I've spoken those words many times, but then, who can speak logically when love's involved? Truthfully? Not I! Words are like so many masks we wear. We speak words that bear no resemblance to what our hearts hide. No matter what words I have uttered, my heart is true to Yvonne, and she knows it. I could sit here forever and it would not be long enough for me to tell you how much Yvonne means to me. Yvonne is my life. Without her there is nothing."

David gave Melvyn an unexpectedly bewildered look. "Are you in a hurry to get to the party? I'd like to stay here a little longer and clear my mind. It seems a long time since we've been able to speak to each other. The past three weeks have been hell. There were times when I thought I was losing my mind. Doubt is a terrible thing. Like scorpions darting my mind, threatening to drive me insane with their poisonous sting." He reached for the bottle. "Here, your glass is empty."

"No, I don't think I should drink any more. Yvonne won't like it. I think we'd better pack it up."

"You see? There you start again. Fuck what Yvonne likes or dislikes! You're drinking with me and we're baring our souls. Or rather, I am. And you want to go to mama! Yvonne's a hot-blooded woman, and you want a mother. Jesus! You bring on the shits! Oh well, come'n, let's push before your precious Yvonne comes a'searching for her baby."

David struggled to his feet, and the last few books he had piled up in front of him clattered down onto the floor. He sniggered drunkenly and said, "So much for self-improvement!"

190

"You're drunk!" Melvyn reproached him.

David screwed up his already narrowed eyes and peered at him. "What an absolutely brillant deduction, young Lochinvar. It would be damn strange, after savouring almost a full bottle of your delightful Frontinac, to still be altogether sober. Yet I beg to differ. My legs might be slightly unsteady but I'm far from drunk. My mind is wonderfully alive. Every word that we're spoken, I can recall."

David held himself stiffly as they walked through the dining room. Melvyn's father was now absorbed in the rugby commentary coming from the radio, a bottle of wine on the table next to him. Mrs Francis was seated on the other side of the room, fingers industriously plying knitting needles.

"A pleasant night to you, Mr Francis, and also to you, Mrs Francis. We're off to the ball where young Melvyn will cut a fancy figure."

The disapproving look that spoiled the pleasant face of Mrs Francis delighted David. He should have expected it, Melvyn had once told him that his mother considered him a bad influence on her son. He turned to her husband: "Ah, Mr Francis, I see that you're well fortified for the night. Do you think I could have a wee one for the road? The road home is quite short, but any old road turns into a long road if one does not fortify the inner man." With a puckish look he added: "Isn't that so, Mrs Francis?"

Mr Francis was not quite sure that David was not mocking him, but obligingly, to Melvyn's disgust, poured him a glass.

"Good old Libby," David said. "There's nothing fancy about it and it serves its purpose admirably."

Melvyn glared at him from the doorway, muttering, "I want to go!"

"Wine's for lingering. Don't rush me," David replied. Then to Mr Francis: "I ask your pardon for your son's impetuosity. He's young and has other things on his mind." He placed the glass on the table. "The wine was nice. The company better, but we must leave."

Outside, Melvyn complained about the delay.

"Yes, it was necessary for me to drink with your old man. It would've been unseemly if I had left without partaking of his wine. I drank with the son and I shall drink with the father. You've told me that your mother finds my presence unsettling, but her son is welcome at my place no matter what time of the day. He's more than welcome. He is, in fact, a member of the family."

They walked on in silence.

Melvyn looked at David. His shirt looked like he had slept in it; one shoelace had come undone and trailed in the dust; his hair was awry and his face shone with sweat. He stumbled as he walked.

David returned his scrutiny, then jerked his eyes from Melvyn's face. That's right, he thought. Dolled up like a gigolo. Fancy clothes, fancy talk, fancy man. God's gift to frustrated housewives – the Barrymore of the bundu.

Chubby Checker blared them a welcome as they passed through the gate to David's house. Through the open window they had glimpses of figures bobbing and weaving.

David's spirit was lifted by the beat. "Let's have ourselves a ball," he said. Then they were inside.

Girls in tight-fitting slacks and clinging sweaters were twisting with men in shirtsleeves, all caught up in the frenzied cajoling of the singer whose lung-power was further amplified by the stereo player. The women's flashing limbs created a kaleidoscopic effect.

A plait of hair stung David's face. He grabbed at it and tugged. The owner swung around and faced him, her body still responding to the beat. David sagged at the knees and started swaying his body in time to the music. The young woman, surprised, matched his movement. With one last shout, the record came to an end. He followed the woman to the wall.

"I don't recall ever seeing you here," David remarked, glimpsing Melvyn on his way to the kitchen. "What's your name?"

"Charmaine."

"Yes, any other name would've been a mistake. It's indeed charmed I am. Tell me, Charmaine, are you truely as charming as you appear?"

The girl gave an embarrassed giggle and looked across the room for deliverance from this strange man who paid her compliments with such mock seriousness.

As if on cue, Hester appeared next to them.

"David, I've been waiting for you all evening. Oh, I see you've met Charmaine."

"Yes, I've met charming Charmaine but we've not been properly introduced."

"Charmaine, this is Mr David Patterson," Hester said. "I've told you about him."

They shook hands and David held onto her hand, his thumb lightly rubbing the soft flesh of her palm.

"I'm to blame for the delay. Had I known that you had invited such a charmer, I would've been here sooner. Have you invited more girls?"

"There are five of us, all teachers. Two brought boyfriends – I hope you don't mind?"

192

"Well, if it can't be helped, it can't be helped. As long as the rest of your delegation of teachers are as beautiful as Charmaine."

"I'm sure they are, Mr Patterson," Charmaine laughed, tossing her hair so that the plait bounced up and down.

"Do that again, Chairmaine."

She complied and David explained, "With your hair tossed like that, and your wild-eyed look, you're a filly in flight across the meadow on a summer's morn."

"David, I'm jealous," Hester cut in. "It's my party and you haven't said anything nice to *me*."

"Hester, Hester, can there be anything nicer than having you here tonight? Please enlighten me as to what calls for all this merriment so that I can congratulate you."

"It's my birthday. But don't ask me my age. I absolutely refuse to tell you. So there!"

"But Hester, age with you is of no consequence. The passing years can only make you lovelier."

Hester gave him a light peck on the cheek.

"Your perfume reeks of wickedness," he swooned with half-closed eyes. "Pity the poor man caught in your spell."

"It's you I want to trap," she teased. "But you're already caught. And now I'd better see to the rest of my guests. After all, I'm the hostess." She turned from him. "Someone put on a record," she ordered imperiously.

This time it was a blues number and someone switched the lights off. David took Charmaine in his arms and slowly circled the room with her, his hands caressing her back. Her breasts were soft against on his chest. "Charmaine," he whispered in her ear, deliciously intoxicated by her nearness.

But the record ended, the lights were turned on and someone pushed a tray in front of him. He reached for a glass.

"I don't drink, Mr Patterson," Charmaine said as he reached for another glass.

"More's the pity but we must remedy that before the night is done. Also, this 'mister' business - I'm David and you are Charmaine. It's as simple as that. Now, tell me where have you been all my life?"

"Here and there, David."

He stepped back and took a good look at her.

"Catto, you're mit it. You know the rules. Tonight, you're going to be my catto and I'd like to meet the son of a bitch that says no!" He emptied his glass. "Don't go away. I need a refill."

In a corner David noticed Eddie talking to a tall girl in a clinging green corduroy dress. Her skin was very fair, almost too pale, and the black hair piled on top of her head made her look even taller. Eddie seemed very pleased with himself.

He restrained David as he walked past. "My dear," he said to the tall girl, "let me introduce you to the gentleman of the house. Lavonia, this is Mr Patterson." And to David: "What do you think of my Grecian beauty, huh?"

"Not bad. She's almost as charming as my Charmaine. Where's Rebecca?"

"She'll be along. Later."

"You'd better make the most of it, then."

By now the room was too small for all of them and David had to push his way through the crowd of bodies to reach the kitchen. He stopped several times to speak to someone.

He stopped in the doorway. Melvyn was crouched on the kitchen floor, a tomato crate between his legs and a hammer in his hands. Yvonne, not yet dressed for the party, was perched on the side of the table, looking on.

Anger flared up inside David.

He strode across the floor and jerked the crate from Melvyn's grasp. "I'm not taking any more of this shit!" he yelled. "This is my house and I'll let you know if I can't run it. Get the hell to the front room."

Melvyn looked at him, and then at Yvonne. He left the kitchen without a word.

Yvonne did not change her position, coolly watching David attack the crate. The hammer slipped and caught the side of his hand. He swore loudly and tossed the hammer aside and commenced to break open the crate with his hands.

"I warn you, David. If you going to act like this, I leave you. I'm not going to take your shit any more!"

"Yes, you're not going to take my shit but I must be shamed with the shit you two are feeding me. There's nothing wrong with that, is there? Go'n, get dressed. What do you want me to do with these damn tomatoes?"

"Put them in the fridge. Hester can cut it up herself. She's no madam! It's not my party and I'm not going to put myself out. The people she invited is her friends and she can look after them herself!"

While putting the tomatoes in the fridge, David discovered three bottles of vermouth next to a bottle of milk. He peered at the labels, opened one and filled a glass to the brim.

The frenetic beat of the music was calling out to him but Melvyn's solicitousness towards Yvonne had spoilt his mood. He preferred to drink.

Hester found him propping up the refrigerator. "Come'n," she said, "the girls have been asking after you."

He allowed himself to be led inside.

"I'm sorry for neglecting you and your guests. There was a small job I had to do."

Hester guided him to Charmaine, who greeted him with an eager smile. Her jolliness was infectious and soon he responded to her banter and invitation to dance, Yvonne temporarily banished from his thoughts. But when the dance ended, Chairmaine was claimed by another partner and he looked around the room.

Melvyn was slouched against the wall near the kitchen door.

I suppose the other women are not good enough for him? David thought.

Sensing that someone was staring at him, Melvyn raised his head to look straight into David's challenging eyes. He held David's gaze for a few seconds, then wavered and averted his head.

The lights were switched off again and David pushed his way from the room. He rapped impatiently on the locked bedroom door.

"Who's it?"

"Come'n, open up, Yvonne!"

Yvonne stood in front of the mirror, dabbing perfume behind her ears, from which huge earrings dangled. She had changed her dress and now had on a pair of tight shocking-pink slacks and a low-cut white satin blouse. A white lace mantilla lay on the bed.

David blinked. He had never seen any of it. Yvonne had always steadfastly refused to wear slacks, insisting that it was garb for teenagers. She had always shown him every bit of clothing she bought. What was this?

"Where did you get that from?" he demanded, pointing at the shiny blouse. Only then did he notice the perfume on the dressing table. The Flower Mist looked more expensive than the Goya he had bought. "And that?"

Yvonne finished putting on lipstick before she turned to face him.

"I bought the clothes." Her eyes flickered to the mantilla on the bed, which Melvyn had bought. "And Melvyn bought the perfume. Do you mind?"

It was not the words but the way they were said that tore the curtain of restraint to which he had been clinging. He stared at her, nostrils flaring, his mind whirring with Eddie's insinuations and his own paranoia.

"Where's the perfume I bought you?"

She pointed to the bedside table. The perfume was still in its wrapper.

"What's wrong with it?"

"Look, did I tell you to buy it for me?"

"No. But you're wearing someone else's perfume. Did he give you what you've got on?" He could not get himself to say "Melvyn".

She planted her hands on her hips.

"No concern of yours. I told you everything's over for us. I'm your wife only in name. I'm ready to leave the day Melvyn say so."

A red haze filled his mind. Without registering, he raised his hand and slapped her.

Yvonne fell across the bed, the print of his hand vivid on her cheek.

From the front room came the sound of a combo hotting it up.

His heart racing, David screamed, "Besides being a liar and a cheat, have you also turned yourself into a whore? Have you slept with him?" He could stand the uncertainty no longer.

"Why don't you ask him?"

Her taunting was too much. His hand dug into her hair, pulling her towards him. Just as the music reached a crescendo, his free hand lashed out and landed on her face with the thud of someone hitting a drum.

Yvonne did not hear any sound throughout the barrage of blows, her head rolling from side to side, a rivulet of blood starting to trickle down her chin.

David stood with his hand raised, aghast at the scarlet spattering on her white blouse and partly-covered breasts. He let go of her hair and sank down on his knees beside her. "Yvonne. Yvonne. Please forgive me. I didn't mean to do it!"

She pushed aside his fluttering hands. Half in a daze she got up and walked over to the mirror. One side of her face was already showing signs of swelling. Her lower lip was puffed up. With some tissues, she wiped the blood from her chin and carefully draped the mantilla over her head and shoulders so that it concealed the bruise marks.

David still sat on the floor, his eyes following her every movement.

She put Melvyn's bottle of perfume in her handbag, walked to David, slowly bent over and spat in his face. "I hate you, you bastard!" she hissed.

The door slammed and he was left sitting on the floor, tears washing away the saliva on his cheek.

Yvonne hurried through the hallway before anyone could catch a glimpse of her. But in her haste she bumped into Terence as as he came out of the kitchen. He caught at her shoulder to steady himself and the mantilla slipped from her head.

"Yvonne, what in heaven's name happened?" he gasped.

"It's David! He did it to me, the swine! I'm leaving him! Is Melvyn inside?"

196

"He's sitting on the doorstep, out in front."

She skirted Terence and left by the back door.

"Don't do it, don't leave David!" Terence called after her.

The pounding beat of a rock group finally stirred David into action. He didn't mean to hit her, he must tell her. He staggered up.

Hester and Steward were in the kitchen loading a tray with glasses of wine.

"Where's Yvonne?" Hester asked David. "I haven't seen her all evening."

David raised his eyebrows in bewilderment, his hand groping for one of the glasses.

"Is anything wrong?" Steward asked.

"No, no."

He drained his glass and moved to the front room.

"Come'n, all you twisters," the record urged.

Charmaine bobbed up in front of David.

"This is our dance, David."

He murmured an apology and returned to the kitchen, leaving Charmaine staring after him with an open mouth.

There was still one bottle of vermouth left and without bothering about a glass, he held it to his mouth. Liquid splashed onto his chest when he removed it. Bottle in hand, he stumbled from the kitchen, almost tripping over Terence who sat huddled at the side of the house.

"She's gone, David," he said. "Why did you do it? God, her face!"

David pulled at Terence's shoulder. "Gone? Gone where?" he groaned.

"She's gone off with Melvyn. She said she's leaving you, that she was never coming back."

David sank down on the sand, still clutching the bottle.

"What are you going to do, David?"

The liquor he had been drinking all evening took possession of him, changing his contrition into contempt, not for himself, but for Yvonne who had turned herself into a willing whore – what else? – and for Melvyn who had betrayed him in the guise of friendship.

He raised the bottle to his lips and took a deep draught. "Shit on Yvonne and Melvyn!" he slurred. "I'm going to get drunk. That's what I'm going to do!"

He thrust the bottle at Terence. "Here. Drink!"